The Sundering of t|

Jacob Bower is a young author living in the small town of Towcester, in England. He attended the local secondary school after which he started working at Towcester Racecourse. While working there Jacob embraced his long passion of literature and began work on The Escape from Humanity. A fifty-page handwritten novel, that soon grew into the wider Ilmgral universe.

Jacob Bower

<u>The Knights of Earth Saga.</u>

Book One: The Escape From Humanity.
Book Two: Vengeance of the Gods.

<u>The History of Ilmgral.</u>

Volume 1: The Sundering of the Two moons.

All books available as a Kindle E-Book or paper back through the Amazon store.

The Sundering of the two moons.

THE SUNDERING OF THE TWO MOONS

BY JACOB BOWER

Jacob Bower

Copyright © 2018 Jacob Bower

All characters in this novel are fictitious and solely from the author's imagination. Any resemblance to persons living or dead is purely coincidental.

Cover artwork by Emily Mortimer.

The Sundering of the two moons.

Authors notes.

Not much is known about the worlds beyond our solar system. The worlds that until recently we did not know existed. Chance has allowed me to study in the great libraries of Ilmgral, to see its vast history that Earth has now become a part of. For that reason, I have created this story, to show you the long tapestry of events that would one day bring universal war to Earth.
In this volume I cover the early years of the Ilma, from the creation of the universe to the most tragic event of those ancient years.
From the libraries of Dragor, I have translated these tales, so that we may better understand the role that has come to us.

Jacob Bower

Book One- The Holy Quadrant.

By The Church of Holy Quadrant

Book Foreword.
The holy quadrant is a religious text similar to the bible and other religious texts of Earth. It was written during the kingless times, in the hope that a better understanding of the Gods would release the Ilma from their punishment. The First volume begins at the Blessing of the Ilma, for it concerns their rise to power and though many of the stories told after, are mentioned in The Holy Quadrant, I have taken only its first few passages.

The Sundering of the two moons.

The Holy Quadrant of Brin Halana (The Three plains)

In the universe before, at a time of great strife, the vassals, servants of the Gods, did war upon their creators and the people of the universe were used as pawns in that war. Long was the strife and in the last day, the powers met in final battle and the universe was torn apart.

In his last breath, the God of doom decreed to the dying universe, "Never again shall the Gods dictate all that happens. In the land that follows our folly, new Gods will be born, and new vassals will nurture their worlds, but mortal life will have its own protectors. These Ilma will have the power of the Gods and they will rule the mortal peoples and allow the universe to reach its full potential."

Then in fire and storm the old universe was consumed, the Gods and the vassals with it and what remained was a timeless void. Power cannot be destroyed however and in that void the power of the old universe was unleashed in a great explosion. That explosion created the three plains of existence.

Livinden, the realm of light, was formed first. Its power is eternal, like light itself and it sustains the powers of the realm that is. Here light formed a figure that was both beautiful and majestic, a woman of the stars. Livella Remain, the light maiden. In her, the power of Livinden was held and in that realm of light she fashioned for herself a home and created many things composed of light, but she felt a loneliness for this world that only she could endure.

Livella began to wander in her youth and in a time she came to Besan Gretan, the realm that is, and she was amazed for suddenly she took a physical form. Like a woman of the Ilma she was, with golden hair. Her skin was flawless and pale, and she was garbed in a simple robe of pure light. She was amazed with her physical form and understanding came into her mind of the realm that is, where matter is whole, and all things exist for only a short time.

Besan Gretan was empty at this time, a black void and for that Livella was sad, wishing to bring the light of Livinden for those that may follow to marvel at. She lifted her right hand and beheld between her fingers the light of Livinden, and she took that light and formed then the first stars of this universe and she gave them physical form and these nine stars, larger than any that now exist, brought light to the realm that is. As the ninth star was positioned, Livella mused that she thought she heard a voice or many voices, from somewhere beyond Besan Gretan and those voices were lifted in song. In their melody she worked and around her great stars she formed lesser stars and arranged these into galaxies and all the while the melody continued. The voices soon began a song of praise to the new stars and called to see them with their own eyes and Livella followed the singing voices that filled her mind with sorrow, and she passed from Besan Gretan into a world of shadow.

Her light seemed subdued in that place but she was enthralled by the sound of voices and so she wandered in the land of shadow and came to a hall,

The Sundering of the two moons.

where she found the singers.
Ghostly spirits stood before her, singing under the order of a composer who stood like she, a figure beyond the three plains. He was hooded and robed but golden burning eyes could be seen, and he seemed to be nurturing souls, aiding them in their singing and growth. Golden eyes turned upon Livella and in a musical voice, he spoke, "Welcome light maiden, bringer of the stars. You come to Agraldin, the realm of the souls, where life is nurtured. Beyond the doors of my church lies the flame of life and from that flame Besan Gretan will be full."
At his words, the spirits sang. All different shapes they were, creatures of fir, scales, those that walked on two legs and others on thousands.
"What will you do with them?" Livella asked and was shocked, for never had she spoken but the singing voices put the words in her heart.
"They wait for you mother of the stars." The figure said, "A sacrifice you must give, to birth the earth and form a union to water the lands so that life may flourish for a time in the realm that is."
Livella left the hall in wonder and came again into Besan Gretan and stared at her great stars and the galaxies that swirled around them, but it was a tainted love she held for them now. For those stars were formed from the light of Livinden, where no mortal life could live and though these stars would provide for those of mortal being, they could not hold them. She came then to a star that burnt with a pure white light, the first she had formed and much of the majesty of Livinden was held within it. As she

approached, the song from Agraldin came again and understanding came into her mind of things that were to come.

"From my sacrifice." She said and the universe trembled at the first words spoken there, "I bring life to the universe." With a cry she plunged her right hand into the star. So great was her cry of anguish that the other eight stars erupted into a fire that consumed much of the galaxies that surrounded them. The matter of the stars collapsed into themselves and became things new and heavy, that gave off no light and became separate from the realm of Livinden.

She withdrew her arm, but her physical form was changed, and her right arm was gone from the shoulder and her shining form was blackened there. In pain she wept, and her tear lingered by the star that now burnt a vibrant red. In a great explosion it erupted and Livella was tossed far across the universe, but she stared in wonder, for in the place of the star, a child lingered.

He was grey of skin, with coarse hair covering him but his hands were stone and veins of ore glittered across his body in the light of the stars that remained. Livella came to the child and words of the mortals named him Orna and she nurtured him. Quickly he grew and the elements of the destroyed stars became his plaything and together Livella and Orna began to re-order the universe. From her lost stars, she fashioned new ones. These were smaller and less majestic, for her sacrificed stopped her from pulling anymore light from Livinden. Around these lesser stars, Orna formed

The Sundering of the two moons.

planets. Worlds of swirling rock he formed, or giants of gas that nurtured great storms. Again, the voices of Agraldin sang in a majestic tone for the glory of the Gods and their creations but still no life came.

Soon Livella became weary of the realm that is as she felt no love now that her stars had been destroyed and she returned to Livinden, but Orna could not linger long in that realm of light. He was born in Besan Gretan, and he was bound to it. Orna now loved Livella, and he wished to ease her hurt and so coming to the area of his birth, he collected the remnants of the star that birthed him and formed a new world. All his power he poured into Ilmgral, and he fashioned continents for the coming of life and dreamt of great oceans where life would start but this thing he could not create. In the attempt, he formed rivers of molten rock and the world became a mass of flames and poisonous fumes that spread to many of his creations, and he roared in his anger.

Livella heard his cry and came from Livinden and looked upon the world of fire and was saddened and yet she shed no tear, for only two tears would she ever shed. One at her sacrifice and one more at the final day. The tear of her sacrifice lingered still by the world Orna had created. Reaching out she grabbed it and feeling the power within she laid it on the world. It glowed for a second and then the rivers of molten rock were calmed and from fissures great oceans formed. Clouds lifted above the world and the first raindrops fell in gentle tears onto the mountains. Water flowed into great bowls of the earth that overflowed and ran in many streams and rivers back

to the sea.
The amazement of Livella and Orna was great, but Livella moved, and her radiance was veiled so that the oceans froze, the rivers became glaciers and the voices of Agraldin lamented. At their call, a fist hammered under the frozen ocean.
Livella moved quickly and she pulled towards her a star and Orna placed Ilmgral in orbit around it and set it to turn so that equally the heat of her star could fall upon it. The oceans thawed and rivers flowed again. From the great sea a figure rose in splendour. He was tall and nimble, with a skin partly like scales of fish that mirror him. His eyes were blue with hints of green and he regarded his parents with love, "You have given life to me from your sacrifice's and from me the beginnings of life shall come. They will need guiding by starlight and moonlight." Thera, they named him, and he parted the sea at his feet and revealed a mountain like a red sunset and another of silver. These Orna took and he shaped them and placed them as moons over the planet like silent guardians to move the tides and aid with the nurturing of life.

Together the God's worked, forming solar systems of planets, some blessed with water and perfect light but always, as is the way in Besan Gretan, the works of Thera and Orna strived against eachother but that was as necessary as the passing of time.
Only on some worlds was these three in harmony. On some, the light of Livella's stars scorched the earth and boiled the seas, while on others the light could not reach, and the waters froze. Only on those that

The Sundering of the two moons.

life could be sustained, could the music of Agraldin be heard and with that, the Gods were contented. Travelling back to Ilmgral, as was her want, Livella beheld a planet grown green and the oceans brought forth rain that sustained things that now grew upon the soil. Slowly she descended and she came to a point where two rivers met and beheld a forest around her, and that forest glowed with her presence. At her feet flowers of red and blue bloomed, basking in the light of her sun. She stayed there, and watched, as the sun of her making became colder and the leaves turned to silver grey and fell to litter the floor, while the flowers withered and died at her feet. Livella despaired, feeling that these things had died in just a second of her mind, whereas the things of her creation lasted years beyond counting and in Livinden, nothing perished.

Her despair was ill-founded, for in the next second the trees began to bud, and flowers grew anew from the canopy of fallen leaves and the sun came again to full strength. So beautiful was the decay and re-birth that filled Besan Gretan, that Livella's heart was moved even greater by the voices of Agraldin. Voices of those who wished to touch the realm that is for whatever short time was allotted to them and her immortality became a frightening thing, "They wish for the gift of mortality now." Livella said to a budding red flower, "But soon they will wish for more time and that I cannot give them."

"Do not despair light maiden." Said a voice and before her walked the figure from Agraldin but he was no longer cloaked. He was garbed in cloth that changed colour as he moved. At times it was a vibrant green, at others the dark red of dusk and even at times as though he was dressed in the night sky. His face bore no relation to the creatures that would come after or maybe he was all of them, but Livella only saw a mirror of the Gods, vibrant eyes full of knowledge and a face flawless, cast in the same shadow of Agraldin. "Gadrika I am named." He said at Livella's shocked glance, "I come from the realm of spirit and in my halls, I nurture and preserve a balance for the universe, to see it steered to proper course. That requires life and life I gift to Besan Gretan with my flame so that all our realms may grow more beautiful, and we can finally achieve what all those who came before us failed at." His form seemed to shift, and he became then one of the Ilma, tall and magnificent, with golden eyes and no red scales, "In me all life shall live in Besan Gretan, but they shall be free of will, guided by the tapestry of those who came before. Here on this world will come the Ilma and they will be as children of you and in them your image will be seen. They also will have power, power to control their will and though we be Gods, we will be subject to them and to them will the dominion of Besan Gretan be granted. They will see it rise to proper station, protected from the greed and taint of those who are immortal" Gadrika smiled, and he grew shorter, and red scales now covered his cheeks, "With them shall be the Graul, the servant race. Like the vassals shall be to us so shall be the Graul to the Ilma and they will serve them in all their endeavours." Livella smiled and words from the God of doom of the

The Sundering of the two moons.

universe before ringed in her ears, but she also became cold. She had sacrificed to bring Besan Gretan to this part and she wished to guide the people of the world and be worshipped for the power that she was. She saw also the corruption of power that would come with the Ilma and the chance of hurt to all their works.

Gadrika spoke no more, and he became a brokin, white furred, with golden horns and he galloped across the meadow and faded from sight. Livella looked upon Ilmgral and in the years that passed she saw creatures come and go, growing and changing at the design of Gadrika and the weaving tapestry. Livella departed to Livinden, to await the coming of the Ilma, the guardians of Besan Gretan.

The Counsel of Gadrika.

Through years uncounted, the tapestry in the hall of Agraldin was woven. Through many creatures the Ilma came into being and the souls of the Ilma were nurtured by Gadrika and language he gifted them. Knowledge was woven into the tapestry so that the Ilma and Graul advanced swiftly but always was the Ilma the foremost. Through all the continents of Ilmgral the Graul and Ilma flourished, but never in equal numbers and upon the great continent the Ilma came little. That land passed out of the love of the Gods for many years, until a high king of the Ilma would unite all the lands.

Livella watched the beginnings of this fledgling people and once again thought of guiding them further than the tapestry, that put knowledge in their minds but no understanding. With the help of Orna she began again the re-ordering of the universe, and it stands now as it did then. She moved the stars and created a tapestry of her own that only on Ilmgral, in Brinsita, could it be truly perceived. The constellation of separation she formed and the red mountain star. The constellation of the Island she placed so that always it sat on the horizon, resting over lake or sea. All these things she had seen in the tapestry, woven before even the first Ilma had spoken word, but she knew not the tragedies that would lead to these events or how the weave would reach them. Maybe then the path was not set but these events were guided by the music of Gadrika and his flame of life. After her toil, Livella departed for a time to the realm

The Sundering of the two moons.

of light but Orna and Thera, now enamoured with Besan Gretan and the creatures born to the universe, set to work on other worlds. They worked tirelessly on the habitation of new worlds and in the hope for new creatures to live upon them. Creatures that would one day serve the Ilma and for a time Ilmgral was neglected.

This troubled Gadrika, as disasters long held back by the Gods began being weaved into the tapestry and the advancements became less and the Ilma stalled. Gadrika took new counsel and felt then the tug of the old universe. He remembered in deep thought, the wars of that universe and how the Gods played mortal against mortal until the universe was consumed. He thought of the Ilma, who would need to come into their power, and he went to the hall of sanctuary and found purpose there.

He called the Gods back to Agraldin and gave them counsel before the doors of sanctuary, "Long have we toiled on common purpose." He said to them, "And soon shall the Ilma inherit the power that I foretold but the things of our craft go astray. Disasters threaten the Ilma, maybe unto their uttermost doom. I decree then, that we should pick some of the Ilma to inherit a greater power than any shall afterward, and they shall be our vassals and should live upon the world for a time and serve as our hands upon Ilmgral."

The Gods were all in agreement and Gadrika led them into the hall of nurturing and the souls of Ilmgral were assembled, ready for their touch. As had always been the way, Orna and Livella walked together hand in hand and they found two souls who were like brothers, though one was clearly more advanced than the other.

The older, with hair like copper and fire in his golden eyes, Livella touched and said, "He shall be the first, as the fire of the red mountain star and he shall read my tapestry to the Ilma, and they will understand their meaning." She looked into Orna's eyes, "And yet I perceive that it shall be against your creations that his fate will be sealed."

Orna smiled, with grey eyes bright and turned to the younger, who was bigger in stature, meant for hardy toil, "And so then my vassal shall come and he shall wander until he comes upon the people of your child and like here now, they shall have friendship and he will pay back the debt that I owe you."

Part of their power they bestowed upon the pair and they left the hall of sanctuary and came to the room of weaving and saw then that already weaves were beginning for their vassals. In that weave a great mountain erupted in the north of the land of Cambane and Orna knew indeed that his vassal would have to repay the debt.

Thera long travelled the hall of sanctuary and in time he came to a group apart from the rest, who sang a song that sounded to him like the waves and among them, one voice sang clearer than all the rest. Thera's heart was moved by the maiden, and he became enamoured with her beauty, "I shall not touch you in this hall." He said bitterly, "For then danger would surely come to you, and I would not see such a beautiful voice be wasted in lethal toil." Then he sung

The Sundering of the two moons.

and the souls seemed to turn a crystal blue and the love of the sea was put into their hearts and the heart of the maiden. Thera left and went back to Besan Gretan, to linger by the shores of the great continent and await the maiden to be born upon the world.

Long had been this plan for Gadrika and he nurtured two souls from their formation. As twins they would be, equal and opposite, his truest servants. To these he said, "Your strife will be hard, and your need will not be on Besan Gretan but serving me here in Agraldin. Your children will serve the greater cause and from them the Ilma may find salvation in the terrible events that are to come to pass." He touched the souls, and one became like polished silver, but the other was tainted by greed and jealousy.
Gadrika was concerned by this, and he sang to the two souls. He sang of their place in the universe and the brothers sang with him but not in harmony and they squabbled to out sing the other and Gadrika bowed his head, knowing then that he must leave them to their quarrying and he hoped that physical form would see them both to better purpose.
At that time, the voices of the souls of nurturing came into song and weavers wove the vassals into the events of the world and the Gods retreated to await the coming of their children.

Of Drage Livella

In the north of the realm of Cambane, a lone mountain erupted in sudden flame and the ground trembled. From the mountain great fires reached into the heavens and a dark and cold summer followed from the cloud that blacked out the sun. Those of Cambane repented to Orna and prayed to Thera for the seas to rise and strike at the mountain and many feared that the Gods had abandoned them.
That same summer, in the white walled city of Scaraden, a child was born, and such fire was in his spirit that his mother was consumed, and she died in childbirth. The church of Gadrika took him and due to the fire of his eyes they named him Drage, and they nurtured him, for they perceived that he was a child of Livella. In form he seemed as she had when she had come in dreams to the heralds of the Ilma. His skin was perfect white scales, without blemish or mark, his hair like polished copper and his eyes burnt like the noon day sun, so much so that it was hard to keep his gaze.
Into his early teenage years, he developed the power to control and create fire at will and lamps would burst into life at his presence. The church knew then that the herald of Livella had indeed come at last.
To the church, Drage gave knowledge of the stars. He named the constellations as though Livella herself was speaking through him and many came to hear his wisdom. Passage of time was marked by the stars and years were counted from the birth of Drage, a sign of

The Sundering of the two moons.

the coming elevation for the Ilma.
Drage was happy to show them the gift bestowed upon him, but he asked not for money or power. His gift had taken his mother and it was to be shared not horded.
Late into his seventeenth year, Drage was invited to the home of the lord of Scaraden and Drage performed for him as he had for many other honoured guests of the church. Butterflies of fire he made, and he juggled flame, as was the want of the lord. When Drage offered to counsel him, the lord was un-moved as he was a sinful man, who believed more in the strength of iron than he did in worship or prayer, and he wanted this subject of Livella to serve him.
"Come child." He said and Drage approached, the light of his golden eyes falling onto the lord. Drage did not bow and there were some murmurings from the court, but the lord paid little heed to such things and instead he lifted a gnarled hand in Drage's direction, "Kiss the ring of your lord." A blue crystal on the lord's hand caught the fire of Drage's eyes but the vassal did not move.
Murmurings began but with a bow of his head, Drage spoke with a voice that crackled like a fire in a hearth, "I apologise sir." He said softly, "But I have only one lord, Livella Remain, maiden of light, creator of the stars. Her power runs through me and I am her servant."
The wicked lord's face darkened, and his eyes narrowed, a gesture of his gnarled hands made weapons of bronze be drawn but Drage did not move to defend himself.

"You live on my land." The lord began, "You eat the food that I provide and yet you will not show me the courtesy of my title."

Fire crept in Drage's veins as he saw the hatred in the eyes of the Graul who bore weapons against him, as those of lesser race felt anger to those more worthy and Drage prepared for their inevitable assault, "The land belongs to Orna as do the metals that forge such hateful weapons. The food comes from that land by the blessing of Gadrika and it is Thera who waters it. To claim un-rightful ownership of them is nothing but vanity and pride. Pride only the Gods can show."

All at once, the un-holey Graul began their assault but at a look from Drage's eyes, their bronze swords became weapons of fire and each sprang from the hands of the wielder, who in their pain bowed to the child of Livella. The court stared in wonder, for the body of Drage shimmered like the sun's rays off a still pool and the lord quailed from the brightness of his eyes but from somewhere a bolt was fired. Drage winced as an arrowhead pierced the flesh of his arm. The fire within him was quenched and he fled into the streets of Scaraden.

Reverence turned to fear in that time. The true power of the Gods was revealed to the Ilma and in their naivety of the gift that they would soon possess, they attacked. Great crowds surrounded the church of Gadrika and all attempts at peace were unfruitful.

"You must leave." The head of the church instructed to Drage, whose heart was filled with regret, for in his show and in his power, he had become as prideful as the lord and had brought this doom upon the church,

The Sundering of the two moons.

"Or you will be forced to kill with the power Livella gifted you."
"No." Drage said, "They are innocent and not what my inner power was gifted for. Their fear is born from their naivety."
"North you must go." The man said, "For nowhere in this southern realm will you find comfort. In the land of Cambane, in the wood of light, you will find the town of Brinsita and there in ages passed Livella would come and in her church, you will find peace."
Then Drage departed, and he went in secret from the city of Scaraden and walked long roads for many months. He found rest and welcome wherever he could, and he passed through the middle lands, where people were scarce, and he followed the red mountain star northward until he came to a woodland that seemed to glimmer with starlight. He felt the power of his mother and he prayed to thank her for her guidance and a voice heard his whisperings.
"Hail friend." The voice said and Drage lifted his eyes and saw men stood by a tall bridge over a deep, slow moving, river, "You come at night, but day travel would suit you better. It seems you have lost the path."
"Kind men." Drage said to the guards, who were Graul by their stature, "I admire the woods. Tell me, is this the land between the three rivers? I seek guidance and shelter. I am a hunted man in the southern realm and am in need of a home."
Understanding filled the eyes of the Graul and Drage's eyes illuminated a polished star on each of their breastplates.

One spoke, "Proof shall be needed. Any may enter Brinsita, but if you are indeed the one we have been ordered to watch for, then you will need to take the swiftest road."

Drage removed the black cloak that covered him, and his radiance shone in the night and the trees took his light and gifted it back tenfold so that it was like a bright summer morning. Fire danced around Drage's body, and the guards dropped to one knee to bow before him, "Behold." Drage said and they cast their eyes onto him, "I am the one the church of Gadrika spoke. I beg you guardians of light, help me."

The guards stared in mesmerised fear, but they let him pass and they gifted him a brokin so that he could ride the final miles. As dawn broke over the town, he came to the church of Brinsita. It was built of red stone, with a roof of domed glass so that as it caught the sun as it did now, it shimmered like a rainbow. Drage was welcomed by the leaders of the church, and they fed him from their table and all the land of Cambane grew stronger by his presence. In the two years that followed, many great works were written but Drage could feel the coming of darker days and on the winter of his twentieth year, a fell storm came to the northern realm.

Drage was warming himself in the winter sun when he noticed a caravan arriving and he bowed his head for the coffin carried upon a wagon. At the head of the carriage, a great lord sat on a brokin of pure white fur but beside him a girl sat, head bowed, and she was garbed all in black. The members of the church welcomed the lord of Cambane, and they took the

The Sundering of the two moons.

coffin. In the halls beneath the church, they prepared the old lord for his trip to river, where lords of the northern realm would sail to the sea, to rest under the stars until Livella took them to Agraldin.

A harsh wind came that night from the north and the stars shone brightly but no warmth came, and the river froze to the despair of all.

Drage came down to the river's edge and at his feet the ground warmed and the ice melted. Gasps rang out amongst the onlookers as he plunged himself into the river and where he stood, the ice was thawed, and the flowing river lapped at his waist.

The lord of Cambane stared at him in wonder, "You are the one that I have heard rumours of good child." The lord smiled, "Thanks be to Livella that she has sent you amongst us and I vow that no harm should come to you while you remain within my realm."

Drage bowed to the edge of the water, "I thank you lord and I wish that I could walk across all the river, even to the mouth of the sea. That way I could guide your father to the endless shore, but I fear that beyond my warmth, the ice lies thick for many miles, and it will not lessen till spring comes again."

"It is not your fault, son of Livella." The lord began, "You cannot bring the stars themselves down to warm the waters."

The bowed head of the woman at his side, lifted her eyes and they met with Drage's, and such love fell upon him for the sadness of them, that his heart was moved, "Not the stars but maybe I can do something." He said and turning to a member of the church, he asked for a lamp.

A lamp of metal was brought for him and inside Drage made a fire that burnt so brightly that none but him could bare the sight of it, but they could feel its warmth. This lamp, Drage mounted to the front of the boat and the waters around it were warmed from the light and then, like a call had come from Thera, the river current was roused. The boat lurched into the centre of the river and with Drage's lamp at its head, the ice melted before it. Long did that lamp last and many who lived by riverside saw it as it moved towards the sea and all bowed their heads in reverence for Livella.

That night a great feast was held, as the people prayed to the stars for the end of winter and the coming of the sun's warmth. Late into the celebration, Drage departed. At night he liked to look upon the stars through the domed roof and there see the passage of time as Livella saw it. He stopped upon the threshold, for the lady Cambane was sat in the library, a worn book in her hand. For the first time her hood was thrown backwards and Drage stared at her piercing beauty. Red scales came in tear drops down her face and her hair was as black as the night, long and flowing.
"I am sorry my lady." Drage said and the lady was startled but he offered her a smile, "I shall leave you in peace."
She studied him, "No sir." She said in a quiet, melodic voice, "This place is barred to no one, especially not for one whose Livella's light burns. Come and see the stars with me."

The Sundering of the two moons.

Drage walked towards her slowly and together they sat and watched the stars but always his eyes flickered towards her, a different type of beauty that he had yet to see in the world, "You are grieving my lady." He whispered, "But not just from the loss of your grandfather. The light of the Ilma is almost extinguished in you. Why do you walk in such sorrowful garb and only tread the lands of your home in winter?"

"My lady?" She said questioningly, "Is this not your home and I but a beggar at your door. My name is Bela, and you should call me this." Her sweet voice became sorrowful, "I am tired, servant of Livella as we pray now for the coming of summer, but summers have always haunted me. My mother was killed in the earthquake when the demon awoke in the mountain. My brothers killed two summers past in raiding wars against the kin to our west. Now this summer my grandsire has passed. I can find no peace in the summer sun when so much sorrow is bestowed. I have been humble and prayed to all the Gods and yet they test me so."

Drage listened to her sad words and took her hands in his. The coldness of her touch shocked him, for his hands were warm with the heat of his heart. Slowly he lifted her to her feet and took her to the centre of the church and clear above the dome, the red mountain star shone, with four falling stars beneath it, "Livella lives out there, in the realm of Livinden beyond the stars but she has no control over Ilmgral. Her stars are perfect and without fault but the works of Orna and Thera come from the destruction of those stars and

always their creations go astray. A river may carry your sires to the sea, but they may also flood, destroying crop and homestead. Orna's creations give life to us, yet they come from the fires of the planets core and at times that fire must burst. All of Gadrika's works go astray, for they think with their own mind, but he did not put war in our hearts. We are guided by the Gods and the tapestry they weave but in Besan Gretan, all things are of matter and all matter has its own will." They stared into each other's eyes and light kindled in the ladies and Drage spoke on, "Soon the Ilma will have a power to control these things, to set our own will. They have sent me, and others will follow to see the Ilma to that path. I do not believe that this is a chance meeting beneath the star of the mountain, for these are the stars of the vassals. I believe that my doom comes upon that mountain in the north. I was born at the time of its awakening and always has it filled my dreams." He looked at her, a woman in her prime and he was lost, "I do not know when that doom will come but I would like to bring light to your world for a time, as much as I may."
Bela looked into the eyes of the vassal and her heart was lost and they married in the spring. This began the house of Drage in Cambane and they had three children together who took the name of Drage for their family name and for fifteen years the town of Cambane grew more beautiful with the son of Livella's presence.

Soon rumbles began in the depths and the mountain once again spewed fumes into the northern sky that covered all the way to the middle lands. Ash fell as

The Sundering of the two moons.

snow in the town of Cambane and a pestilence followed it. Rumours began of a demon in the mountain, ready to crush the northern lands.
In sleep, Drage often had visions of this demon. A creature of molten rock it was, with great wings that would soar into the sky and lay all the lands of Ilmgral in ruin. In one dream, Drage wandered in an empty void and then a light flickered, and it formed an image of a woman. She shined like the brightest lamp and her hair was of fire, but she had only one arm, the other a stump shrouded in a veil of light.
"Child." She said with a smile, "Now the time has come, the time that was appointed for you. Only you can tame the power in the mountain that now threatens to crack the world."
Drage despaired, even within his dream, "Why mother? Why did you not make me death or blind? For I have now seen the beauty of the world and heard the sweet voice of the one who I love. Shall I leave her again in despair or my children fatherless?"
Sadness crept onto the face of Livella, "Had I known that I could stop these things, I would have done but only you have the power and without you there will be more widows and more fatherless children. Never again will my light live within another but do not despair for your kin. Ever will you guide them, for those who received my touch become as we and shall live forever in the three plains and all those who bare your lineage shall rest in Livinden after death. Their souls shall become guardians of my stars, to watch over the worlds that hold life. A payment for your debt."

A gentle touch she placed upon his face and with that Drage awoke and though it must have been late morning, the sky was dark, and no sun pierced the black cloud. His eyes wandered to the north, and he saw through the cloud and stared at the black mountain, fires spewing from its mouth.

The touch of his wife's hand brought him back from his vision. She was in a robe of silver, but she seemed sad, "It is time, isn't it?" She asked mournfully.

"Not if you ask me to stay." Drage replied solemnly, "Not if you ask me to remain by your side, to share together whatever doom this mountain brings."

A glint of love appeared in her eyes, "Long have I dreamed that we should grow old together but now that dream changes to people choking in the streets, cities turned to ash and fire. I would not have that for us or our children." She stroked his bronze hair, "Oh child of Livella, cruel is your fate and crueller still for those left behind but worse would be the fate for the world should the vassal of Livella not do his duty. Maybe then the red mountain star will cease to burn, and no more children of the gods will come forth. Maybe the Ilma will fall into a distant memory of the tapestry, never inheriting the power that was promised." She shed a single tear, "Even though I shall walk again in sorrow, I know that you will watch over me from the stars."

Drage nodded and kissed her one last time and said farewell to his children before setting out for the north.

He was fitted in armour of leather and upon his chest they had sown the star of Livella. As night fell, Drage

The Sundering of the two moons.

departed into a starless night. He turned back only once and saw, lit by lamplight, Bela Cambane, once again garbed in black and she watched after him. Wisdom she found in her prayers as she watched him leave and for many long years, she guided her people and the sons of Drage. She told them of the future vassals, preparing her people for the time when one would come among them again.

Drage rode for many weeks and came at a time to the foot of the mountain, and he waded through fields covered in ash until he reached its steep slopes. From its peak, great horned feet gripped at the mountain side and a vast shape, serpent like but formed of molten rock, climbed from it. As it stretched, wings as black as the night spread and eyes like fire stared at Drage.
Drage stared at his doom and wings of fire formed on his back and with the power of Livella, he soared into the sky and brought the doom of the Gods onto the creature.

From Cambane, they saw the sky burst in flame as though a great battle was happening within the cloud and lightnings smote against the ground. The mountain began to crumble, and the sea rose in a tumult and smote at the fires within. Until at last Drage threw down the demon and as its body crashed into the ground, the earth was broken, and the sea swallowed the mountain and the land in the north was changed. Drage perished also and from the mountain, a spirit like a bird of flame soared towards the heavens and to Bela it seemed that it came to the red mountain star, and it burned more brightly every night since.

So came the end of Drage Livella and he passed into Livinden and became a vassal to Livella. Long he has strived in the world as a guardian of light, holding back harsh winters and the fiery tumults of Orna's creation. Often, he came back amongst the living, especially to those who bore his name. When he did, he appeared as a spirit of fire, garbed still in the armour given to him by the people of Cambane and ever after he has served Livella faithfully.

The Sundering of the two moons.

Of Camara Thera

As was told in the Counsel of Gadrika, Thera did not touch a soul in the hall of sanctuary. Instead, his heart fell for a maiden, and he sang to her and her to him. His voice set into the heart of the people around her, the love of the sea and set a seed of change into them.

Through many years, Thera lingered in the oceans of the great continent and at a time he saw the people of his song playing amongst the waves. Members of the Ilma they seemed to be in skin tone, but their eyes were blue and many of their feet were webbed. He appeared to them as one of the Ilma, though the scales of his skin shimmered like fish scales in the sun. All hearkened to him and knew him as the God of the sea by the music of his voice and one sang with him, the maiden from the hall of sanctuary and his heart was lost to her. All that summer he spent among the Ilma, and love blossomed between himself and the maiden. She was blessed to carry his child but that year a plague swept through the Graul of that region and Thera, who had spent much of his youth in the deepest depths, saw for the first time the mortality of those who speak with voices and his heart grew cold and bitter. The loss of all these people shocked Thera and he departed Ilmgral and came there seldom after. Sad was the lot of the maiden of the Thera-ilma, but joy returned when her child was born. Her eyes were crystal blue, and her hair was of silver that flowed into scales that seemed to shimmer slightly. The child's toes were webbed, and the sea moved at her cries. Camara she was called as the northern current that brings warm air to the lands of Kuratex and Scaraden. Swiftly the child of Thera grew, and she spent most of her time amongst the waves and Camara learnt the voices of sea creatures and her people became great mariners under her tutelage. Times were changing though and the Ilma had found no strength upon the great continent, where the Graul were wild, worshiping false idols and following strange beliefs. The plague that they brought upon the continent, created famine and the Graul became desperate for the lands of the Ilma and the crafts they possessed. Thus began the biggest atrocity of the servant race, where across the great continent the Ilma were purged, families cut down in their prime and villages burnt.

Camara was old when this disease of the blessed, came to her village. She had grown in peace and was married with children when the hordes of Graul came down like demons from the underworld, slaughtering all they could find. Camara led her people to the water's edge and as her son and husband brought about the ships for their escape, they were boarded and burned. Many men of the Thera-ilma, who had heard the song of Thera in the hall of sanctuary, were slain.

"Come." Camara cried, "Our only hope is the sea, where Thera lives, and our peace may be found."
Her people hurried to the beach while their homes were destroyed, and that beacon of fire was like a signal to Thera. The sea's rose in a violent tumult and

The Sundering of the two moons.

the ships that were now boarded by the wicked Graul, were cast in ruin and the bodies of the Thera-ilma were saved and found rest at the oceans floor. Yet upon that storm a bitterness came to Camara and wind from the far north brought an icy chill and her powers of the sea became powers of storm and ice. At her feet the sea froze, and she stepped nimbly upon the wave crest, now frozen in time, "Come, come, we must flee."

Dubiously her people stared at her but as the wicked Graul came to hack and slay, they stepped upon the frozen sea and Camara charged further from the coast, the sea turning to ice on command and her people followed her.

The Graul that touched that ice fell and went to the hall of Agraldin and faced punishment for all of time. So came the greatest toil of the Therailma in the early years and they marched across the wide sea in search for a place of sanctuary. Water she pulled, clean and fresh from the sea and fish presented themselves for their food but they ate only what they needed and what the sea could provide.

For nearly a whole year, the people of Camara crossed the vast ocean and some were lost upon the path, killed by disease, cold or hopelessness. These went to the sea to join Thera.

As summer came to this region, they began to see lands, but Camara feared this place and they marched between two continents, like dangers set to either side and as they passed, the ground to their east rumbled and the sea shook in answer, but she ploughed her people onwards.

At one place she stopped, and she stared down to great depths. Thera seemed to speak to her, and she saw the things that were to come and the pain that would follow for the Thera-ilma. For they were new, created by his weakness in the hall of sanctuary and now they were sundered from the chosen Ilma. Tears she shed into the sea, to the despair of her people, "Sweet maiden of the sea." Her handmaid asked, "Why do you cry?"

"Passing this point I see things to come. Our new home draws near but beneath our feet a mountain stands and soon the seas will part, and it will rise and in time it will become our home, our citadel, our sanctuary. My grandsire, Orna, shall fashion it as he fashioned the moons, and the waters of my father will protect it."

"Such a glorious place it shall be." The handmaiden cried but her voice became stern, "Still I see no need for tears."

Camara smiled at her, "Long shall be that path and it will be full of tragedy, for it is clear in my mind that the tragedy in our village was not all that would befall us and some that will come will be our fault. We will be few when we come to this chosen kingdom, a place to wait for our kind to die out from the tapestry, that is ever woven in Agraldin."

Camara moved them again but at this time, they lost many from hopelessness. For some wished to lay in rest upon the mountain she described. So, when they finally came to the land that she had seen, north of the land of Cradlin, only three hundred of her villagers remained to her from the thousand that had lived

The Sundering of the two moons.

there.
The people of that land were amazed by the newcomers, but they were a pious lot and the lord had received an audience from Drage and he saw in Camara and her people, the toil and power that could only come from a vassal and they offered land for her rest. Camara's power had changed since she had swum in the tropical waters of her home and she had become cold and cold was now her power, so she settled to the far north of Cradlin, where ice covered bays in winter and the sea creatures were large and wonderous.
Havens the Thera-ilma built and from them also came the Thera-graul, whose appearance changed in the years after and they became taller, with webbed feet and bright blue eyes.
Camara though sensed the coming of age, for though she was child of a God, she was born from the womb of an Ilma, and mortality remained while her spirit lingered in such a body. So, now crumbled by grief, she said farewell to her people and departed for the sea and she swam among the creatures of the deep. Her body faded and from it her spirit lingered in the sea. Great and sorrowful was the song of the Therailma, who sang as they did in the halls of sanctuary, but their voices soon lifted in celebration. As the red mountain star came over the sea, her spirit seemed to swim across the horizon and in a sparkle of blue light, the world turned and beneath the red mountain star, a blue star now hung, part of the stars of the vassal's.
Camara became guardian of the waves, but she kept

her power over the weathers of the world and often her grief and anger came out in her power and the winters of the four realms became harsher. She loved her people and came among them at times of great hardship, and she resembled much her father. Her skin was covered in the scales of fish and her hair was silver, that gleamed like the sun upon a still lake.

The Sundering of the two moons.

Of Crio Orna.

In the middle lands between Cambane and Scaraden, while Camara led her people across the wide sea, a roaming caravan of nomadic people were woken by a great earthquake that rumbled in the lands around them. When they awoke, the lands were cracked and in the morning light they heard the cry of a child and coming forward they found, on a pedestal of stone, a small boy.
They believed he had been abandoned by his mother for the strangeness of his appearance. His eyes were of silver grey and his skin was hard and tough. Since they found him upon a bed of ores, they named him Crio, and he lived among the nomadic people.
He grew in stature quickly, but he was shorter than the Ilma around him and he was broad and found work in the blacksmiths of the travelling caravan. He developed a love of stone and ores and could work them at will, without the need for hammer or pickaxe. The world had grown dark in the lands south of their routes, where wars raged for lordship of the realm of Scaraden. The Graul of that land, under orders, hunted for what had become of Drage long passed and for anyone else that might hold the power of the Gods.
So Crio left his people and desire for the northern lands of Drage came into his heart. He walked northward, earning keep wherever he could with his powers. Following a hidden path to the land of Brinsita, he was assailed by a great train of riders. He stared at the Ilma on tall brokin, wearing armour of

hard leather, dyed a deep and violent red.

"Hold sir." Said the lead of the train and Crio cowered under the gaze of his golden eyes that burnt like fire. As the knight jumped from his brokin, Crio bowed, for the lord was tall, taller than the Ilma he had lived amongst and much taller than Crio and his hair was like a crown of flames, "Who are you and where have you come from?" The lord asked in a deep voice, "Winter is approaching and if you have a home you should return to it. Camara has not long entered the sea, but the winters have already grown colder from it."

"I am Crio." He said in reply and the lord's eyes seemed to soften, "And I have travelled north to save my people from the persecution of the gifts that I possess."

The lord stared at him intently, "Gift?" He asked. Crio raised a thin hand, and a stone came with it. To Crio's shock, the lord smiled, and he beckoned for food and water, and he presented it to Crio, "Powers such as these have meaning in this part." The lord said, "Lucky chance, if chance this is. I am Dusan Drage, heir to the house of Dragor and it was my grandsire who defeated the mountain of the north. He often spoke of the powers he was given and foretold of those that would follow. Clearly you are one." He pointed at Crio's eyes, "For the eyes of all Ilma are gold, apart from those touched in the hall of sanctuary."

So Crio, who had been nurtured beside Drage in the hall of sanctuary and had formed friendship with him, found the people of Drage's lineage and fondness

The Sundering of the two moons.

formed swiftly in Crio's heart.

"Let him approach." Said a voice from a black carriage, pulled by two dark brokin.

"Approach sir." Dusan said happily, "You have no need now for fight or flight, the house of Drage protects you."

With a nod, Crio approached the caravan and a wrinkled hand helped him into the carriage. He bowed his head to the old lady of the Ilma, whose face was gaunt, golden eyes cloudy and grey hair thin. She seemed noble though and faded red tear drops showed the sadness that seemed to fill her at his presence, "I am Bela." She said, "And my husband, now long passed, spoke to me often of the vassals that would follow. Come, tell me of your gift so that I may puzzle out which God birthed you."

With that, Crio fell under the protection of the house of Drage, and he was called Crio Minton, for his work with iron but Bela died in the summer of the next year and unlike the others of her house, she was buried in the town of Amoradrage. On the coast of the north that town was built, where the mountain had been swallowed by the sea. The youngest son of Drage founded the town and Bela was buried upon the edge of the cliff, so she could look for her love. A year Crio spent with Dusan in the northern town and their friendship blossomed and Crio taught the people there how to mine the black obsidian cliffs. From that rock, he helped build the lighthouse of Amoradrage, and from its top, the peak of the mountain could be seen, crumbled under the waves.

Bring, son of Drage, became high lord then. Crio built for him, from the same black rock, the dragon gate and the keep of Dragor. Turning the town that was once Cambane, into a place of strength. For the lord, Crio also forged a sword. The blade was formed from the black stone of the mountain and the handle a sturdy bone, studded with gems.

Crio married at this time and his wife bore to him two sons who were also broad in stature, and they played amongst the children of Dusan, and the friendship of their house was great.

Bring, now growing old and scared of his mortality, used his new strength to war upon the borders of the land of the Thera-ilma and in a pointless skirmish the last son of Camara was slain. The vassal of the sea came to Ilmgral in great anger, and she brought a storm from the northern ice sheets down upon the realm of Dragor. The sea of Amoradrage froze and many were killed in the first onslaught, but the storm did not abate, and all began to flee south.

Soon snow began to fall in Dragor as refugees filled its streets, but the cold was un-relenting and Bring ordered the evacuation, but many were too old or too fragile to travel on the southward road and these he tried to send by ship to the coast.

All those that were able, including Crio and Dusan, began to march southward, trying to stay ahead of the chasing storm. Riders they sent and messages were carried by the wings of the karmain to all the southern lands. Soon replies returned and to the shock of Dusan, Scaraden agreed to send a fleet to the coast of Dragor, to collect the refugees they had

The Sundering of the two moons.

left behind.
For weeks and months, they marched through a frozen spring and the beginnings of a sunless summer. They lit great bonfires to keep out the cold but always they found more of their company frozen by Camara's rage and always the storm followed them. The nomadic tribes of the middle lands, and the small towns there, were abandoned and they joined the refugees.

Bring knew that this storm was meant for him, to lay low the people of Dragor, who in their vanity, had stretched beyond their path. The red mountain star was veiled to them, and no prayer was answered by Drage, the vassal of light.

During this march, Crio remained silent, for he felt a swelling power inside himself, that only grew as they crossed the middle lands and in that place, he split the land and the fires of the earth warmed the caravan.

In the morning karmain brought darks words from the south. The ships of Scaraden had been burnt by rebel lords, bent on seeing the destruction of the house of Drage. Crio prayed for the souls of those they had left behind and Bring cursed the land of Scaraden.

Dusan and Crio came to Bring and Dusan spoke, "Lord, this storm does not abate, and we will find no love in the southern lands, unless we go far beyond the borders of the maps we have drawn."

"We must march." Crio said, "By day and night. We must pass through the middle lands where maybe hope can be found."

Bring agreed and again many died in that last desperate effort, and it was a weary, desperate, and footsore folk, that at last came to the realm of Scaraden. The camp was cheerless, seeing that the storm still followed and Crio kissed his wife goodbye and came to Dusan, "I must go my lord." He said to him, "For there is power in the middle lands but it is a power only I can bring forth. The voice of Orna, my father, calls me back there, to stop the wickedness of his granddaughter."

Dusan despaired to hear it, but he knew of the sacrifice of the vassals and why they had come. So, he nodded and Crio continued, "I ask you to look after my family and to give them lands so that they may rule themselves and live-in happiness for the rest of their years."

So Crio left in the darkness of night and again he marched through the middle lands of his youth. The ground groaned and from a great fissure a figure climbed. As tall as a mountain he stood, grey skinned, covered in coarse hair, with hands like stone. Orna, God of the earth, had come.

"Crio." He said in a deep voice, as hard as the earth, like an avalanche of falling stones down a mountain, "The daughter of my son is wrathful. Too powerful is she and her power cannot be contained by the seasons of Ilmgral. Beneath this land lies the defence against her powers but I need your help to raise them."

"If this works." Crio said, "Will my family be safe and the people of Drage?"

Orna nodded his great head, "They will be safe from all the destructions of the world and shall have gems uncounted and will love the stone of your creation."

The Sundering of the two moons.

Crio smiled grimly, "Then my lord, I give you my body."
A great roar went up and Crio felt the power of the earth beneath him and Orna fashioned a rope around the earth and together they pulled it. Great mountains rose from their toil and the middle lands were uprooted, green pastures becoming peaks that reached towards the heavens. In those mountains they trapped the storm of Camara and part of her power with it, so that the peaks of the mountain became instantly covered in snow. A great height those mountains reached but love for his family and that of the people of Drage ran through all that Crio designed and a great labyrinth he made within the mountains for those trapped to the south.

The caravan awoke that night to the ground rumbling as though the Gods warred beneath them and when dawn crept upon the world, and the rumbles died away, they found themselves in the shadow of a great mountain range. Snow-capped peaks caught the red light of the sun, that broke through the clouds at the destruction of Camara's storm. East to west the mountains stretched, a natural guard against her power.
In amazement the caravan went north and at the base of the nearest mountain, Dusan wept, "Saddened am I now for our saving. With this, I fear Crio has returned to his master and in his sacrifice, we are trapped in a land that does not love us."
But Bring, his father, came to his side and pointed towards a breach in the mountain, where a dark but

grand chasm stood, "Have no fear, for that door was made for us and it is wide enough for all our caravan." Bring began to climb towards the door, "Come, Camara's storm will trouble us no longer."

Through the cavern the caravan went. They found that it was indeed a path made for them and it opened into a hall that looked like it had been carved by a thousand of the Ilma for a hundred years. Many more of these halls did they find, ready for habitation and those who had lost their homes in the middle lands, settled in these but they paid homage ever to the family of Drage, who had brought them south and sheltered them.

Long was the march of the caravan and always many went through great paths between mountains and through them, to new homes but the people of Drage continued northward. On the fourth day of their march, they came to a great opening and before them a bridge spanned between two mountains. Far below lay a great valley, like a mountain had been hewed down just to form that walkway but at its centre, a large piece of rock remained and sat beside it, a figure could be seen.

Dusan approached without fear, already guessing who the figure would be.

"Ah finally you have come." The figure said, cloudy eyes looking up at Dusan who knelt beside him. Sadness filled the son of Drage, as he took the hand of Crio, who was aged almost to the point of death.

"The five days since last we met lie heavy on you, my friend." Dusan said and wept but Crio laughed.

"I have toiled many years of the Ilma in one night but

The Sundering of the two moons.

behold my works." He gestured to the mountains, "My lands shall protect the north and should harm befall Dragor from the south, more of my children will come." Crio pointed to the northward arch at the end of the bridge, "Before you lies Sikaorna. Gift it to one who you will but I ask that the lands to the west, where gem and ore are to be found, you give to my family, in payment for my sacrifice. Through them will our friendship be held."

Dusan nodded, "Of course my friend and they will be our allies but shall be subject to no one."

Crio nodded and Dusan beckoned for his family to come and in the arms of his wife he departed the world, and his spirit went into the mountains to serve Orna again.

In a chamber built into that spot, they buried him and workers after fashioned a statue in the likeness of Crio who was buried there. They spent the night in that high place and as the stars wheeled, they saw the red mountain star and the star of the sea beneath, that seemed to weep and then, giving off its own silver light, the star of iron burnt brightly.

In joy, the caravan of Drage departed and soon they came to the grand hall of Sikaorna, and this Bring gifted to his daughter and her followers remained there.

Coming back into the north, the people of Drage basked in a summer come at last.

Crio's family left then and took those that remained of the middle lands, and they fashioned for themselves, homes to the west.

The snow had melted, and life slowly returned to the

northern land. Dusan worried what they would find in Dragor but again the power of Crio saved them. For in the Dragon keep, built of the black stone of Amoradrage, those who could not escape, were protected from the storm. There was much celebration for the return of the lord and ever after they celebrated the rising of the mountains in spring and remembered Crio who died to save them.

The Sundering of the two moons.

Of The vassals of Life and Death

Some years after the dividing mountains were raised, the people of the Ilma looked towards the red mountain star, with the star of the sea and the star of iron falling beneath it. Yet they saw still, the stars of the twins, dimmed by the light of the other stars of the vassals and they waited patiently.

In the year 164 A.V, a great drought came from the deserts of the southern great continent and was borne upon the Camara stream to the lands of Calerou. Famine came in that burning summer and many of the Ilma starved. A pestilence seemed to have befallen the land.

In the town of Burnda, two children were born, and they were known at once as souls that Gadrika had touched in the hall of Sanctuary, for both seemed to shine with an un-natural light and power was held in their golden eyes.

The first born was strong even in birth and he cried with a voice of power. His skin was almost perfect white, with almost none of the scale lines of the Ilma. His mother, seeing him in full vigour, named him Krim. Expecting a second child of strength, they were shocked when Krim's twin was borne sickly. Though he had the same almost perfect skin, it hung loosely off the child's frame and his pupils were so dilated that the golden irises were almost hidden. He cried in a weak voice and many despaired that the second child of Gadrika would not live beyond a couple of days.

In despair, they named him Agral, that in the years before was the word for hope as the hope that was weaved into the tapestry of Agraldin. Though it is a name whispered with despair now. The power of Gadrika could not be so easily slain though and both children lived and came quickly into childhood.

Krim was ever the foremost and he was strong in body and kind in mind and although Agral was weaker in body, he was quick to learn, and his mind was far superior to his brothers.

There was great love between the brothers, but jealousy and resentment was ever in Agral's heart and even young, at the age of eight, the brothers clashed and the power inside Agral was revealed.

As the universe lies in a balance of life and decay, as did these brothers and while Krim was meant to give aid and healing, Agral was meant to give wisdom and comfort and cleanse pestilence from the world but in his resentment, he took pestilence and stored it, mutating it until his powers became a dark and wicked thing. So, as he fought with his brother, his power came through and a sickness fell on Krim. Oil flowed in the waters around Burnda, and fish died. Tree and flower became rotten, their sap pungent, flowers poisonous.

Only around Krim, who lay in stupor upon his bed, was the pestilence of Agral kept at bay and through his power, the sickness relented. Rising from his bed, Krim saw the devastation of his brother and revealed his power. No want of glory was in his mind, and he saw the goodness in all things and all people. He sang

The Sundering of the two moons.

and the oil vanished from the water and the fish were cleared of their taint. The trees bloomed again, and the flowers lost their pestilence but to Agral he did nothing, seeing then the opposites of their power. Krim could heal some wounds but only in giving strength for things to heal themselves and he could cure a small grove of disease, but Agral could heal all if he wished and could remove pestilence rather than create it, if guided properly.

People now feared Agral, and his name was spoken ever after as a word of death. His mother ferreted Agral away to the fort of Lersatomen, but Krim lived with his father and together they went across the dividing sea and was welcomed by the lord of Scaraden. Long had been the wars of Scaraden with the vassals of the northern realms but in their wish for the gift of immortality, they loved Gadrika and seeing Krim, who seemed to be a perfect image of what the Ilma would become, they welcomed him and in a tower of white stone they let him live.

Agral grew tall but slender in his years at that fort and being locked away made his resentment grow and his powers changed greater from their course. At first he had helped heal people from torments of the body and mind, now he only gave them in jest and scorn. So great was the fear of Agral in that time, that the lords now wished for an end to him. They came to his chamber late at night and drew blades of metal to strike him down. He awoke swiftly and the would-be murderers were stricken dumb. Then Agral's power changed completely. All of a sudden, he was in

Agraldin, to the realm of those yet to be born, but he was in a dark place, full of shadows. There, voices of those who had done ill cried in their torment. This power and darkness Agral tapped into, and he became now separate from Gadrika, a true vassal of death.

Returning to Besan Gretan, Agral killed his would-be attackers. Their souls he corrupted, and he forbid them access to Agraldin and bound them to that tower so that their howls of pain were heard ever after.

Agral brought shadow out of Agraldin and fled into the night. Long he travelled across the southern land, killing animals to sustain himself while he worked on his newfound power. He found himself passage over the ocean and came in time to the land of Scaraden.

Krim had grown strong as well, but humble in his power and many flocked to his banner. He took a wife and had two children. Krun, like his father, was tall and bold. He was also touched in the hall of sanctuary, and he was born with dark green eyes. Roots came from below his eyes and leaves grew within his hair. From him came the Krun-ilma, for the people that lived among him were changed by his power.

Mina was his daughter. She was beautiful as a flower in bloom and as slender as a stalk. She loved all the plants and insects that fed upon them and when she sang, flowers bloomed, and creatures came to listen to her song.

Agral came to the tower of Krim late in the night, but he was welcomed by his brother and Krim took Agral

The Sundering of the two moons.

to live within the tower. Agral lovingly received this offer, but his heart became cold as he saw all that his brother had, that he never could.

Bitterness grew again in Agral's heart and at a time he snapped, and he took Krim's wife for his own and in the anger at her scream of rejection, she died, and her spirit fled to Agraldin. In his torment, shadow surrounded the tower and Krim fled in fear with his two children, who could not yet defend themselves. Rage grew in Krim's heart for the death of his wife, and he planned his vengeance for one he loved dearly. Now she sits in the hall of weaving, and she weaves mostly to heal the world and Krim comes to her still and Mina weaves flowers in her hair.

So again, Krim fled his home, and he came in time to the realm of Krunmelkin, where he became a great lord. Krun, now come to manhood and burdened by grief, took his followers into the great wood on the edge of this land and formed many dwellings. Those who lived within the wood began to change and under Krun, they became the Krun-ilma.

Mina lived with her father until she was married, and she formed many beautiful gardens, but Krim was restless, for he had not forgotten the beauty of his wife or the one responsible for her death.

News soon began to reach him of the lord of death. Agral had become mighty indeed and had declared himself a herald of the Gods. Many flocked to him to learn of their fate and Agral ever twisted their desires to fit his need. In the end he had the ears of all the great lords of that land. Through dark acts he fathered children and these he abandoned but set in their hearts a dark desire for power, that would follow them ever after.

Learning of this set a fire in the heart of Krim and he began the mustering of men and sharp weapons were fashioned for the march of war but on the eve of battle a messenger arrived at the gates of Tukaorna. He was brought before Krim, who was arrayed in armour of perfect white bone and at his side he carried a gleaming sword. Krim welcomed the man and to his nature he offered him bread and a seat at his table, but the figure shook his head, and a flick of his hand dismissed all the servants in the chamber. Krim reached for his sword but gasped, heart filling with joy. The hood was lowered and before him stood Gadrika, the God of life and protector of the hall of sanctuary.

Krim bowed deeply but a hand, neither hot nor cold, lifted his chin so that Krim stared into the eyes of life itself, "You are troubled child." Gadrika said in a musical voice.

Krim nodded, "I am my lord." He replied, "For I believe I have part of your power within me, as does my brother, but it seems fated that one must do war upon the other."

"It is not fated so." Said Gadrika softly, "Not unless Agral has seen it in his mind to work these things. All of the children we have touched have had the free will to go astray, to abandon true course for their own desires but as yet, only Agral has done so and that has twisted his power. I come to warn you, that not by your living hand will Agral die and in going to meet him, you will only join me closer than your allotted

time and many darker deeds will come from it."
"I understand my lord." Krim said solemnly, "Yet it is clear in my heart that you knew something of this. None of the other children of vassals hold powers and yet your touch has lingered on my children. Their powers are meant for the healing of those who cannot defend themselves and they will heal the hurt done by Agral. For me, I can only end his suffering of men, either on the Ilmgral or beyond it."
Gadrika nodded and he took from his back his white cloak and he fastened it onto Krim's back, "Then I can aid you no longer child, but I will also not forsake you. You shall sit with me as your brother should have and you shall sing in the hall of sanctuary, to set into the mind of the Ilma the study of health, to the betterment of all."
Gadrika seemed to fade and then Krim was alone. In the early hours, his army set forth and the cloak that Krim was given, was on his standard and though it was but white cloth, it held all who saw it in thrall. By the power of that standard, the waters of Camara did not hinder them and no army came from Scaraden to stop their landing.
Krim led them eventually to the tower of Agralita, which Agral had turned into a wicked place, and they besieged it, but a separate battle took place that none could see. Krim put out all his power of healing and it fought against the pestilence of Agral for dominion of the land. Feeling that challenge, Agral came forth and his forces followed him, urged on by his strength. In that onslaught the banner of Gadrika was ripped apart, and the cloak was taken by a mournful wind.

On that battlefield, where Ilma slew Ilma, the brothers were re-united and while they battled, their minds connected, and unspoken words echoed in each other's thoughts.

"Why brother?" Krim asked as the brothers grew closer, their powers driving against eachother, neither giving an inch but a sword Agral drew, and it rested upon Krim's heart.

Krim stared at it and for a second his power was nearly overcome, "Have I not treated you with kindness? Why do you persist to cause harm to me and the world?"

"Kindness." Agral spat, his eyes burning with rage, "Look at me." Krim did and his brother's repulsiveness shocked him. Haggard, rotting, skin hung off his bony frame. His hair was falling out in clumps but still Krim pitied him, "You took all the power for yourself." Agral continued, "We were meant to be equal, but you stole everything from me."

"And so you took my wife from me?" Krim became like a flame then, heart kindled with rage and his power overcame Agral. A healing power Krim sent and at once his brother changed. He grew tall and strong, with skin of perfect white scales and his pupils receded, showing brilliant golden eyes, "See what you could be brother." Krim begged, "Call back your forces, relent from this venomous dream and be as a brother to me again."

The sight of what he might have been only enraged Agral more and as his dark power once again overcame Krim's, he was more gruesome than ever.

The Sundering of the two moons.

He drove forward and such rage was in his spirit, that no power of Krim could stop him and he drove his sword between his brother's breast and the blade broke at the hilt.

The skies wept for the passing of Krim, and his forces were swept away by the hordes of Agral. The banner of Gadrika returned on a swift breeze and lay upon the body of Krim. A light blinded Agral and as he pulled the cloak away, Krim was no more. In his anger he threw the cloak back to the air and the wind picked up to take it. Across the sea the cloak flew, across the green pastures and the gardens of Mina, before it came to Elmlin in the great wood, and it drifted towards Krun's palace amongst the trees. It landed with feet and Krim stood before Krun, yet he was no longer of this world.

He shone with a golden light and light was in his eyes. The cloak he now wore upon his back and at his side, sheafed, was the broken blade that had killed him.

"Do not weep son." Krim whispered in a voice like the songs sang in Agraldin, "And do not turn to rage, for I am now doing the task that was appointed to me and I am the guardian for the souls of those who will do good upon the world."

"But father tell me?" Krun yelled as he drew his sword and he looked a lord indeed, mighty and strong, a leader that the Ilma would follow, "How can rage not fill my heart. My uncle has taken both my parents and yet Agral walks free upon the land. Is this Gadrika's fairness?"

"Do not question the thought of Gadrika, for he sees what is woven in the tapestry. He tried to stay my hand, but I went for my own selfish revenge. Your uncles time will come, and he shall face judgement for all his sins. Flourish with your people, for my blood shall protect you." Then Krim departed to Agraldin but the houses of Krun and Mina flourished, and their people knew no sickness or disease.

In Agralita, Agral grew even more sickly, and he sent out vast pestilences that crippled the lands around him. He also touched into Agraldin, and he dragged souls from their rest and gave them the bodies of those dead, but he chose only the worst to fill his ranks.

This was the worse deed of Agral, for Gadrika purposed those souls could only inhabit Besan Gretan for a short while, less they grow stale and bitter of the world, and he knew that this was done in mockery of himself.

Then, for the first time in all of existence, anger festered in the heart of Gadrika, who could not touch Besan Gretan truly, nor could he bring death to those who inhabited it. Krim, he sent to his son, who sat now as a king of the Krun-ilma.

"My son." He told Krun, "Now is the time. Gadrika has given his blessing and it is time now for your uncle to end his tyrannical hold on the world and to go to serve penance in the halls of Agraldin."

Krun looked down and Krim perceived that his son had grown into the role indeed, for he appeared sad at this fate and there was no want for vengeance in his eyes, "But Father." He said sadly, "You could not best him, so why should I now?"

Krim smiled, "You go not to best him but to cleanse

The Sundering of the two moons.

the land of his taint once he is bested, to bring balance back to Besan Gretan. Your uncle has pulled himself thin and the power he now has drags him to his death. His hold on the powers that Gadrika gave him are faltering. Go with the blessing of the quadrant and all those who go free."
With that, his father departed and Krun set to work gathering his host. Many of the Krun-graul and Krun-ilma marched with him and Mina called great lords of the Ilma, and she rode at the head of a great host and many animals marched at her side.
This great army crossed the sea and like his father, he was nearly unchallenged in the land of Scaraden, and the small host sent against them was swiftly swept aside. Soon the host came to the fortress of Agralita and many of the soldiers became sickened as they drank from the corrupted streams or ate the food of that land. All had fallen under Agral's sickness and only the power of Mina kept those affected in the lands of the living.
Long the siege lasted and during it, Krun brought great trees that sucked the poison from the streams and lands, and the corpses of those trees decayed swiftly and gave fresh soil for the growing of many flowers that Mina cultivated.
Soon Agral's power began to waver and the fear of him lessened and the doors of Agralita were opened. Krun came then to the chamber of a dark tower where his uncle lay in rest and from a scabbard, he drew a knife. Sharply the eyes of Agral opened and he thrust with his power, but it was weak and Krun was young, come now into full manhood and his power

surrounded Agral.

"Yield." Krun ordered, "And I may find mercy in my heart for the killing of my mother and father."

Agral laughed, and the sound was sickeningly seductive, "Mercy." He spat, "You are like your father, weak, destined to stay in the line painted for you by the Gods. The Ilma are to be a higher power, custodians of the universe, under no dominion of the Gods."

Like a cornered animal Agral struck but the blade he had concealed, caught meekly in Krun's armour of thick bark, "You have no power now that can overcome that of Gadrika's." Krun said in a deep and commanding voice, "Now Kneel."

Then Agral knelt and in his bow, he revealed that he was garbed in thick chain mail, even while he slept and at his waist was a sword hilt, but the blade had been broken from it. Krun then drew his own blade and anger overcame his sense, but his hand was stayed by a deep voice.

It was the pure voice of Krim, "This is not your murder." The vassal of life then came to stand in front of his brother, "I pardon you brother. You shall serve Gadrika still, to lead those who follow in your folly to a better task and to use them to heal the wounds of the tapestry that your treachery has caused."

With a flash, Krim cut his brothers throat and while Agral writhed on the floor, Krim tore the cloak of Gadrika in two and one half he clasped to his shoulder and the other he lay on his brother's now motionless body. The white cloak became almost black with the blood that stained it, but a wind picked up and lifted it

The Sundering of the two moons.

and with it, came Agral's spirit.
More like the Ilma he looked in death, but he was still tormented. Chain mail he wore ever after and in guilt he bore the sword hilt that killed his brother. The stars of twins shone brightly that night, Krim's a bright gold and Agral's a silver that flared often, showing the torment within himself.

His body, Krun took back to Krunmelkin, and he buried him in a grave in Ashanitakrun, where the land was held in winter ever after. Then he gave up his sword and became a great songwriter and he lived to a great age before giving himself over to the trees of his home. He became then a vassal for all the forests of Ilmgral and the creatures that lived in them carried his song after.

Mina did not grow old, while young she forsook the world, and went into the service of her father and served him on Ilmgral. She guided souls in the tasks of healing so that wisdom carried in the minds of the Ilma to undo the taint of Agral. Her kin were ever the targets of his scorn and he desperately aimed to destroy that house.

With the passing of Krun, the vassal's of Ilmgral were complete and the power within the Ilma was ready to come to full bloom.

That ends the story of the vassals of the holy quadrant. Now we divert from the tales in that book, for although many of the stories to come are told within that work, many lies are told in their telling and the Graul were often treated to harshly.

There was one more vassal not mentioned in the book of the Holy Quadrant and he does not feature in the red mountain star, for he was of the Graul. Karomin of the great continent had once served a member of the Ilma, slain by the rebellious Graul and he took to saving as many of the Ilma as he could but in her rage, Camara mistook his intent and drowned him. In great sorrow did she come to Agraldin and beg the forgiveness of Gadrika. Hearing this plea, Thera pulled Karomin's ship from the depths and Gadrika hallowed his soul, and he serves now as the vassal of the southern oceans, the only Graul to ever be gifted such an honour.

The Sundering of the two moons.

Of The Coming of the Powers and the Unification of Scaraden.

With the passing of the vassals, the Ilma became ready for their gifts. It began not long after the passing of Agral. The Ilma born, soon developed powers over the elements and in gaining that power they became mighty lords, placed even higher than the Graul, who became more subservient to the blessed people.
As the powers became apparent, lords in Scaraden took it as a sign of the Ilma's separation from the Gods and of their right to rule the universe. Long had Agral resided in this land and his whisperings against the Gods festered in the hearts of the Ilma there. His children also lived still in this land, and they took no lordship but whispered words ever in the lord's ears.
In the year 300 A.V Lord Lidon of Scaraden, who had been touched by Agral in the hall of Sanctuary, grew dark and terrible and Colda, heir of Agral, whispered in his ear of kingship. He built in reverence of Agral and the immortality that he promised, a great four towered church and declared himself king of that southern realm. Many great wars he fought in his conquest and many dark deeds were done, cementing Agral's hold over that land. Lord Lidon, with Colda his advisor, would become the first king of Scaraden and the first king in the lands of Ilmgral. A deed that angered Gadrika greatly. Ever would Agral's whispering be heard in that land and from there would the division of Ilmgral be sown.

Book Two- Notes as both squire and Lord.

By Bruska Crud.

Preview.
One of the oldest known journals from those who served in the early days of Ilmgral. Bruska rose from a squire to a high lord of the realm of Cradlin and served in some of the darkest days of those early years. The story focuses greatly on Selosa Aquitex. Maybe one of the greatest warriors of this time, though her full story is a sad one and not much is remembered of it.

The Sundering of the two moons.

Chapter One- Who I must serve.

I woke for my first day early, nerves filling me from head to toe. The sun was bright outside as it shone upon the walled city of my home. Cradlin, the city of two towers and it was those towers that met me as I stepped from my door. The tower of Umoria to the left, its silver walls reflecting the sun, while the tower of Aradtoria to the right, cast the streets in an eerie red hew. I was dressed as expected of me, a shirt of the green colours of my house, with sturdy leather trousers.

The streets were full of Graul, working as was their place. I was of the Ilma, and though I came from a house of little wealth or position, I still held the power of that race. I walked awkwardly, partly through my nerves, and partly from the scabbard at my waist. It was my fathers, a decorative piece, made of bone from an age when our ancestors had fought with such things. The Ilma were weapons now, but customs remained from that uncivilised time.

My walk took me through the market of Cradlin, where here and there foreigners talked in dialects strange to my ears. Children stared at the Krun-ilma, so garish in their appearance, but they came often in late summer, to work off trade debt at harvest time. No one stared at the Thera-ilma who walked the streets. Regal and splendid they looked, cloth of blue matching their eyes. They lived to the north of the city; in havens they were gifted in years past when Camara had crossed the sea in search of a home.

As I approached a hall between the two towers, my nerves grew rapidly. Brokin of great size, with huge curling horns, grazed in a stable by the guard's quarters. Swift steeds and battle steeds were crowded within. I swallowed hard as I took my place beside other Ilma stood to attention there. All I had schooled with, played with but now no one looked at eachother.

Today was the day when our futures would be decided. Harvest was approaching and at this time new lords were given rank. These lords, and the lords they stopped serving, would need squires to attend them, to learn from them. My two older brothers had passed through this ceremony. They had earnt renown as squires of great lords and had become lords of lands themselves when their years of service were up.

I rubbed a hand at my face, a face that made me nervous. I could have passed for one of the Graul with the amount of red my face carried. Long brown hair covered what it could but bright red scales on my bulbous nose showed clearly. I was of the Ilma though, and I deserved my place here.

I and the four other squires waited until the bells of Umoria chimed and the guard captain of Cradlin stepped towards us. He was of the Graul, but he was strong and steadfast, enabling him to rise to the highest rank that a Graul could.

One by one, the squires were called and told to report to their new lords. One, would squire for the lord of Cradlin. That was expected as he was son of the high lord of Lianosuta. Two others would be travelling to

The Sundering of the two moons.

the borders of the land of Dragor. That was a high honour due to the trade that flourished in those parts. The fourth I pitied, for he went to serve in a small town near the Thera-ilma, where the land was frozen. That pity lasted for only a second though, "Bruska Crud." The Graul said and I stepped forward hesitantly, "Report to lady Aquitex."
My heart sunk. I had expected better than that. Mr oldest brother had squired for the lord of Carano and had earnt great renown during the Graul rebellion. My other brother now ruled in a new southern fort, near to the western forest. I had expected better than Selosa Aquitex. She was a warrior, an exceptional leader of troops but no true lady. She governed a village to the west, which was nothing more than a few small farms and inns. I wanted to learn trade, culture, how best to form laws and increase the power of my hold. Under Selosa, I would learn only how to fight. Something I had no intention of doing. Suddenly the reason for this charge became clear. My oldest brother had married Selosa's sister, this was a family affair.
I tried to hide my disappointment as I came to the hall beneath the tower of the dusk moon. I could see Selosa sitting at a table, laughing with other lords. Most ladies who ruled homesteads dressed regally in fine clothes. Selosa though wore armour even in the city. Plates of bone were intertwined and covered in orange leather, that was scuffed and damaged from many battles. The first of which I remembered well. Selosa was young during the Graul rebellion, still three years away from her right time as a squire. During that

terrible week, when Ilma had been slaughtered in their beds, she had rescued the lord of Cradlin and rallied a large defence of the city, of which my brother aided. She had been made a squire that week and studied under the greatest generals the lord of Cradlin had. She was the best now.

She was not unattractive for all that. She was covered in muscles, but her face was delicate, her golden eyes large and red scales touched only at the bottom of her neck.

I stood by the table and waited patiently for her to notice me, which she did immediately, and her gentle smile caught me by surprise. She was actually beautiful, with her big eyes, small nose and stunning smile. That made serving her even scarier. I bowed and she laughed heartily before she stood. She did not even come up to my chin, but her arms dwarfed mine.

"Bruska." She said in a voice that was soft but commanding.

"My lady." I replied, and I could feel the sweat on my hands.

Her eyes turned hard, "Lady?" She asked, "Do I look like a lady of the court, married to some fat lord?"

Panic filled me, "No."

"I am general Selosa Aquitex, commander of the western marches." I saw a glint in her eyes, "You should call me sir. A more befitting title for my rank."

"Yes sir." I said meekly and the lords on the table snickered. This would be worse than I thought. Not only would I serve a woman, but I would also be admonished by one as well.

"Do you have a brokin?"

The Sundering of the two moons.

"Yes." I did, a soft and gentle steed.
"Then saddle yours and mine. I have spent too long preparing the Graul of the west march should we ride to war, and I wish to be back at my homestead by nightfall."
Gingerly I nodded my head and left. The stable hand directed me to Selosa's brokin and I took it to a nearby stable where my own mare was housed. Selosa's brokin dwarfed my own. It was nimble, but tall, with white fur and long, broad, curling horns. I knew that it must have come from the plains of Kuratex and at a large price. Mine was a sturdy beast of these northern lands, covered in thick brown fir and with only little horns. A brokin made for a hard day's work.
Her saddle surprised me, for it was covered in flecks of metal, sharpened into small arrow heads. The Ilma rarely wore metal, for all the Ilma held some power over it. I had seen lords of Scaraden covered in plate armour once, but it was said that they lived in it most of their lives and learnt great control over it. The armies of Scaraden also wore metal but that was for a worse reason, to keep the Graul that wore it as slaves to their Ilma generals.
Once I had saddled the brokin, I waited for Selosa. She came to me swiftly, still wearing her armour, but I saw many little metal knives at her belt. She noticed my curios glance.
"No one I have met can best me in control over metal and so it becomes my greatest weapon." She said and took my hand in a firm embrace, "I know you are well trained Bruska, yet I may ask you to die in my name.

You may at times need to address me as sir but in private I ask that you use my name, or Sel if it suits you better."

My voice came out in a whisper, "Thank you."

Together we rode out of the walled city. Fields of golden crop lay before us, ripe and ready for the coming harvest. In just two weeks these fields would be barren and the granaries of Cradlin would be full. Then Camara's harsh winter would begin and the streets of Cradlin would be covered in snow. I almost regretted that I would miss that but playing in the snow was a child's game and I could be considered a child no longer. We rode along a hard stone path that soon gave way to cracked dirt the further away from the city we came. The fields changed also, becoming now meadows of grazing trillon or thick woodland.

"I am right in thinking that your brother married my sister?" She said after an hour of silent riding.

I urged Dwell, my brokin, to ride alongside her war steed, "Yes." I murmured, "Just after the rebellion."

Her gaze considered me, "I do not remember you at the wedding."

I felt flushed by her large eyes, "I was there, and I remember you. You wore a suit of dark green."

She laughed harshly, "That fool father of mine wanted me in a dress." She laughed again and it was cruel. I felt I would be scared to hear that laugh in battle.

"Battle." I whispered. That was surely where this path would lead me. Some fool would start a rebellion and Selosa would be sent to quell it with me by her side. We rode in silence again and as we crept over a hill; a small collection of houses came into view. It was an

The Sundering of the two moons.

exceedingly small village. Farmhouses dotted the landscape but in the village proper there were no more than a dozen houses, made of brick, with thatched roofs. An inn stood in its centre, but it was smaller than even the smallest in Cradlin. Selosa led us to the centre of the village, where a large house stood. Five Graul came out of the house as soon as we approached. Three were women, though one could only be barely called that. The other two were men, one wiry the other strong. The strong one approached first. He was armed with a small shruda. He nodded to Selosa and then to me, "No trouble to report." He said swiftly, "There was a dispute between two farmers that was handled and travellers from Minton caused a brawl in the inn but there were no wounds." "Good work. You may retire Anka." Selosa said and the man nodded and made his way towards the inn, humming happily. Selosa turnt to me, "Even the smallest village must have guards." She explained, "A dispute in a village could see many murdered and everyone in a village plays a crucial role."
The second man approached, her scribe and he delivered notes and spoke of the prospected harvest in the area. All was good news. His wife came over and told me that my rooms had been readied and that their daughter, who was older than myself, but still smiled flirtatiously, would show me to my room. The last girl, maybe my age, her blonde hair ragged, and her face covered in red spots, was not introduced but she hurried after the maid, and I saw her carrying out many chores.
I dismounted and took the reins of both our brokin.

The stable at the back of the inn took them and I made sure they were both well fed and groomed before I retired myself.

That night I waited on Selosa and before bed, I cleaned her armour and became acquainted with the village. By the time my head rested upon my hard bed, I was exhausted beyond reason.
I woke to screams. It was late night now and Umoria and Aradtoria shone almost to their full in the night sky. Only in my tunic and shorts, I ran down the stairs. A flame, kindled within my hand, guided me. The cries came from the kitchen. The sight of the maid made me slow. Pity was in her eyes as she gestured towards the kitchen. I walked slowly as the cries became gentle sobs. It was the young girl. She was sobbing, eyes shut tight as Selosa gently cradled her. Selosa nodded to the hearth and my flames shot towards the still smouldering wood. It caught in an instant and flames reflected off the two girl's white scales.
"She has nightmares." Selosa explained, "Her family served in Cradlin until the rebellion. Her family were killed in front of her, so I took her into my service. She still dreams of that night." She cradled the girl and waited on her, until the girl cried herself to sleep. Then I carried her to her bed. By this time the sun was rising, and I had no thought for my own bed. I took breakfast of flat bread and cheese before making a fresh broth for Selosa. In that time the girl appeared, and her eyes darted to the floor at the sight of me.
"How are you feeling?" I asked and her lips quivered.
"Fine." She replied nervously.

The Sundering of the two moons.

"What is your name?"
"Sand." she replied in a slow voice, before adding hastily, "My lord."
I laughed, maybe to her shock, "I am no lord."
"But you are of the Ilma."
"Not all Ilma are lords. My name is Bruska, and you should call me thus, for we are both servants in this house." I lifted my hand and a pan rose from its place on the fire, "Though my tasks may be slightly easier."
The smile fell from her face, "I'm sorry I kept you awake."
"What troubles your dreams Sand?"
"My mother was taken by men not my father. The same fate may have befallen me if it was not for the lady knight. I dream of that."
All my mirth went. I remembered the horrors of that night. Ilma had stirred the Graul up. Rebel Ilma who stole lands and set the Graul to bad causes. We had locked our doors and not opened them until the all clear had been sounded but many were buried in the days that followed.
Sand was soon ushered to her chores and Selosa woke not long after. She ate her broth with bread and ordered me to share some with her. Then we went about tasks, giving orders for excess grain to be sold in Cradlin, taxed by her of course.
As the sun approached midday, she turned to me, "Do you hunt?"
"I have at times sir." I replied, thinking of the one time I had gone with my brothers.
"Then we shall go hunting." She smiled, "I must purchase dried fish from my uncle. I would send my

scribe, but he would charge double, and I hope that a trade of grain from here may sweeten the deal. There will be a chance to go hunting along the road." She stood and stuffed a last soggy piece of bread into her mouth as she did, "Go and see Anka. Ask for ten shruda's, then have the brokin saddled."

I did as commanded and found ten shruda's, their shafts no longer than a foot, with leaf shaped blade's almost as long. These were metal, used for throwing by the Ilma. I strapped five of these onto Selosa's saddle and did the same with my own. Selosa soon appeared in a dark green tunic. She mounted swiftly before examining the shruda on her saddle.

"Is it far sir?" I asked as I mounted Dwell.

"Three days at a steady pace. The roads are well cared for and we shall make good time." She pulled from her back a shruda that glinted in the sun. It was amazingly engraved, and as it caught the light, it appeared as though fire ran through it. She relaxed her hand, and the blade hovered a few inches over it and turned from her power. I gasped as she flicked her wrist and the shruda shot through the air, landing with a thud in the side of a wagon. She winked at me and with another movement of her wrist, the shruda returned.

I marvelled at her control. I could throw a shruda, I had trained ever since my powers had first developed but my control over metal was weak. Water was my domain, I even felt I could best the Thera-ilma in my control of that.

We started off late that afternoon with provisions for four days of travel. I knew my maps and knew that

The Sundering of the two moons.

several small towns and villages covered here to the coast, but Selosa had little intention of staying in inns. She wanted to camp out under the stars before winter came and snow settled on these hills.
We rode across the rolling fields of the north, passed ripe crops and grazing fields or meadows left to the creatures of Mina. We rode all the way until the sun sunk below the horizon and although summer still held, the air became cold. We camped on the edge of a wood a short distance from the road. I collected wood and set to starting a fire, which was no problem for one of the Ilma. Flames formed in my hand and these I sent in a long stream to the wood. The fire was soon blazing, and we warmed ourselves by it. That night was clear and silent apart from the occasional wagon that went along the road or the cries of night birds. It was clear that Selosa had spent much of her time in situations like this, either on her own or with bands of soldiers.
She told me of the stars and their histories, and of those whose stories had not yet been woven into the tapestry. It surprised me how much she knew of the holy quadrant. I had studied it little. It was then that I noticed a pin on her cloak, bearing four tall peaks,
"You follow Orna." I said in my surprise.
In these lands it was often Livella who was most loved, and many lords took passage to Brinsita when they died, to travel by river to the sea. Orna, the god of the earth, was most loved in the lands of the dividing mountains or to the west in the kingdom of Kuratex.
"I follow all of the Gods." She said, "But my strength

comes from my command of the metals he created. It is in his creations that I hold my trust in battle."
"I had never thought of it like that." I admit.
My family, like many, worshiped Livella the most and went only to the church of Livella in Cradlin. If I followed her belief, then it should be a phial of sea water that I carried with me, in reverence of Thera. We slept under the stars that night and when we woke, the ground was covered in white frost. I was miserable as I ate dried meat and a collection of oats while I needlessly tended a fire that would be no trouble to relite. Selosa though had woken in good spirits and had vanished with first light. She came back with a small rodent, with two small horns and a spiked tail. She instructed me in the gutting and preparing of the tularp, that I had only eaten farmed and well cooked. She did not waste time on the animal that I would usually have eaten stewed or roasted. Instead, she took out a sharp knife and sliced pieces of fatty flesh into a pan. All that was left was a skeleton that she tossed towards the two brokin. Dwell, who had never eaten much meat, turned his nose up at it but Grald, the war brokin, chomped on the bones happily, blood mingling with his white fur.

We rode again all that day, not stopping to do any hunting but to my delight we rested in a small village, in an inn that was warm and the food filling. The next day clouds came on a swift breeze from the sea and brought with it damp rain from the realm of Krunmelkin. That was the worse day in the saddle, using my power over water to fend off the rain. I did

The Sundering of the two moons.

so in the camp that night as well and did not sleep
until dawn crept on the horizon and the wind carried
away the rain clouds to reveal the dawn stars.

"Wake up Bruska." Selosa yelled at me, and my eyes
slowly opened. It felt like I had only just closed them,
but the sun was already high in the sky, "I have done
your job and prepared breakfast and ridden into my
uncle's town to warn him that we are hunting in his
region. Eat and prepare or the gupin's will all be back
in their dens before we arrive."
I sat up slowly and began rolling my blankets, "I am
sorry sir. I should have woken sooner."
To my surprise, Selosa gave me a sad smile, "At times
of war I may grow angry that you oversleep and then
you will crave your bed, but this is a time of peace,
and we are in a fair country at the end of summer.
Sleep is a precious thing at times like these."
I ate quickly and then we rode into the woodland
nearby. Dwell whinnied at the sound of crunching
fauna beneath his feet, but I kept him on, following
Grald who seemed to take everything in his stride.
Suddenly Selosa stopped. She dismounted and ran her
hand across some wet mud, "The gupin have been
near here but they have now moved off to the fields
beyond. Come Bruska, we shall find easy sport in the
fine sunshine."
In a flash she was back in her saddle, her heels digging
into Grald, who lifted his horned head and charged.
Dwell followed and we broke through the trees into
an unkept field, full of tufted grasses and fallen trees.
There gupin grazed happily. I had never seen wild

gupin so big, their large fatty bodies covered in white winter fir and big teeth protruding from their snout like noses. Grald lifted his head again and with a smile Selosa egged him on. I followed behind and mirrored Selosa as she pulled a shruda from her back. A foot away from her, the shruda followed Grald, completely in her control. I held my shruda in my hand, fearful of my own control.

The gupin looked at us and with a cry they dispersed. Selosa spotted one that hobbled as it ran. She lifted her hand and the shruda went high above her. She then threw her hand forward and the shruda followed but the gupin turned at the last minute and the shruda shot into the ground, quivering.

The gupin turned towards me and I opened my palm. The shruda quivered above it and with a cry I let it fly. My throw was off, but I gave a triumphant yell as it embedded in the gupin's rear end.

"Good hit." Selosa cried as she turned swiftly, blonde hair billowing behind her as another shruda hovered at her side. She ran towards the now crippled gupin and her shruda sped true towards the target, taking the creature behind its neck, and killing it cleanly. Grald came to a halt beside the motionless creature and Selosa dismounted, her power pulling both shruda's from it, "A successful hunt." She smiled, "This will be some gift for my uncle's dinner table." She looked at me, "You need some work with that shruda though." Then she laughed, "Wait with this, I will go into town and request a cart. Not even Grald could carry such a beast."

The Sundering of the two moons.

It did not take long for Selosa to return with a cart driven by two poor looking Graul, with long matted hair and dirt across their faces.
With their help, they lifted the gupin onto the cart and the two Graul butchered a leg, that would feed their families well or they could sell it for grain to last the winter. We followed the cart and then coming over the hilltop, I saw the most magnificent thing I had ever seen, the sea. I had thought of it, imagined it but nothing could compare to its vastness and its majesty. On the edge of a cliff, I could see a town, but my eyes could not focus on it. Instead, they were drawn to the horizon where I wondered what lay beyond.
"Wait." I said, halting both Selosa and the cart. My eyes strained towards that line between sea and sky. There we many ships on the clear ocean but the sails that appeared then, filled me with fear.
"What is it?" Selosa asked, looking between me and the sea.
"Ships." I pointed towards the now growing number of sails that were coming into view.
The Graul beside me laughed, "There are many ships in the ocean my lord. We trade much with the great continent. The wheat and gupin of our land is well sort after."
Selosa looked hard now and her voice became stern, "These are no trading ships." She said, "Trading ships do not move in formation or in such great number."
My heart seemed to drop. Hundreds of sails could be seen now, so many so that it was like an island was moving towards us on a strong breeze, "That is an

invasion." I whispered, fearing something I had never truly seen, war.

"Take the gupin." Selosa yelled, "Ride now, ride for the nearest village towards Cradlin and have them send out their fastest riders and whatever birds can send messages."

The two Graul nodded, knowing now the truth of those ships. Their wagon turned and disappeared down the hill, kicking up dust as it did. Suddenly the coast seemed to ring with the sound of bells and signal fires burst into life. Selosa sped off upon Grald and I did my best to follow.

"What are we going to do?" I asked and pulled the wind to carry my words towards her.

"My uncle is no warrior." She explained, "He will try and defend the coast, where many good soldiers will be killed. If we do not rally to one point, then the armies of Melkin will ravage our lands before they besiege Cradlin. Lianosuta to the north will hold for a while but that is why they do not sail towards those treacherous seas."

We rode into the coastal town that was now in a state of panic, with people hurriedly collecting bundles and arms-men waiting for orders. I waited outside the manor house and when Selosa returned from speaking with her uncle, she bellowed to the crowd, her power magnifying her voice, "ALL MEN ABLE TO BARE ARMS MUST HEAD TO THE ARMOURY AT ONCE. WAR HAS COME TO CRADLIN. WOMEN AND CHILDREN MUST GO WITH ALL SPEED TO THE CITY." She smiled in an evil way, "STAND WITH YOUR LORD AT THE CROSSROADS TO THE EAST. THERE NO

The Sundering of the two moons.

INVADER SHALL PASS. RISE NOW. RISE NOW PEOPLE OF CRADLIN."

The male Graul, who knew their place, left their loved ones and moved sullenly to the armoury. I did not pity or envy them, for my path most likely led to the same place as theirs.

"What now sir?" I asked Selosa as she came back to me and the two brokin.

"We head back to my homestead, to get my people ready for war. Then Bruska of house Crud, we ride to battle."

Chapter Two- The Battle of the crossroads.

We rode hard for the next two days, stopping rarely for brief rests until night came. Every town we passed, Selosa rallied a Graul militia and before we left for the next, sullen men took up whatever weapons they could find.

We arrived in Cradlin in the early morning on the third day and news of the invasion had spread before us. Outside of the gates, lines of tents housed soldiers from all the nearby towns and banners swung in a breeze, bearing the crests of many Ilma lords.

Selosa took me within the tower of Umoria, where lord Livinor Cradlin held his war council. The high lord of the realm of Cradlin did not look overly regal. His brown hair was held back in a ponytail while red scales under his eyes always made him look tired, but he was strong and tall. He was dressed in robes of a dark green, but he had a long lucrax perched under his arm and he stroked it like he was familiarising himself with its feel. Selosa went to the congregation of lords, but I held back.

"Do we hold here?" Livinor asked, "Can we hold here?"

"Nay." Said one. He was young, probably a couple of years older than me and he wore orange armour that showed him as a lord of the city of Carano, "Already our lord is bringing his forces and that army is set to fight an open battle and not a siege."

"I agree." Said another, a general from Cradlin, "The Harvest is not yet completed, and we have not the provisions to feed an army in a long siege. The armies of Melkin will find the fields here ripe for their picking. If we stay within these walls, we will feed the armies of Aginor and leave the coast undefended for their reinforcements."

"Why now?" Livinor asked.

"Aginor Diactra has only recently been crowned king of that land." I heard one of the lord's spit, "It is said one of the children of Agral's house is his advisor." My throat tightened at the name of the vassal of death, "He has put the thought of becoming the first king of the world in his mind. Kuratex will come under his sway if he can mount a successful incursion into our lands."

"My lord." Selosa's soft voice seemed strange compared to the deep voice of the male lords, but she spoke with no less conviction, "My uncle and all the homesteads between here and the sea are gathering their Graul. They will hold the crossroads northwest of here. If we gather our forces there, we may be able to hold until the army from Lianosuta can strike them from behind."

Livinor nodded, "A wise choice but I will not leave this city and the people here undefended should our holding action fail"

The young lord from Carano stepped forward, "My lord, do we not have an alliance with the four other realms of this land, just for this purpose? Have riders been sent to our friends?"

"They have." Livinor replied, "and I wish they would arrive sooner but the lands of Minton and Drage are far away, and we cannot wait for them to arrive and aid us. By the time they have mustered and marched here, we would be already well besieged."

"I do not suggest we wait for them my lord." The lord from Carano spoke again, "I suggest we get the armies of Drage and Minton to march here, to create a defensive siege around the city. That will be the prize Aginor seeks. If he holds Cradlin, then he will open up all these lands."

Selosa nodded, "I agree. The armies of Drage will pass through the vast farms of Grinlavine and bring enough provision to aid our people while the armies of Minton will move unlooked for from the south. The Thera-ilma though, should travel west first and march with the army of Liano."

"Agreed." The lord of Cradlin nodded, "Ride my lords, gather the armies. No man who can weild a weapon should be left behind."

The rest of the day the preparations began. Riders returned from Minton and from Dragor late in the evening. The armies were readying and would march the day after next. Weeks of constant march it would take for them to arrive, by that time many of the people of Cradlin, myself included, could be dead. The night before we marched, Selosa took me into the city and into the workers area where blacksmith hammers were ringing constantly.

"I do not know whether you are ready for war my friend and I am saddened that it has come so soon for you in my service." She said to me.

"Thank you, sir." I replied in a small voice as I tried not to think about the battle that awaited me.

The Sundering of the two moons.

"Come, I have something for you."
She walked into the bustling street, the wind bringing with it the warm heat of the furnaces. I looked at her, bathed in the red light of the fires. There was no gleam in her eyes, no smile on her lips. I knew then why she took the path she did. This was what she was meant for, she was a warrior to her core.
Here and there, those who the day before had been farmers or shop keepers, now clumsily thrust bone shruda's into the air, or checked loose fitting leather tunics. Many looked petrified and I was sure if I could see myself, I would have looked the same. Among them was the trained soldiers. Graul who had sort for more than meagre livings on a farm, but these were too few, not enough to hold back the full might of the kingdom of Krunmelkin. Selosa led me to the back of one armourer. It was the largest and it bore the crest of the house of Cradlin, the militaries armourer. There would be no brokin shoes or broken farm tools in there.
An old man, who was clearly one of the Ilma by his height, was running his hand along a blade that glowed hot from the fire he poured into it. He smiled at Selosa before plunging the glowing blade into a water bucket. When he pulled it out, the blackened blade was placed on the anvil. I knew how lucky I was to be blessed with coming from a house of the Ilma with some power and position. Not all Ilma were that lucky. Many were weak, barely able to hold their power, and these found work doing what little they could, only slightly favoured over their Graul counterparts.

"Selosa." The old man smiled, and my eyebrows raised at the lack of title given to the lady, "I have just finished off that piece you asked for."
She seemed to ignore the slight on her honour, "How is business Kortan?"
"Was steady till this morning. You would have thought war would better the position of a one powered Ilma, but I am too old for such things now."
"Will you ride with us?" Selosa asked, showing him great respect. I realised I still had a lot to learn.
The old man reached behind him and put on the table a tunic of green leather over light but strong plates of bone, "I shall, and I may earn some renown and money for my retirement, though a grave seems more likely. My sons ride in the lords Caravan so at least I know my house will be secure." He gave me a small smile that I hastily returned.
"One Ilma is worth a hundred Graul on the battlefield my friend. It would be an honour to fight alongside you. How much do I owe you for the work?"
The old man placed a gnarled hand on the armour, "Pay me when we return sir Selosa. I hope it fits the young lad."
I looked at the tunic, my eyes widening before Selosa patted me hard on the back, "I had not the time to measure my young ward this morning, but it will serve him, I'm sure." Her hand pushed me forward, "Take it, you will need it."
My heart raced as I picked up the armour and quickly pulled it over my head. The weight of it was strange but as I examined it, I could tell it was well made and it would be a burden I would carry thankfully, "I cannot

The Sundering of the two moons.

thank you enough sir." I said as me and Selosa left the busy street.

She laughed to my shock, "You may thank us both when the battle begins but for now, we go to rest. Forget your night tasks, for we march at first light." As we walked, many Graul came up to ask permission to march within her ranks. Many she accepted, apart from those too young or too old. The women who offered, she rejected outright but to these she said, "You may find renown fighting here to defend your home as I once did. War is not just fought on the battlefield, and you may need to fight in a different way, doing the tasks of those who do not return."

We spent that night in a crowded hall in the tower of Aradtoria. I was amazed that even with the noise of many other sleepers and the looming threat of battle, I slept soundly that night. A sleep of peace and undisturbed dreams.

As dawn approached, the bells tolled solemnly, and we rose from our blankets. I walked with Selosa, and we marched onto the plains beyond Cradlin, where soldiers were lined in rank. We walked to a line underneath the banner of her house, two crossed and bloodied shruda. There were some Ilma who followed her, members of her father's household and they each commanded one of the groups lined up behind her banner. Slowly Selosa examined the troops and gave them some provisions. Some she sent away, due to a look in their eye or a deformity in their body. These did not return to the walled city but instead were given camp jobs. Many tradesmen followed the lines of troops, spared from combat. Weaponsmiths and farriers were among them. Healers, engineers, and scribes also.

At the back marched two groups of male and female Graul and Ilma. One group was dressed in white. The order of Gadrika were healers and followed armies at times of war, never taking sides in a conflict. The others were dressed in black, and their heads were bowed. The order of Agral would tend those who had died and make sure they found passage to the halls of Agraldin. To me they were a foreboding sight. My first true idea of what was to come.

Horns rang clear on the breeze and a great shout went up from the troops. Across the field, soldiers marched under the banner of two mugs. The banner of the house of Carano. This almost doubled our numbers and I searched among the armoured men for a sight of my brother, who would march as one of the lords of Carano's bannermen.

We set forth to a rousing song that filled my heart with joy. Slowly, rank by rank, the soldiers began to march along the great road out of Cradlin. I heeled Dwell and followed behind Selosa, the sound of many marching feet following me.

We marched all that first day, a slow march but we stopped for no meal. My legs were cramping by the time I stepped from the saddle. At once the camp workers began setting up tents and the soldiers picketed the horses in orderly lines. I waited on Selosa in her tent but as night fell, I went in search of food. Footsteps approached and I turned, delight filling my

The Sundering of the two moons.

eyes, "Brother." I said as we embraced eachother. I had not seen Losa since the spring, when he came in a caravan with the lord of Carano for a feast. He wore the colours of Carano, a tunic of sunset orange. We did not resemble eachother much. Red scales still covered his face, but his jaw was stronger and his nose less pronounced than my own, "I had not expected to see you." I said quickly.
"I came searching for you." Losa said solemnly, "Are you nervous?"
I looked down, my face probably revealing the nerves that were welling up inside of me, "It would be a lie to say I truly understand the situation." I replied, "But I am ready to do my duty."
His golden eyes stared into mine, "That is the reason I came. If you would like, I will relieve you from Selosa's service. You can serve as my squire, in my caravan."
I felt touched by my brothers care and part of my mind wished for that but something else grew in the back of my mind. I had only just joined Selosa's service but already I knew that I loved her and would follow her wherever she led me, "I thank you, but my place is by Selosa and that is where I will stay."
He smiled at me, and I thought for the first time that he may have considered me his equal. His strong hand gripped my shoulder, "Very well brother. I hope that we may meet on the battlefield and when we do, the brothers of house Crud shall earn great renown."
I heard the soft footsteps of Selosa approaching behind me and turned to smile at her. She returned it, but her eyes were on Losa, "Lord Crud. How fares you and your men?"

My brother nodded, "Sir Selosa. They are well as am I and we are eager to defend the lands of our home. Your soldiers seem ready for battle."
"Thank you sir."
Losa again grasped my shoulder, "I will leave you both to your tasks."
He departed without another hug or piece of affection. With the newfound respect, came the truth that I was now a man full grown, on the eve of my first battle and there was now no place for such things.
Selosa approached me slowly as I wiped a solitary tear from my eyes, "He asked you into his service, did he not?"
I could not lie to her, "He did sir."
A sad smile formed upon her lips. She looked no longer like the warrior but more like the lady who had cradled Sand to sleep, "I would allow such a thing. If you would ask it."
"No sir." I said without hesitation, "I am your servant, and I would not abandon you so swiftly. We are in this together and I shall do many great deeds in your service. Cowardice would lead me to my brother's caravan. There I know I would be protected, shielded far away from the battle. That would be a terrible day for myself, especially were something then to befall you, who I already love like family."
She seemed stunned, her golden eyes regarding me differently as she ran a hand through her blonde hair. Suddenly she laughed heartily and pulled me into a swift embrace. When she released me, her smile was full.

The Sundering of the two moons.

"A fine speech." She said gayly, "If I knew you had such strength, I may have looked at you differently Bruska. You shall fight beside me when the battle comes and if you become a lord yourself, then I shall marry you."
I laughed, knowing the jest of her words. Marriage would not have suited her. That night we ate and drank as equals before I fell into a restless sleep that did not reinvigorate me.

The camp was torn down in an instant and the regiments had re-assembled before the sun had crept high above the horizon. We marched on, down roads and through fields, hooves and feet moving to a sombre tune.
Behind us walked the soldiers under Selosa. Seven hundred militia from the villages around Cradlin, including her own homestead. These would be the ones doing the dyeing this day. Behind came the trained infantry, wearing the green armour of Cradlin, each carrying a large lucrax, with its curved bone blade and long wooden shaft. Each held many bone shruda's as well.
Behind them marched the cavalry, the guard of house Aquitex. Picked and trained from an early age to ride the best and strongest brokin. These also wielded lucrax, bone blades for the Graul and metal for the Ilma. All told, Selosa commanded nearly a thousand Graul and thirty of the Ilma.
To our front, the lord of Cradlin rode. He had two full battalions of cavalry and rank upon rank of Lucraxia. He also had two battalions of archers, wielding the

long range brinlon. Many Ilma he had in service as well. Those of small families, who did not have the luxury of squiring but could earn money and maybe position serving in the army.
Behind our lines, the armies of Carano marched, with a thousand militia, archers, and infantry. Our army could not have numbered much more than four thousand. Nothing like the ten thousand that had been spotted by scouts in the armies of Melkin. I knew the odds. Without the armies of Lianosuta or the Thera-ilma, this holding action would not work.
"We are lucky in a way." Selosa said and I looked at her in surprise, "If the armies of Melkin went and besieged Lianosuta, then he would already have a haven to land men and fodder, but Aginor is inexperienced. He wishes to take Cradlin early and did not want to risk a lengthy sea siege."
I stayed silent, staring into the lines of men in front of me.

Late in the afternoon we arrived at the crossroads and found another thousand men. The militia that Selosa's uncle had assembled. Others had marched to Lianosuta and would be hopefully marching with the army from there.
Slowly our soldiers began to be arranged along the flat plain of the crossroads. The camp workers set up a mile behind, but Selosa told me that few would return to use such a camp. In the distance, dust showed the approaching forces of Melkin. Now nerves nearly overcame me and I said every prayer that I knew. Songs and prayers were fluttered by the

soldiers also but many of these faltered before completion.

It was an agonising hour before I caught my first sight of the armies of Melkin. We were lined up on the right flank of our army, behind a deep line of lucraxia. In front of us, a huge amount of infantry appeared and behind them came cavalry. Horn calls rang out amongst our camp. I felt like we were standing on the edge of a knife. No one was talking, or even breathing it seemed. I looked up as men from Melkin began to fly into the air. I had seen wind riders from Melk before but that was in shows. Now they looked like swarming carrion birds, swerving over the battlefield at the commands of the Ilma flight masters below.

I saw no hope for our victory and my eyes strayed constantly to the northwest, where the armies of Lianosuta would appear from.

All at once the calm was broken. From the enemy line, a rain of arrows launched into the air. Shields were raised but as the arrows fell into our soldiers, screams and shouts rang out in such a chorus that it was almost deafening. I was at no risk from these arrows, out of range as I was but I felt for those who waited on our orders, knowing that soon another swarm would be launched towards them.

"Be strong Bruska." Selosa said, a smile on her lips but steely determination in her eyes, "Now is the time to be strong."

I nodded, my voice catching in my throat. Soon our own archers answered and screams, and shouts came from the armies of Melkin, and I felt my blood rise at that. A horn blew and the infantry advanced in one long line. Wind riders soared over them as they marched, dropping stones darts, or at times burning oil over our ranks. A volley of arrow fire peppered the wind riders, and many were skewered, crumpling in their wingsuits before hurtling into the ground with a sickening thud.

The armies of Melkin charged and the two lines of infantry crashed with the sound of thunder.

I looked up as the battle seemed to turn into chaos. One of the wind riders were heading for our line but I saw the glint of metal, as one of Selosa's shruda soared into the air. It caught the wind rider hard in the chest and he crashed to the floor at the hooves of Dwell, who reared and growled.

"READY NOW!" Selosa yelled as she turned Grald to the side, "Lucraxia, long line." She shouted and the soldiers in front of us spread into a line, one hundred Graul long, five rows deep. The cavalry of Melkin was approaching and they crashed hard into our line of lucraxia. Many brokin and men fell but a few of our enemy broke through. Water formed around my hands, and I launched it at the nearest rider. Graul and brokin collapsed to the floor, before a lucrax was driven through their armour. The cavalry withdrew and then charged again; each time more breaking through the line of lucraxia.

A shout went up to our left. I looked across and saw lines of cavalry pouring through the soldiers from Carano, who were vastly outnumbered and were being swiftly overwhelmed. I said a silent prayer for my brother.

Selosa suddenly sat up high upon Grald, "Now is the

The Sundering of the two moons.

time, flank them, flank them." She drove her heels into Grald's side and charged, the rest of the cavalry moving with her. I spurred Dwell on, doing my best to keep pace. Dwell responded to all my movements and pride welled up in me for the beast, "I will make a war steed of you yet." I cried over the crashing hooves. The riders in front of me crashed into the enemy first, breaking them like water upon rocks. I saw none of those our stampede trampled. Suddenly I found myself at the head of the column of riders and I pulled from the ground, a great swirl of water that charged ahead of me and Dwell. I yelled as we struck hard into the line of infantry. Shruda's flew in front of me, crashing into our enemy while my wave threw others off their feet. I had never killed before, but I felt no shame in that moment. Blood lust filled me as I heeled Dwell to go faster. It seemed to me that maybe our cavalry charge would win the day, but a horn call signalled our doom. We were charging headlong into the cavalry of Melkin. Two speeding walls approached eachother, neither able to turn aside. The thud as brokin hit brokin was horrendous. Horn's ripped skin or knocked rider from steed. No weapons were used, our brokin were our weapons. Steeds doomed to die. I hit the line late, and my water pummelled into a brokin, knocking it aside and toppling its rider, who screamed as hooves surrounded him. Then I suddenly lunged sidewards. I stared into the face of my enemy, mad rage in his golden eyes. Before his bone shruda could strike, I formed fire in my hand and the bright burning spear split his mouth.
He slumped over the saddle and his brokin reared,

charging hard into Dwell. Then we were both falling, and the ground came up to surround us both from the still charging armies of brokin. Air fell out of my lungs as I hit the ground hard, but I rose and looked down at Dwell. She whimpered, the horn of our attacker, broken, sticking from her side. Blood fell steaming onto the floor and then Dwell fell silent and rage forced swirling fire to surround me. No war steed was Dwell, but she died on fields she had never grazed on, in a war she could not comprehend. My fire scattered brokin and ignoring my hurts, I climbed from my earth walled sanctuary.

The battle had now turned to utter chaos. Infantry from both sides were mixed with the now stationary brokin. Weapons wielded in all directions struck whoever they could. Again, I controlled my strongest weapon and anyone I saw in the dark green colours of Melkin, I struck with it.

I searched for the white fur of Grald and Selosa amidst the chaos. A shadowed loomed above me and my eyes turned skyward. One of the wind riders was stalking, his face showing that he was of the Ilma and in his hands he wielded fire.

instinctively my water struck him, and he went limp in the air. He came down with a sickening crash and I lost him in the foray of brokin and Graul. My heart skipped several beats at that. Killing one of the Graul was fine, but one of the Ilma, one of the chosen people. That was something dark, works only Agral could sow.

In that moment it seemed like more of the Ilma joined the battle and one pressed me hard. Fire, wielded like

The Sundering of the two moons.

a whip, cracked in my direction and all I could do was bring water from the dead around me to block the blows. Steam surrounded the battlefield and I lost sight of my enemy for a second. A glint of bone was all I saw, and I screamed as it skimmed against my cheek. Rage filled me again and in a sudden wind the steam cleared. The Ilma was charging, shruda in his hand but I was quicker. Water crashed into his stomach, and I ripped the shruda from his grasp. I collapsed on top of him, screaming in my blood lust as I thrust again and again.

By the time I moved the battle had passed me by. To my left stood the un-used ranks of Melkin and to my right, the battle raged on. Again, I heard the twang of arrow fire and the earth lifted to protect me from that volley. Thuds echoed into my barricade and as the earth fell, I stared at the next line of cavalry, charging swiftly towards me. Fire formed in my hands, ready for death that rode on galloping hooves. Suddenly I ducked as hooves came from either side. Cavalry in the orange of Carano swept passed and in another thunderous charge they collided with the armies of Melkin.

"The battle turns ill." Losa said to my right. His orange armour was covered in blood. On his head he wore the skull of a trillon, fashioned into a helmet, "Your lady fights still on the right flank. You should go to her." Around my brother, lords on great brokin appeared, every one of the Ilma. My brother joined them, and their hands lifted as they heeled their steeds. Fire formed in a great wall in front of them and they cried as they charged into the commanding lines of Melkin.

I turned away from my brother to stare at the armies still fighting behind me. Selosa was in there and I had to reach her. I charged back into the enemy, a great wall of water surrounding me. This knocked many of my enemies to the floor, who fell easily then.

I saw Selosa, fighting in a great open space against one the Ilma. She was true in her mastery of metal. Knives or shruda's she sent straight into the Ilma, who deflected them with fire, water, or whatever other power he could manage but never did the blades waver when he lifted his hand.

Heedless of anything else, I charged into him. His fire wound around my arm and I responded with water and both of us went crashing in opposite directions. I saw the glint of the metal shruda as Selosa threw it, but it went wide and skimmed only the arm of the lord. He smiled triumphantly as a great snake of fire launched towards me. My arm reached out, the shruda quivered and just as the snake went to strike, the Ilma lord was struck dead, the shruda protruding from his back.

The fire dispersed in a second and I laid on the floor, breathing hard.

Selosa pulled me quickly to my feet, "We are surrounded." She said, "Our defeat is imminent. We have the better soldiers but not the numbers."

Fire from myself and Selosa, kept the enemy at bay for a time but I felt myself tiring. It would not have been long before I could not muster a tear let alone anything else. I saw a break in the line and vain hope of flight filled me but across the field I could see militia

The Sundering of the two moons.

Graul fleeing, pursued, and run down by the brokin of Melkin.
Just as despair filled me, the sun set, and it seemed like the woods beyond the lines of Melkin were ablaze. Then there was a blaze. A great swirling wall of fire that spread from the woods to the lines of our enemy. Cavalry and Graul charged through the flames, crashing into the back line of Melkin who hurried suddenly forward.
The new soldiers broke upon the hierarchy of Melkin, surrounding them in a swirling ring of fire and water while the other forces continued to ferry the army into those already fighting. Me and Selosa held our ground and slew any Graul that approached. Then the line of new cavalry passed us and grabbing two riderless brokin, we mounted and joined the onslaught. As I rode, I looked to my left at the Graul beside me and what was in his hand. Delight and pride welled inside of me at the sight of it. On a long pole he bore a standard. The moons of Umoria and Aradtoria over a blue sea, glimmered in the light of the Ilma's fire. The army of Lianosuta had arrived.
As we rode many of the Graul of Melkin dropped their weapons and cowered where they could and slowly the call for mercy spread amongst them. By a miracle and good timing, I had survived.

Chapter Three- The True Price of War.

I wandered the battlefield, stepping over the bodies of Ilma, Graul and brokin, that lay there. Many were still, motionless eyes staring towards the night sky. Carrion birds crowed everywhere while Graul in dark black began instructing in the care of the dead.
I ignored the order of Agral and marched the battlefield, searching for the place where Dwell lay. As I walked, I stared at the bodies of those fallen, wondering if any had been by my own hand.
I tried to feel something inside of myself. Beyond the sickness of the smell of the battlefield, I felt only one other thing, shame. Shame that I had so quickly fallen into such a baseless act and participated in such a fruitless endeavour.
I looked up at the stars. They were veiled by a thin whisp of high cloud, like Livella herself had called it too withhold her wisdom from us, who had strayed so easily. Out of nowhere I find Dwell, laying where I had left her in her protective mound of earth. Some Graul lay upon her, but I do not move either. I knelt beside Dwell and pulled the horn from her side, and I prayed that she may find some meadow in the land of Agraldin where she could graze in peace.
Slowly I left Dwell, and with my last goodbye, I went to leave the battlefield. Back towards the camp I stumbled upon Selosa, knelt beside a body. It was the armour smith who lay there, the earth around him was scorched but he was pierced by many bone shruda. I looked down at the bone tunic he had made

me. It was burnt and grazed from blows I had not even noticed, "His work protected me and yet we will not have the chance to pay him for it.

Selosa looked up at me, golden eyes glistening with tears, "We will repay him in the security and safety of his family."

The night air was becoming chill, and I could feel my eyes threatening to drop, "We should head back to camp sir. We will have a long day tomorrow."

She stood slowly, and we walked silently back to the camp and her tent that had been erected for her. I made her a simple supper of bread and dried meats that we both ate slowly; our bodies close to exhaustion now. Then we slept and I slept like never before, my body on the point of exhaustion but I woke early. I stumbled around the camp, preparing a fire for Selosa when she gave a cry. I ran to the tent but stopped in the threshold. The young lord of Carano, from the war council, stood at her side. Selosa's eyes turned towards me, tears streaming down her face. Before I knew what was happening, I was on the floor, screaming, pounding my fists into the dirt. Selosa ran towards me, gripping me as I screamed. Through teary eyes I looked at the lord. In his hands was the skull of a Trillon, fashioned into a helmet and I knew it well.

Selosa was speaking to me, but the words never sunk in.

"Where is he?" I asked.

The young man coughed, "In his tent." He looked down, "He was alive when we found him, but he has succumbed to his wounds."

The words hit me worse than anything had in the battle. I turned and buried my head into Selosa's chest and cried. She held me tightly, like she did to Sand back in her house, but I was not that young girl. I was soon to be a lord, I had to show strength. Slowly I forced the tears to stop, forced everything to stop. I pulled myself away from her and stood, hoping my feet would support me.
"With your permission sir, I would like to go and see my brother." I said sternly.
Selosa seemed put off by my sudden turn, "Of course." She whispered.
I walked out of the tent, into the bright sunshine of the morning. A few questions took me to my destination. I walked in but stopped dead.
"I'm sorry my lord." I said in a whisper.
The lord of Carano turned towards me, golden eyes regarding me carefully. His blonde hair was cut short, framing his strong face. Red scales swam around his jaw. He looked kingly and I knew then why my brother had so easily joined his service, "What do you need?" He said, his voice not stern but musical.
My eyes instinctively went to my brother. He lay on a bed, arms folded upon his breast. On his head lay a disk with a mirror placed within, on his mouth a phial of clear water, on his breast a disk bearing the star of Livella and on his stomach a disk of many different metals. A woman, garbed in black, stood at his head, her eyes cast towards the floor. These were the funeral rituals of my lands. I never thought I would see it upon my brother.
The lord's eyes softened, "You must be Bruska."

The Sundering of the two moons.

"I'm sorry for disturbing you, my lord." I said slowly and went to turn but his voice stopped me.
"No Bruska. It is a sad day to lose a brother, for that is also how I thought of him." He beckoned me forward, "Come and pray for one we have lost."
I walked over and stood beside the lord, who placed a hand on my shoulder, "Were you close?" He asked me.
From there I could see the stomach wound that had killed my brother. It appeared to have been done by a burning brand, but it had clearly festered. I turned my eyes instead to the mirror on his forehead, watching myself reflected upon it, "We were separated by many years, but he always wanted to protect me. I fear that may have even been his last act."
Lord Aila Cardon shook his head, "It was folly, that last charge of my caravan. If we knew we were that close to victory, I never would have sent them."
I look down. The fact that they did, meant that our roles were not reversed. That was a debt I could never repay my brother, "We fought the battle to kill as many of our enemy as we could, not for hope of victory. I see that now. We fought so that Cradlin may have had a greater chance to defend itself. We could never have known that the army of Lianosuta was so close."
Aila smiled at me, "You have a sharp mind. A trait of your family."
My eyes turned to the disk filled with water, the mark of Thera and a thought suddenly struck me, "There were no Thera-ilma? None have come since; did they abandon us?"

"A council will be held to discuss such matters." He seemed frustrated, "But there is tension between us and the Thera-ilma. Further disputes over land."

"My brother's helmet." I said then, changing the subject swiftly, "It was a gift from yourself, wasn't it? I will bring it to your tent."

"No need." Aila said, "For now it is a gift to you, to keep the friendship of our houses."

I was touched but could find no words. We prayed for Losa and after, the disks were collected from his body.

Aila gave me a smile, "I shall leave you now, for we must all grieve in our own way." He walked to the edge of the tent but then stopped, "Bruska. There will be a seat missing at the council tonight. I would be honoured if you were to take it."

"I should serve Selosa." I said in shock.

"I shall speak to her and If I know her like I do, then she will not deny this request. House Crud, who have lost a son, should have a say on the future." With a nod he left.

Then I was alone with my brother and the woman of the order of Agral. The Graul would tend my brother until he was put in a boat for his final voyage to the sea. There he would be taken by Krim to the halls of Agraldin, to weave the tapestry for the ages to come.

I arrived back at Selosa's tent, and she offered me a small smile, "I have been told you are coming to the council tonight." She said, no emotion in her voice.

"If you ask it sir, I shall wait upon you. I feel that is too lofty of a place for myself."

The Sundering of the two moons.

"Nay." Her eyes became cold, "You fought well yesterday and have earnt the honour to represent your house."

The rest of the day I spent working, taking guard of prisoners as they began to pile up the dead. Some would return to Cradlin, to be sent to Agraldin in whatever way the families saw fit, but most would remain here. Ilma members of both the order of Agral and the order of Gadrika, separated the earth to create two deep pits. In one was buried those of the armies of Melkin and in the other, the soldiers of Cradlin and Carano. These mounds were then covered with earth and stood like two hills either side of the crossroads. A reminder for all of time of the battle I fought in.

When I returned to the camp, I was allowed a rare luxury. I bathed in water heated by my power and scrubbed the dirt and dried blood from my body. Then I dressed in a green shirt and trousers, fastened by a buckle in the shape of brokin horns. They made me think of Dwell and my mood was solemn as I walked alongside Selosa to the council of high lords.

Many men were already seated, and I took my place beside Aila Cardon, with Selosa to my right.

High lord Livinor Cradlin entered, and he looked truly regal now, in a coat of dark green, finished with gold trim around the wrist. Behind him came lord Aginor Diactra, dressed in rags, with four young squires behind him, all of them Ilma. Murmurings began at once among the lords and Aginor looked angrily at us all. My eyes turned towards the floor, afraid to meet the almost mad gaze of the man who had brought all this upon us. I guessed he must have held great power. It was rumoured all those of the line of Diactra did, but he looked pitiful now. I examined him slowly, doing my best to not let it show. Although he looked vicious, his golden eyes were bloodshot, and his breaths were ragged. Guards stood behind him, Ilma also and one had his hand positioned towards Aginor, most likely restricting the prisoners flow of blood. The debate began at once. Lords voiced their opinions on what was to happen to Aginor and his soldiers. Some suggested mercy, others asked that all the soldiers should be held prisoner, unless a ransom could be paid to release them. The consensus though, was that the soldiers should remain to aid in the harvest before they would be sent back to their homes defeated but alive. I had stayed silent, as I watched Aginor rage at every single suggestion made. I thought I should have felt more anger towards the man, whose war had seen the death of my brother, but I was cold, and I felt nothing for the man, or the fate that awaited him.

There was no agreement on what was to be done with him and the debate had turned nasty between rival factions, some wanting peace while others wanted blood. Lord Livinor watched the debate silently, hands rubbing at tired eyes. Then he rose, and all voices became silent, "We have all lost a lot over the last two days." He said in a commanding voice, "And we have all voiced our opinions. All saved one." I faltered under the gaze of his piercing eyes, "One among us also lost a brother this day but has not yet spoken. Stand lord Crud."

The Sundering of the two moons.

I looked between Aila and Selosa, who both nodded their heads and I stood slowly.
"You lost deeply at this man's hand." He beckoned towards Aginor who snarled at me as spit fell from his mouth that I realised was full of air, gagging him, "What do you believe should be done with this fool?"
Before I could speak, Selosa stood, her hand reaching for my wrist, "I ask your forgiveness lord Cradlin. My ward is young, and grief is in his heart. He has not yet the clear mind for such counsel. Do not put your decision upon his shoulders."
A wave of Livinor's hand forced Selosa to bow and sit. Livinor's eyes never left mine, "He stands here not as your ward, sir Aquitex but as one of house Crud and I would hear what they would make of such a situation."
Finally I felt something, hatred. Aginor was smiling at me, maybe sensing the weakness that I sensed in myself at the time but then I smiled. Aginor was bound, a captive and it seemed his life was in my hands. I could show him something, that the lies of Agral did not touch this land, "My lord." My voice was cold, "We won a victory yesterday, a victory we should never have had to win. We were asked to defend our homes from savages." Nods of agreement came from the lords seated around me, but I tried to ignore them, "I think our greatest victory remains in compassion." Now there was stunned silence but in the corner of my eye, I saw Aila smile and Selosa gripped my wrist tightly again. Livinor just regarded me carefully, "We do not take lofty kings to rule us. We do not kill for fun or sport, and we have homed

three vassals within our lands. We are the chosen Ilma, us of Cradlin, Minton and Drage, who have held these vassals. We are the best that our race can be, and we will show our savage cousins that we are the chosen of the Gods. My lord I speak for my family and my brother who was taken from me, that true victory will be shown with mercy."

The stunned silence continued. Everyone looked at Livinor. Flushed, I sat back down in my seat. Selosa smiled at me and Aila grasped my shoulder affectionately.

Livinor finally nodded, "For one who has lost much to show mercy, must truly be the will of the Gods." His gaze strayed to the prisoner, "Aginor Diactra, of the house of Mina. What folly have you shown, to fall so far from such a noble house? You will go free back to your land and will pay tribute to us for the remainder of your days and agree never again to attack these lands. To secure this, your wards will remain here, for one is your son. No ransom will free them, and should you ever again seek war against us, then they will be put to death."

The wards, most no older than myself, gave a shriek but Aginor looked despondent and nodded in swift agreement. He was led away, and his wards were pushed in the opposite direction. Soon they would be given clothes and would serve Livinor for the rest of their lives. This ended the council and that night we drank heavily of fruit mixed with shaving of potent fungi. I went to bed merry as colours danced in front of my eyes and I fell asleep to the noise of party in the camp.

The Sundering of the two moons.

I woke early to a dry mouth and head pounding from the drink. I went about my morning tasks, even with Selosa rising much later than myself. Then I saddled Grald, and we prepared for the march back to Cradlin. That ride took two days and I cried at my first sight of the city as I rode upon the carriage bearing my brother's body. The two towers looked beautiful in the morning sun but what astounded me more was the many tents and barricades erected around the town. Flags of bright red swung among the camp, the symbol of a dragon upon them.

Fearful that we had been broken, the lord of Dragor had not waited to muster an army in Grinlavine but ordered all troops to march at once towards Cradlin. Some had arrived even as we had begun to battle at the crossroads and more had poured in during the following days, creating a defensive siege around the city.

That night there was another great feast and debate was held between the lord of Dragor and Livinor, but I was not privy to such things. I spent the night in the church of Livella, with my parents and many other mourners.

The next morning me and Selosa rode back to her homestead, to continue my service.

Chapter Four- Treachery in the storm.

Two years of service passed swiftly for me as I served Selosa and grew in stature and mind. In those two years, Selosa taught me much of her control over metal and what she knew of governing, which was much more than I had once expected.
A year into the service, her uncle died and without an heir, Selosa took lordship of the coastal town. This meant I spent a great deal of time by the sea. Under Selosa the town swelled and a great sea facing fort was built and the town was renamed, Melkamorasuta.
Autumn of my second and final year of service was swiftly approaching, when me and Selosa returned to the fields near our coastal fort. There was a solemn edge to our march, knowing that it may be the last time we went on a hunt of Gupin like we had that afternoon. Already talk of my new role as a lord in the service of Cradlin was being discussed and as winter approached, Selosa would find herself another squire.
"You seem down Bruska." Selosa smiled at me as she rode on Grald beside me.
I rode now a large brokin of dark fur. Bruga, he was called, and he came from the Langorn Valley to the south and must have cost Selosa a small fortune. No breed of brokin were valued higher. He was not as affectionate as Dwell, but he served the purposes of what I would now need in a steed.
"I am well sir." I said with a nod, "Just remembering."
"There is little time for that." She said and she laughed in her boyish way, "This will be a warm night

for so late in the year. Shall we camp under the stars one more time?"

I looked towards the sea. The town of Melkamorasuta sat on the edge of it, no more than a couple of miles away but we would probably never have the chance again, "Yes." I said finally.

With delight, Selosa lead the way to a small thicket of trees and dismounted.

She had grown much in her two years of serious governing. The winter after the battle had been harsh and the one the year after was long, so much so that people questioned whether Camara held some ill intent towards us. Rumours suggested relations between Livinor and the clan heads of the Thera-ilma were at an all-time low and always did Selosa hear rumours of skirmishes in the northern borders.

"You hunt dinner." Selosa ordered, "I shall set up the camp."

I nodded and jumped off of Bluga's back. I removed his saddle and tied him to a tree with enough slack for him to happily graze. Then from my bag I pulled out five steel darts. These hovered above my hand as I crawled through the nearby thicket, my eyes searching for clues of my quarry. I stalked cautiously towards a small family of tularp, and my eyes lingered on a large male. My fingers barely twitched as one of the darts launched forward. The tularp scattered, all but one. The male threw itself to the ground and twitched for only a second.

I walked over to my kill and pulled the dart from it. A quick flick of my wrist cleared the glistening blood before I pocketed them all. This tularp would easily

feed both me and Selosa.
A fire was raging at our camp as I approached and Selosa nodded affectionately at my kill.
"You have come far from the small lad who grimaced at the sight of my tularp." She laughed heartily, watching me as I began to prep the small creature.
"What a week that was." I said absently. That week had seen me join and kill in her service.
We were mostly silent as we ate our tularp but as the stars came into view and a three-quarter full Umoria rose into the sky, basking us in its silver light, the mood turned solemn.
"You will make a good lord Bruska." Her golden eyes regarded me, sharpened by the light of the fire, "What you have learned will make you a great governor. Far away from the life I live."
I smiled; she would have me take her place if she could. She felt like war was coming and she wanted to be out leading troops, not taking in trade documents. That would likely not be my life. No Crud, before my brothers, had been lords of their own holds. My family had always presided over a specific trade in the big cities, mostly in the movement of grain. House Crud may have risen slightly higher in my generation but not enough to be trusted with a newly come city and sea fort.
I tried to lighten the tone, "Thank you. It is the wife that worries me."
Selosa laughed in a boyish way, "She will be very pretty and will nag you always."
I wondered whether she could see my scowl in the darkness, "And when you are summoned to court,

The Sundering of the two moons.

you will laugh at me."
She did laugh at me. Then we sang songs and told some stories before laying out under the stars. That had become second nature to me and at that time the air was warm, though I could feel the wind changing. During the day it had come from the south but now it blew over from Krunmelkin and by the morning it would come down from the frozen north. Selosa fell asleep almost at once, but I laid awake for a while, watching the stars. The two moons covered the stars of the vassals, but the stars of separation were clear to the north. As I lay facing the sea, the star of the island sat just above the horizon, glimmering with a blue light. I fell asleep wondering what Thera had said to Livella in the forging of that star, for surely it was his.

The wind had changed, and, in the morning, we woke up to a frost. Unusual for the time of year but not unheard of. We returned at once to the city and Selosa spent the day going over what she had missed. More rightly I went over what she had missed. I spent much of the day down at the port, checking over the goods that were arriving from Krunmelkin, Kuratex and the great continent. Making sure the goods were well kept for the winter. As afternoon came, the wind rose and outside of the harbour, the seas crashed violently against the cliffs. The wind brought with it hail and a biting cold that even my power was hard pressed to stop. Then as night fell, snow came in a blizzard and the roadways became covered in ice while icicles hung from the rooftops. This was very

strange, considering we had only just entered autumn.
I found myself running back through the streets, my powers clearing the way in front of me as I stumbled back to the keep where Selosa had her residence,
"Damn." I said, as I came to Selosa's study, "Camara must really be angered to bring snows here this early in the year."
Selosa cocked an eye, "What is happening?" She was reading a book, her favourite pass time.
"I have closed the port. The winds are treacherous, and I fear a wreck should any craft set sail." I said to her slowly as I used my power to remove the rain from my clothes.
Selosa nodded but she seemed distant. I noticed the book she was reading. It was memoirs of those who had travelled across the sea with Camara, "The lady of the waves seems angered." She said as she closed the book.
"Camara is often reckless." I replied and closed my eyes, "Thera forgive my blasphemy, but it is true."
"Maybe." Selosa mused as she moved to a large window that looked out over the harbour. It rattled with the power of the wind and snow whipped passed it.
"What is wrong sir?"
She looked like she had before the battle, like she was ready for a fight, "Something is stirring in this land of ours." She said slowly, "We have had skirmishes in the past but have fought no large wars like the other four realms. We are beset by enemies. Those from over the mountains and across the sea. We are at threat from

those who listen to lofty kings and those who dream of empires. I fear though, that the Thera-ilma are our greatest threat. Bitterness is in their hearts for all that has befallen them in the past. They have not forgiven Dragor for the sacking of their cities and with the power of Camara, they may seek to control us."
"But we gave them lands." I said, trying to understand her logic.
"And they have paid for them many times over." She looked down, "Imagine if they could bring a winter that never ended again. Never ended unless we paid a ransom. The Thera-ilma could name a king without having to fight a battle."
"Then they would doom themselves. The Thera-ilma are few."
She turned towards me, a sad smile on her lips, "Perhaps it is just the gloom of this day, but I see dark things coming this winter."
I moved to the fire and stoked it high. Her power would keep her warm, but she would also gain energy from the flames, "Do you need anything sir?"
"No Bruska but wake early. We will need something warm. Ask the cooks to prepare a stew."
I left her study and walked to the kitchens. I started the fire for the struggling cook and gave our order for the morning before retiring to my own rooms that Sand had kept warm for me. She had grown to and was now married, trying to undo the damage done to her.
The next day passed much the same, with driving snow and freezing temperatures but the second morning I woke to a blue sky and calm seas. Out of my

window I could see the town blanketed in white snow, creating a strange transition to the blue sea. Me and Selosa ate before watching the children play in the streets with most commerce now ground to a halt.

In the snow, under the sunshine, the storm of Camara seemed like a good thing, perhaps a gift for the delight of the children. The dark mood that had brooded in Selosa during the storm had vanished, but it would not last.

The first thing I knew of the dark events that had taken place was the warning bells ringing throughout the town. Instinctively my eyes turned seaward but only the trading ships could be seen, finally setting out for their destinations. The bells sounded again, and I realised that they rang behind us, on the landward side of the town.

"Come Bruska." Selosa ordered and I jumped up to follow her as she trudged through the snow-covered streets to the main gates. Two towers of wood stood as its protectors, and it was from there that the bells tolled. At sight of us they ceased and the pair of us climbed the steps to stand upon the pinnacle.

A guard dressed in light green, with sleeves of blue, saluted to Selosa with a hand upon his abdomen.

"What is it?" She ordered sternly.

"In the distance sir." The guard said, pointing eastward along the coastal road, "There are travellers from Cradlin."

Selosa's face showed her confusion, "Travellers come often between our towns."

I strained my eyes but can barely make out the

The Sundering of the two moons.

people. Only a bright red standard was clearly visible. "They fly the red flag my lady." The guard said in a panicked tone and my eyes turned to Selosa. Her eyes dilated in fear as she strained to see the figures.
"Red flag?" I asked, my own eyes turning back to the white blanket of snow and the figures moving slowly closer.
"A sign." Selosa mumbled, "A secret message used by high lords to show that their hold has fallen to the enemy." Suddenly she jumped into the air and across the wind I heard her yell, "Come Bruska."
Her power allowed her to land gracefully on the floor below and she charged towards the figures.
I did not hesitate as I launched myself over the barricade. Cold wind whistled passed me and I held my hands towards the earth, slowing my descent. I landed in the soft snow and charged through the trench Selosa had made in front of me. I could see clearly now the two towers of Cradlin borne upon the unusual red standard. Fear for my parents filled me and I ran faster, watching as the man at the front of the train collapsed into the snow and was almost enveloped by it. Screams of help began at once and the pair of us launched into the air, pulling at the earth to cross the remaining distance.
We landed by them as they desperately pulled the tall Ilma out of the snow. My heart stopped. "Please." One yelled, "The lord is dying."
Both myself and Selosa were stunned into motionless as the Ilma lord was heaved over. He no longer looked regal. His face was sickly, his eyes feverish but I still recognised Livinor Cradlin.

"What happened?" I asked as I turned to the standard bearer.
With a groan Selosa hauled Livinor up and began examining him. Her features paled at the wound to his stomach. Other than the standard bearer and the lord, there was another man, wounded as well and five women, one who carried a bundle to her chest like it was something extremely precious.
"The storm." The standard bearer said slowly, "It was a feint. The Thera-ilma entered under the cloak of the storm and killed the tower guards. They brought the sea with them and are using it to keep the city under hostage. They have rounded up the Ilma within the tower of Umoria."
I felt heat rising in me. I would have charged off at once to Cradlin if it weren't for the lord giving a desperate cry. I aided Selosa in sitting him in the snow and together we created a fire to warm him, "Why?" I asked.
A lady answered. She was of the Ilma as well, but she could barely lift her hands, let alone use her powers, "They came to court two weeks ago, asking for full sovereignty and control of all the northern coasts, including Lianosuta. They threatened a harsh winter, with ships locked in the harbour if we refused." She coughed and I spotted blood mixed with her breath, "The lord did not like the threat and sent them packing but took a hostage for their insult."
"How did you escape?" I asked but Selosa stopped me.
"These questions can wait." She lifted the earth and a great slab supported Livinor. Fire surrounded it, not

The Sundering of the two moons.

large flames but enough to warm the air around him, "The lord is dying but he might yet be saved." Her eyes turned to me, "Head back to town. Clear the meeting room and prepare it for these people. It will be warm and have hot food sent there. Then find a healer and bring him to my chambers."

I nodded and held my hands to the floor. I launched upwards, striding further than six strides in one leap, and continued to do so until I came to the gates. They opened for me, and the guard yelled down from the gantry, "What is happening?"

I paused, "Leave the gates open but do not look upon those who enter and ring no bells of warning."

The guard nodded, and I continued through the snow-covered streets. I found Selosa's scribe outside the fort and gave my orders for the meeting hall to be cleared before I ran to the church of Gadrika and found their a few of the white clad priests. None in all the land were so adept with healing and they followed me to the hall. Selosa had just arrived, bearing the lord on the stone slab and at once the order of Gadrika set to work treating them.

I prayed to Gadrika, begging that my next order would not be to go to the church of Agral, and call one of them to my service.

I went to the meeting hall and was happy to see the refugees eating and warming themselves by the fire. The wounded man was being tended by Selosa's handmaid. A child cried and I looked as the bundle in one of the woman's arms stirred. A child, we had saved a child in that storm. Fearing for my family, I sat away from the refugees, afraid of what news I may

hear in their conversation. It was not long though before Selosa returned, a smile upon her face, "He will live if his fever breaks this night. I am sorry for crude words, but I must learn what has happened." She pointed at the standard bearer. The Graul looked younger than me. Red marks covered most of his face and arms. His nose had been broken it seemed and his eyes were swollen. He stood and walked towards me and Selosa.
"What is your name?" Selosa asked.
He swallowed, "Anda, my lady."
Selosa smiled at him and beckoned him to sit. My mouth was dry, fearful of the news he would bring.
"Tell me what happened Anda." She ordered.
He swallowed again, "The storm came in the morning so that there was no sunrise. We knew it was one of Camara's games, but we did not know the true reason for the storm. The Thera-ilma were dressed all in white and were nearly invisible in the snowstorm. The Thera-graul took the walls, slaying many of the guards, the wind masking the sound. A group assaulted the tower and took the lord's wife and children hostage. Luckily, the lord himself was holding a meeting with local traders. Others of the Thera-ilma began capturing the other lords and ladies, surrounding them in the sea and moving them to the tower of Umoria. The lord tried to fight his way there and that was when we found him, just as he was overcome. My captain, an Ilma, died so we could escape." My jaw grew tight at his words, and I could feel my nails digging into my skin as my hands balled into fists, "We grabbed the lord and escaped through tunnels under the towers.

The Sundering of the two moons.

As we did, I took up the red banner. The tunnels lead to the stables where brokin for errant riders were held. These we took and in the cover of the storm we escaped." He looked down, "The brokin died early this morning on the border of your land. The poor beasts could go no further."
"Why come here?" Selosa asked, "Carano is closer."
Anda nodded, "The tunnel took us out on the western side, and we dared not pass the city. The storm had also come from the northeast, and we feared to enter further into it."
I thought of my family and of Livinor's. His oldest son was only a couple of years older than me, his daughter a year younger. I had played with them growing up, "So his whole family is held?"
Anda nodded but turned his eyes back to the table, "All but the baby." He said, "By luck the child was under the care of Lalia." He pointed to the Graul woman, who cuddled the babe closely, "She was hid in the tunnels when we found her."
Selosa nodded, "Return to the fire and your meal Anda." She said, "You have done a valiant thing and your family will be great captains in the lands of Cradlin, when I tell your lord what you have done."
Anda nodded and returned to his meal. I could feel Selosa's eyes on me, studying, waiting for my reaction, "I'm sure your family are fine." She said.
I had to believe they were, "What do we do?" A ransom for his family is more than we could ever pay and how many men would it take to storm the gates of Cradlin?"
Selosa considered for a second, "Send riders to

Lianosuta. Ask for every fighting Ilma lord to come here at once and to form an army behind them. I do not think we could save Cradlin through strength but maybe in stealth we could release those trapped."
I set to work at once, sending out the riders with written letters from Selosa. That night I did not sleep but I instead aided in the tending of Livinor, who spoke in murmurs as his skin burnt. He remained that way for the next day until his fever broke over-night. Then he fell into a restful sleep. On the second day demands came from the Thera-ilma, who would give up the city if Livinor was turned over to them as captive and Lianosuta abandoned. Selosa gave no answer to their demands. I did not ask her for the return of my family, not while there was still a chance at saving everyone. The next day a boat sailed into the harbour from Lianosuta, bearing five lords and a sixth entered the city hooded and cloaked. All these Selosa welcomed in her study. I watched the hooded man wearily, always ready on the point of attack should I see the blue eyes of the Thera-ilma shining from under his hood.
"This is an outrage." A young lord called Druga yelled as he read the demands of the Thera-ilma, "The land of Liano has always been held by those loyal to the Cradlin's. We should rally our troops and ride to their haven of Fasurasuta and take it by force."
"We cannot risk it." An old lord, the brother of the lord of Lianosuta, said, "The hostages will be slaughtered as soon as our forces crossed the border."
The cloaked figure stood, and all eyes went towards

The Sundering of the two moons.

him. I saw Selosa, hand stretched out to the shruda by her side, but her arm fell as the Ilma dropped his hood. My heart caught in my throat. Aila Cardon regarded us all with a grim expression. He looked less regal than I remembered, dressed in black as he was but his eyes still held the same dark intensity.
"My lord. I did not realise you had come." Selosa stuttered.
He smiled, "I am known to be one of the most powerful Ilma of this time. I did not want my close presence known unless it should force their hand. I have come from the walls of Cradlin." He said, "I was travelling there the day of the storm and was able to slip upon its walls. I went inside the sacked city but could not find strength during the storm to counter the Thera-ilma. The Graul are in a panic. Shops have been looted and crime is rife in the poorer areas of the city." His eyes went towards me, and I faltered, "I wanted to know how they could hold so many of the Ilma captive."
"The bannerman said they had brought the sea." Selosa scoffed but Aila nodded.
"Not an exaggeration. Around the tower of Umoria the sea spins. A great ball of water controlled by the Thera-ilma within. Should anyone move, they will drown those held captive and most of the city with it." His voice faltered, "Never before have I seen such strength. I tried to breach the wave but their control over the waters is far too strong."
"What do we do then?" Druga asked, his high voice strange next to the commanding musical voice of Aila, "Do we pay the ransom and give him the lord."

Aila stared harshly at him, but it was Selosa who spoke, "No." She said suddenly, "To do so we give up our strength. The Thera-ilma would just be enlivened by their victory. Our winters will grow harsher with every demand we then refused. In our weakness, other enemies may strike. Even Aginor may see his chance to exact his vengeance."

Mr heart skips again, "Aginor." I whispered before speaking out of turn, "What of his son? If he was to be harmed or set free, our peace will be destroyed."

Selosa and Aila shuffled awkwardly, "There is no fear of that." Aila said, "For he did not stay with Livinor. The threat of rescue would be too high for that. He resides with the family of Dragor as the lord's squire."

"Livella shines light on your judgement." A large man said. His golden eyes showed tints of grey, showing his relation, however distant, to the vassal Crio. He was rumoured to be a great master of the earth and that showed in his size. I found his name, Borgarinda, fitted his girth and demeanour, "Now let us bring the mountain down upon the Thera-ilma as Crio did to Camara so long ago."

"What then must we do?" The old lord asked.

There was silence. Aila paced the room, trying to form some plan in his head. Selosa looked to the sky, hoping to find an answer. She was the first to speak, "We have only one choice." She said menacingly, "We cannot break the sack of Cradlin by force without being seen by our enemy and risking harm to those inside. We must get into Cradlin unseen, get into the tower of Umoria and take control of the wave ourselves. Only in a secret mission can we find

The Sundering of the two moons.

victory." She looked down, "I will not force any of you to come."
Borgarinda laughed heartily, "The rock does not fear the wave." He boomed, "I shall go with you."
Aila nodded, "I think all who stand in this room will go with you. I have some control over water. More than most I would think but not nearly enough to break the control of the Thera-ilma."
I sat listening to his words and then I lost myself to them. I could feel all the moisture exhaled through his lungs, the water in her blood as it pulsed heavily through Selosa's body. I could feel the baths in the rooms above and if I searched, I could sense the waves of the sea, in my control even from that distance. For the first time in my life, I did feel like one of the chosen people, "I do." I said, cutting off their discussion. All eyes turned towards me, apart from Selosa's, who stared at the floor, and I felt the tears in her eyes, "I am average with everything else, but I think in water I may equal the Thera-ilma."
There were no laughs like I expected from the lord's. Most had sat in the meeting when Aginor's fate was decided and knew my worth from there. Aila stared at me intently, a smile creeping onto his lips, "Selosa. It seems your choice in squire may not have been simple chance. Twice now he has found himself in the middle of a war and twice has he found the answers that us old lords are lacking."
Selosa's voice was melancholy, "I believe he makes it up."
I laughed, "That I do sir."
Selosa's eyes went to the floor again but when she

lifted them, they were stone cold. She was the warrior again, "We ride at first light." She said, "We go in black, and we must go swiftly. I will send a well-guarded caravan along the road to Cradlin. They may believe it to be a parley from lord Livinor and that will be our cover. Go and prepare yourselves, we ride as night falls."

The Sundering of the two moons.

Chapter Five- The Sack of Cradlin.

Night approached swiftly and we rode out of the town dressed all in black. In the early evening, Selosa had sent out a well-guarded caravan, that travelled slowly by the eastward road. Throughout the night, we rode through path's un-trodden and did not stop till dawn began to creep into the sky. During the cold autumn day, we rested and set out as dusk came again. We rode faster than we should upon our brokin, but they were good steeds and midway through the third night, we came across Cradlin. The city sat in darkness, but I could see the glow of distant fires burning and a constant smog seemed to sit around the town. We crept up close to the stone walls, using small thickets for cover. We acted together and working against the powers of the Thera-ilma, we brought our own storm and clouds covered the two moons and veiled the stars. Lamps shone now on the walls, but we saw little of the guards patrolling them.

We crawled right to the base of the stone wall and once there, Borgarinda produced steps of earth that hovered all the way up the smooth brick work. I pulled water to me and watched as Selosa and Aila began to climb. Me and Druga followed next. My heart was in my throat as I took each step, waiting every time to hear the sound of alarm. Selosa and Aila had stopped at the walls top, looking over the edge. Borgarinda gave a slightly audible grunt and the rock I rested on rose, coming to a halt beside Selosa.

Nervously I peered over the edge. Two guards stood there, both wearing blue and white, and bearing a brinlon, their blue eyes shining. Selosa and Aila nodded to eachother and slipped silently over the walls. They approached the Graul, and each drove a shruda through the guard's chests. Hands slipped over the Graul's mouth, stopping any scream. A guard further along gave a shout but Druga launched into the air and brought the brick he stood upon crashing down upon the Thera-graul's head.

I slipped over the battlement and stared at what had been my home for the first fifteen years of my life. The two towers were hidden by a great sphere of water. It covered them completely, and it churned endlessly as a great swirling ball. Otherwise, the streets were eerily empty.

"Druga, Sorka." Selosa whispered, "Head to the guard house. Arm as many Graul as you can muster. We need to retake the walls and draw their forces out of the towers."

The two Ilma nodded, smiling as they disappeared over the walls and down the streets. Borgarinda soon appeared over the wall. Selosa led the way down to the streets and then I took over, leading the party towards the two towers. As we approached them, the majesty of the wave astounded me. I wondered about the power it must have taken to bring the wave. Then it hit me. They had spoken of a storm, but the streets were clear of snow, of any sign of snow. I looked at the wave. The storm had been the sea and there was the power of the storm, spinning around the towers of the moons.

The Sundering of the two moons.

We found ourselves under cover, staring despondently at the wave that covered the towers in their entirety, "What do we do?" Selosa asked me. Aila answered, "We could try the tunnels."
I reached out, feeling the wave and my heart sunk, "The tunnels are flooded." I probed the water with my power, "I do not think I can fully break the spell; we should wait for the fighting to begin elsewhere and when they leave the tower, I may be able to hold open the breach."
Almost on que there was a violent crash, and a ball of flame flew into the sky. Bells tolled along the walls and the four of us waited, concealed in the shadows, watching the swirling water. In a gentle sweep, an archway appeared in front of the tower's door. My hand reached out, and I felt the force of the water and I battled some unknown enemy for the dominion of it. Five guards, dressed in blue and white, charged through the door, sweeping towards the fire. The gateway quivered and I worried that I may not be able to hold it but then the door shut, and the opposing force vanished. My hand's trembled as I held open the wave, "Go now." I said in a strained voice.
Selosa, Borgarinda and Aila, charged across the street and slammed through the door. I followed more slowly, desperately trying to keep the archway open. As soon as I passed through the door, I released my hold and the water crashed back down. The change was instant. All noise from outside seemed to become muffled. All I could hear was the sound of churning water and the ferocious battle that was taking place in the hallway. My hands became flame, and I joined

the battle. I launched a great swirl of fire at my enemy and the hallway became covered in steam. I heard Borgarinda laugh and stumbled upon him as his fists crashed into the floor. The Thera-ilma flew upwards, crashing into the ceiling with a sickening thud. Selosa charged passed him, metal darts launching into Thera-ilma and Graul alike.

We fought through hordes of blue eyed Graul, killing most who could do nothing against our strength, until we reached the meeting hall. Borgarinda charged in without thought. I did not see the wave that crushed him until it was too late, nor did I hear the scream as it forced all the air out of his lungs. All I truly heard was the sickening crack as his bones were crushed.

I yelled as anger filled me. My hand crashed into the floor and great stone slabs launched at the attacking Thera-ilma. He fell to the floor, ribs cracked.

Suddenly the Ilma that were trapped there attacked but it stopped at one of our enemy's words, "Release the flood."

My heart stopped, and my breath caught in my throat. I heard Selosa yell and saw the spit coming from her mouth. Borgarinda had power over water, yet he could not stop such a bombardment and I wondered what hope we would then have. Suddenly Selosa's cry seemed to slow. The window's shattered and I could see every shard, see every vibration as people screamed. I looked down at myself, amazed by the blue flames that seemed to dance upon my body. All of a sudden, those blue flames burst forth like a great swirling tornado. My aura charged at the oncoming wave with a crash that shook the tower. I screamed as

The Sundering of the two moons.

the blue flames broke the control of the Thera-ilma, until Selosa and Aila smote them.
The wave crashed to the floor, and I fully released my aura, breaking the wave apart so that it fell harmlessly to the floor as a gentle wave. The hallway became silent as the Thera-ilma and Graul that remained fell to their knees, begging for our mercy.
My eyes scanned the faces of the Ilma held there, falling on one, "Mother." I yelled as I charged towards her and my father. She embraced me, her brown hair falling across my face.
"You stupid boy." She said while she stroked at my hair, "You should not have come."
I laughed as my father looked at me, surprise on his face. What I had unleashed, few of the Ilma could do with control.
Before we could say anything else, Selosa approached, "Where are the lord's children?"
My parents regarded her nervously, "Held at the top of the tower. They are held at the point of shruda's, and we have been warned that they will be killed should anyone attempt a rescue."
Selosa pulled me aside, but my mother held onto my hands, "Can you feel anything?" Selosa asked.
I closed my eyes, feeling through the walls of the tower but other than a few stale wash bowls, I could feel little presence of water, "Nothing." I said slowly.
"We must hurry." She ordered and I pulled my hand away from my mother's grasp,
"Stay Bruska." My mother yelled but I gave her a smile and followed after Selosa who stopped in the middle of the hall, "Any Ilma who can fight should

rally the Graul. We must drive our enemies from this city." She nodded at me and with Aila we charged out of the meeting hall. We climbed the stairs of the tower, moving up many at a time. As we reached the top there was a long desperate scream. Aila burst through the door, but a wave knocked him backwards and he crashed down the stairs, coming to a stop many steps below us. Selosa charged in and I went after her but we both stopped in the threshold. Livinor's son was dead, a gaping wound showing at his chest. Already the Graul was moving towards the lord's wife. A great force of air pushed against us from one of the Thera-ilma and we could only stand motionless as the bone shruda passed through lady Cradlin's chest. Anger blossomed on Selosa's face and with a cry, fire sprang at the man, knocking him backwards so that his wind shield failed. The Graul was charging towards Livinor's daughter. My hand came up, pulling water from the stair well. The Graul's wrist shattered from the force, the bone shruda falling to the floor.

The daughter fled to hide behind the bed. She had power but from the look of her shaking legs and tired eyes, she had not the strength to weild it. Metal glittered as a blade launched in my direction. I ducked, hand forcing it away so that it landed with a dull thud in the wooden floorboards. The Thera-ilma lord went then for Selosa. His hands went to fire, and he launched flame at her, which she pushed back with balls of air. This was a feint though and the man stepped towards the door where the water lay. His arm came up and a jet hit Selosa's stomach, bending

The Sundering of the two moons.

her over. She launched darts from her belt, but each was swallowed by a wave of water.
Exhaustion filled every part of my body from the use of my aura, but I had to find that one last ounce of strength. Water now swirled around the man, using it as a shield against any of Selosa's attacks.
Power surged through me and sparks arced between my fingers, "Get down." I yelled.
Selosa dropped to the floor just as I let the bolt fly. Noise like thunder shook the tower and the man flew backwards, crashing hard into wall beyond, skin burnt and clothes steaming.
Exhaustion filled me from head to toe. I could barely lift my arms and could fight no other enemy if one came but none did.
Quiet filled the room. From outside the sound of fighting came but above that, shouts of, "For Cradlin."
I collapsed to the floor; body finally spent. Livinor's daughter crawled from her hiding place and the cries for her mother tore my heart apart. I tried to quell my exhaustion. I stood and moved on stiff legs to wrap a cloak around the young girl before pulling her, kicking, and screaming out of the room. As her tears faltered, she looked at me, recognition filling her eyes and she fell limp, "Thank you." She whispered.

Victory was soon reached and the Thera-ilma were driven out of the city. Aila took up stewardship and sent messages back to Melkamorasuta of the retaking of Cradlin. Me and Selosa approached him slowly, for rage was in his eyes, "So they are both dead?" He asked, teeth gritted. We nodded and Aila stood, a ball of air crashing into the floor, "Those fools. Those arrogant fools. They have doomed their kind with this act. They took more than Camara's eyes. They took her rage and her recklessness."

"His daughter is safe." Selosa said, "She is being treated by her handmaids. We should return her to her father and get her away from this terrible place."

Aila nodded, massaging the wound to his head, "I agree. I will stay here and see to the restoration of the city but with her I will send a vanguard back to your homestead."

"We shall return also." Selosa said sternly but her voice softened, "If I have your leave?"

Aila nodded, "I am not your commander and I would have asked you to go. The lady will be well looked after with you and Bruska as an escort. Yet you are weary and should rest tonight in comfort."

Selosa nodded in agreement, and we left Aila. I spent that night with my mother and father and slept early, my body drained from the fight. During the night, another violent storm swept across Cradlin, but I knew that no attack would come. Ilma now held the walls. Driven by their will for revenge, they fought against the storm. In the early hours I woke to clear skies above me but beyond the walls hung a wall of ice and cloud, held back by the power of the Ilma.

I waited outside of the tower of Umoria, guarding a carriage being pulled by two brokin that were sturdy and long haired, fit for work. Liven Cradlin walked from the tower, escorted by two guards in dark green. She looked fragile; clothes hidden by a great black cloak. Her golden eyes were bloodshot, her long

The Sundering of the two moons.

brown hair pulled back into a tight bun. Red scales hung around her eyes and framed her nose but her whole skin looked shallow, like she had not washed or slept. She entered the carriage without a word and two brokin were found for me and Selosa. They were both chestnut working steeds from the nearby fields. Selosa nodded to the four Ilma who accompanied us. I knew them to come from low merchant families of little power, yet they could find renown within the lord's personal bodyguard. These were fresh faced recruits though. His true bodyguard had been killed in the assault. A captured Thera-ilma came with us also. He sat in the front of the carriage, one of Selosa's shrudas hovering at his back.

We rode away and entered the wall of ice and snow. The temperature dropped instantly and Selosa ordered the prisoner to part the storm. He did reluctantly and clouds gave way before us, allowing a short view of the road ahead but the rolling fields of my home were obscured by the storm.

I felt like we were being watched. Like inside that wall of cloud, enemies waited. We saw no one though and a mile into our journey the storm broke. It was like stepping through a door into a new world. The sun shone brightly and still carried enough warmth in early autumn to make me sweat. We rode late into the night, and I took my turn guarding the lady's carriage. The next day burnt even hotter as we rode to the crossroads. My eyes went to the floor as we passed the two mounds, now covered in lush grass. As we rode passed that place, the door to the carriage opened and Liven warmed herself in the sunshine, "I never thought I would see the sun again." She whispered slowly.

I smiled, watching her as she breathed deeply, taking in the warm air. Her eyes fell swiftly towards me, a smile appearing on her lips, "I thank you Bruska."

My cheeks heated. I did not think she recognised me. My eyes went to Selosa, who was watching the Thera-ilma intently, "For what my lady?"

"What you did last night." She said, a tear falling from her cheeks.

My heart filled with sadness for her, "I wish we had been quicker."

Her jaw clenched, and sternness came into her eyes. She was beautiful, a high lady completely, destined to rule and this disaster had only reinforced that, "How is my father?" She asked.

"He will live my lady."

"Liven." She said quickly, "Years ago we played together and now you saved my life. I would rather you said my name."

I nodded to her and tried to hold her gaze. Her head tilted, "You have grown under Selosa. My father told me what you did at the battle here and the counsel afterwards. I had not believed that the shy boy of house Crud could have done so much. Then you came and rescued me." Her gaze became distant, "I guess we never know what people are capable of."

I looked down, knowing she did not just mean me. The Thera-ilma had acted without remorse, killing her mother and brother for spite, once they knew the battle was lost. Those people had probably stayed in Cradlin before and eaten food from her father's table.

The Sundering of the two moons.

Words came unbidden to my mouth, "Agral burns hatred into their hearts," I said sadly.
She nodded as she moved further out of the carriage, feeling the breeze, "I want to ride in the sun." She said quietly.
My arm lifted, and words of halt echoed among the Graul and Ilma guards.
"A problem sir Crud?" The carriage driver asked.
I hopped from my brokin and opened the carriage door for Liven, "The lady wants to ride in the sun."
Selosa gave me a small nod. While Liven mounted my brokin, Selosa passed control of the Thera-ilma to another and began to walk beside me. There was no command in her eyes, only affection. She knew, like I did, that the moment I agreed to go on that mission, I was no longer her ward. I could not be. For my effort, the lord of Cradlin would offer me a lordship and a respectable hold. There was no point in hanging onto our previous titles for this return journey.
"What is wrong Sel?" I asked, once the lady had stirred the brokin forward.
"We are beset by enemies." Selosa said sadly, "We are ripe for the pickings by kings of foreign lands. We once had allies but now one has turned against us and will continue to do so with increasing ferocity. Lord Cradlin will have no choice but to strike at the Thera-ilma and strike hard. I fear what evil I shall be asked to do to achieve his vengeance."
"They attacked us." I whispered.
"We are not innocent in this affair. What evil had Livinor done to force their hand to such an act."
I walked in silence beside Selosa then. We camped

again under stars and that night grief overcame Liven. In the morning, her golden eyes were red with the tears she had shed. She did not ride that day, nor did I see her at all. She sat huddled in the carriage, tended by a handmaiden. It was early the next morning when the sea finally came into view, and we reached the wooden walls of Melkamorasuta. We rode through the gates un-hindered and came to the fort at the edge of the cliffs. We hurried the lady inside and I was relieved to see Livinor standing, ready to greet her. News it seemed had not followed us as he looked for his wife and son. In tears he collapsed and together, father and daughter cried. I left them to it and rested in my rooms while Selosa held council with the high lord.

She found me as dusk settled. Her jaw was set and her eyes dark, "The lord has not been idle in our absence. An army has begun being assembled, full of every able Ilma from Lianosuta and the towns north of Cradlin. Never before will so many of the ilma ride in one army." She looked angry, "I tried to calm him, but he has used his right. None, whether they be soldier or not, could refuse his summons. The army is assembling at Siraorna in five days' time.

I looked down. She might not have viewed me as her squire anymore, but I had not yet been risen to lord, "I will prepare our armour."

She shook her head, "There is little need. We do not go to war. A reward for our part, I think. He seeks us to lead the camp followers, to make sure the army is well supplied. The fool seems not to expect a battle. He thinks all men will return and they will need

The Sundering of the two moons.

supplies to last triple what we need."
I was thankful that I was not going fighting. I'd had my fill of that, but it seemed strange that Selosa, one of the greatest generals in our realm, would not be required.
"We shall ride out in the morning." She said before leaving me to my questions.

Chapter Six- The Burning of Fasurasuta.

It took two weeks to march from our home and regroup with the army at Siraorna. During that time raids had hit our northern villages from the havens of the Thera-ilma and hatred had grown even greater towards them.
the army itself seemed smaller than the one that had grouped to fight the armies of Melkin. These were all trained soldiers though; no militia had been gathered from the male Graul. I saw many of the Ilma there, much more than had been present at the battle of the crossroads. They looked towards me and Selosa, before dropping their eyes to the floor, afraid to meet ours. All of this seemed to make Selosa nervous. I could see that we did not have the forces to storm the haven of the Thera-ilma, but I presumed this was just a show of strength from Livinor, a sign that he would not be bullied by the people of Camara.
It took another five days to reach the northern coasts, all the while the air grew colder. While we ordered the erection of our siege of the city, I climbed to a tall hill. White lands lay in front of me, falling away to the ice-covered sea. On the edge of the horizon, I could make out the gentle lapping of waves but soon, winter would see it all covered in ice. Creatures, large and full of fat, rested upon the ice and members of the Thera-ilma herded them. Their eyes looked towards that hilltop, where the banners of Cradlin now hung.
My eyes strayed then to the white city that stood vast against the ice shelf. Fasurasuta, the haven of the

The Sundering of the two moons.

Thera-ilma, it was built after the storm by Crio's kin in an attempt to bring together the two peoples. It was said that in the summer it shone for miles and in winter it became part of the ice itself. Many jewels of the earth and the sea were housed within and from there, the children of Camara's first followers governed. My father had been there to do trade and had said that it was a marvel of the music of the sea. Now though it was silent. Defences lay all around it and there was a sense of coming doom, emanating from its walls.
All that day the siege began. Our small army surrounded the city while me and Selosa watched from a hilltop. The general stood next to us, one of the Ilma from Siraorna and a graul also, a great curved horn in his hand.
"You should tell the ram to advance." Selosa said, "The men are in position. If you wait any longer the Thera-ilma will begin shooting."
The Ilma general turned to the man-at-arms beside him and nodded his head. The Graul put the horn to his lips and gave one loud call. My eyes went back to the city, watching the ram that stayed motionless. Instead, a line of at least a hundred Ilma began to form a semi-circle around the white walls. Selosa looked confused, her eyes staring at the general, "What are they doing?"
The Ilma general nodded again, and another horn call echoed in that empty frozen field. My breath caught in my throat as a great wall of fire rose from the Ilma lords. I could feel the heat of it from my position as it rose higher and higher, blocking out the white walls.

That was when the screams of panic reached my ears. I saw Selosa's eyes widen, "What are they doing?"
The General laughed gruffly, "They had water. We have fire."
"No." Selosa gasped.
I stood rooted to the spot, staring at the vast wall of flame. I hoped it to be a feint, a warning, but we had sent no ransom or given any demand. My heart dropped as I realised the reason for our small army.
"Stop." Selosa begged. Her hand came up and her metal shruda hovered at the neck of the general, gently tickling his windpipe, "This is not how we do war. Stop them."
"These are our orders." The general said, his flickering eyes were the only thing that showed his nerves.
"May Thera protect them." I whispered without thinking.
The general laughed again, "Thera brought these abominations upon us."
"STOP THEM!" Selosa yelled, desperation filling her voice.
"My life is forfeit if I do."
Selosa gave a curse and the shruda fell to the floor. She dug her heels into Grald's flank and the war brokin reared before galloping down the hill. She only made it a few strides before the horn sounded one final time.
She stopped dead and my tongue pressed hard against the roof of my mouth. Slowly the flame moved forward, passing over the white walls and blackening them. Screams came loud on the coastal breeze, that brought a sudden storm down to try and

The Sundering of the two moons.

quench the flames but there was not enough of the Thera-ilma to control it. The Ilma at the walls base continued to push the flame forward, most producing auras of different colour to fuel that deadly fire.
The gates fell and a gap was made in the flames. Thera-ilma and Graul poured through, straight into the warriors waiting to slay them. I fell to my knees, staring as the flame continued through the city, "Livella forgive us for the fire we bring upon them. Orna hallow their walls to protect them. Thera give them strength and Gadrika, lead us who have gone astray to heal these hurts in the hall of Agraldin." Selosa fell from Grald in a sudden faint, and I charged to her side. She cried, fist slamming into the ground. We both cried, till the last screams faded from the city of Fasurasuta, the ice haven of the Thera-ilma. The last true gem of that troubled kind.

Selosa spoke to none of the lords as they returned from their slaughter, nor did she try to fight them. Instead, with me at her side, we left the camp and walked on numb feet towards the ruined city.
My heart broke as we stepped through the shattered gates and began to walk the blackened streets. Women, children, Ilma and Graul lay in heaps as blackened silhouettes in the falling ash. Acrid smoke hung in the air, mixed with the stench of death. Many of the dead had been hewn before the fire had devoured them. All around us Graul soldiers ransacked the city, taking whatever could be found. Above the once white walls, the banner of Cradlin hung, stirred by a strong wind from the sea.

I thought Selosa might have tried to stop the looting, but she marched silently towards the coast, knowing any attempt would be fruitless.
As we reached the harbour, sea ice melted by the fire, crashed against the sea wall. It sounded loud compared to the silence of that dead city. Here my broken heart was torn out of me. In one last desperate attempt, the Thera-ilma had fled here but the coast had offered them no sanctuary. The waves were red as they pounded against the coast.
Then a violent storm blew in from the north, bringing driving rain into myself and Selosa. I watched her, wondering whether she would take those last couple of steps and plunge herself into the violent sea. Instead, she just stared into the storm, golden eyes seeming like they were glazed over.
Slowly she bowed her head and turned away from the sea and without looking in my direction, she started walking out of the city. I followed her and tried to leave that terrible place behind.

The storm did not abate for weeks on our sombre march home. We left before the army and went on a long march down the river of light before passing back into the realm of Cradlin. When we did eventually arrive back to the walled city of Cradlin, we were welcomed by a party of jubilation but neither of us joined in the revelry. I followed by Selosa as she walked to the tower of Umoria, and none stopped her as she charged into Livinor's study.
The lord looked much better now and only a small bulge at his chest showed he had been wounded.

The Sundering of the two moons.

With a flick of his wrist, he dismissed those in the room. Selosa came to his desk, "You fool." She yelled before she collapsed at his feet, "You didn't have to kill them all."
"Sir Selosa." Livinor said coldly. No remorse, no emotion in his voice. His eyes went to me, "You boy, leave us."
I nodded and found myself in one of the taverns of the city. I drank heavily of pungent fruit wine, listening to the returning soldiers showing off their spoils. All my thought was on that white city and the screams that came from it. The drink brought me much needed sleep, but the sleep brought nightmares of fire and crashing waves.
The next morning, I felt less than fresh. Selosa found me and she smiled for the first time since the battle, but I could tell it was forced, "Livinor would like to see you." She said.
I readied myself in my best clothes and was surprised when Selosa ordered me to wear my ceremonial sword.
I followed her to the tower of Umoria, "How did you fare last night?" I asked while we walked.
"I was angry." She admitted, "And am so now. We spoke long into the night, and I understand some of his mind, though I still do not agree with the act. I am no rebel Bruska. I would not betray my lord, but I do not think I could serve this one now and Livinor knows this. He has given me leave, if I want it, to find my own way." Her smile widened, "I smile though, since you now have a way out of the path Livinor has set us upon. A way to never face battle again and for that, I

am thankful."
She could say no more as we finally reached the lord's study. He beckoned us to enter and pointed to a spot in front of the burning hearth.
"Bruska." He said smiling, though this seemed forced as well. His eyes went often to Selosa, "You have served the people of Cradlin well. First at the crossroads and again in the act of saving my daughter." He pointed to the blade at my hip, "Draw your sword."
My mouth began to water, knowing what came next. I drew it and knelt before Livinor; my blade stretched towards him.
"Bruska of house Crud." He said in a stern voice that boomed in the hall, but it was drowned out by my beating heart, "For loyal service and bravery. I lift you up in the name of the holy quadrant. Rise lord Bruska, servant of the realm of Cradlin."
I lifted my sword towards him, "My sword I give to you for all the years of my life, to serve valiantly and righteously, under the guidance of the holy quadrant."
At his beckoning I stood, and he placed his hands on my shoulders, "May Livella light your nights, Orna keep the foundations of your wall, Thera keep your crops watered and Gadrika bless you with many children."
I repeated the line and then Livinor embraced me tightly before kissing the top of my head, where Gadrika's guidance shone the most. When we parted, he smiled at me. I stood beside Selosa as a knight crowned. A lord in my own right, ready to start my

The Sundering of the two moons.

new life in whatever role Livinor asked.
Livinor gave me no orders but instead his eyes turned to Selosa, and the room grew tense, "Sir Selosa. You have served me valiantly. Last night words were spoken between us, many that I would like to take back. In the heat of anger, I gave you leave to serve whatever lord you wished but I revoke that now."
Selosa went to step forward, but his hand stopped her, "I do not ask though, that you remain in my lands if you do not wish. We have crushed one enemy, but rumours speak of another across the sea. Word has reached me that the children of Krun and Mina no longer work in harmony. If you would accept it, I would ask that you leave for the great wood and head to the hall of Elmlin as an ambassador for the realms in alliance. I hope to bring another people into our agreement."
I looked at Selosa. Her eyes were sad, her jaw locked. Then her eyes met mine and her shoulders sagged, "Yes my lord." She bowed her head.
"Worry not for Melkamorasuta. I shall find it a worthy steward. From there a boat will be made ready for you. Before you leave, you may find another ward if it would suit you."
I couldn't stop the slight bit of jealousy from filling me. I thought that I might ask to go with her, but I had my own duty now and I had to forge my own path.
"No thank you." She said, "I go in secrecy and would take no other into a land where we have enemies."
Livinor nodded, "Go and prepare."
Selosa bowed and left. I went to do the same, but Livinor called me back and beckoned me to a seat at

the hearths edge. I sat slowly as his eyes watched me keenly, "You seem confused." He spoke cautiously.
"You sent her away?"
"I did."
My eyes went to the door that Selosa had just left by, "She is not a rebellion threat."
"She is not." Then to my surprise Livinor smiled, "It is not in her nature."
"Why did you not tell her of your plan?" I knew I was stepping over the line but jubilation at my new position had fallen away sharply at the memory of the burning.
"Because she would have tried to find another way." He replied honestly.
"Then why send her at all?"
Livinor shrugged but his eyes were cold, "Do you not think she would have gone anyway. I gave her a task so I did not have to order her to do what she could not. I hoped she would have stayed in the camp and would not have to see it. I did not think she would react as she did."
I felt heat rising inside of me. Before I could help it, I was stood, "HOW DID YOU THINK SHE WOULD REACT?" I stopped, shocked at myself and I took a deep breath, "I am sorry lord, forgive me."
His eyes remained soft, "I sent her on this mission to give her the chance to heal. She is in pain and if she stayed as governor of Melkamorasuta, then she would just sit and brood."
"I hope she finds peace." I said, afraid of what else my emotional mind would say.
"Have you ever been to Elmkrun?" He asked and

The Sundering of the two moons.

when I shook my head he continued, "Oh it is beautiful in spring. The very forest is soothing." Then a wide smile spread across his face, "Maybe one day you will go as a member of my family."
It took me a while to process the words and when I did my eyes went up to the lord nervously.
"Liven has been through much and I see little gain in uniting her with the child lord of Dragor." He smiled, hand reaching out to my shoulder again, "With all that has happened, when she asked, I did not think to refuse. So, lord Bruska of house Crud, would you accept the hand of my daughter?"
I fell to my knees, still cradling my sword, "I shall protect her and all her interests till the end of my days."
He lifted me from the floor and embraced me once more before dismissing me. Selosa waited outside and she threw her arms around me, laughing while she did, "Now you shall have a wife to nag you and one like a princess at that." I was speechless and with true mirth in her eyes she pulled me by the arm, "Come sir, you look like you are in need of a drink."

I watched the ship from the top of the fort as Selosa sailed away from Melkamorasuta. Liven stood beside me. She had been from my side little since the announcement and everyday my fondness for her grew. I was glad for the company. I felt my life would be lonely without Selosa, but I had some comfort from that.
"I wish I could stay here." I whispered to Liven, "So that I could welcome her back."

Liven laughed gayly, clutching my arm affectionately, "My father would never let us live here. He will want you down south."
I smiled, "Far away from harm."
I turned away from the sea and kissed the top of her head before we both walked back into the fort. Outside our brokin were readied. For me, Bruga. For Liven, a small white steed. I mounted and we rode from the coast, ready to start my new life without Selosa.

The Sundering of the two moons.

Chapter Seven- A threat in the woods.

Years passed for me in my new role as lord. In all that time correspondence from Selosa was rare. It did seem though that Livinor was right, and she had found some rest from the trauma of that terrible day. For me, Liven was my healer. That year had nearly broken us both and together we had rebuilt.
We had moved from Cradlin, and I became lord of the small town of Tukanita, on the border between the realm of Cradlin and Minton.
Two years into our life there, Liven bore me a daughter and I named her Sand, in remembrance of the fragile girl in the service of Selosa. In this time and the years that followed, a darkness had seemed to come over the realm of Cradlin. The Thera-ilma were now nearly destroyed, their havens in the hands of either us or Dragor. Their people were persecuted, hunted, forced to beg, and scavenge. At first Camara had stricken the land with strong and deadly winters but with every one, the persecution of her people grew fiercer, until it seemed she had resigned herself to defeat and the winters had calmed.
With the harsh winters, I was happy to be so far south, where warm winds from the great continent kept the climate fair and running into the Thera-ilma was rare. When I did meet them on their now nomadic lives, guilt for my inaction at Fasurasuta filled me and there were murmurings among my retinue for the bread and shelter I offered the refugees.
It saddened me how far we had fallen from that first

speech I had given to the lord of Cradlin. Now we hunted and slew the people of one of the vassals, the daughter of the God that I most cherished.

On a cool spring morning, I looked out over the fields of my home. Tukanita was built upon a flat plain to defend the southern pass. From my balcony, in the tall stone keep, I could see for many miles. On the horizon sat a dark mass of trees. The west wood officially came under my care, being the closest town to their border this far south but I travelled in them seldom. Seeing them made me think of Selosa. Where she was, in the great wood, they had vast cities built within the trees. The Krun-ilma could move whole forests it was said, and I wished to have some of them as my neighbours.

"What troubles you?" Liven asked from behind me.

I turned to face her with a smile. She was even more beautiful now, motherhood suited her well. She held Sand in her arms. The toddler smiled at me with big golden eyes, her hair falling to her shoulders in gentle curls, and it seemed that one of the servants had laced flowers within her hair.

"You should be merry." Liven said, her eyes catching mine, "Aila Cardon will arrive today. Then you can officially mark the festival of the mountains."

I stepped towards her, kissing the two most important people in my life on both of their foreheads, "That cannot come soon enough."

Liven's smile brightened, "Come, they have breakfast ready for us."

It had seemed strange to me to be waited upon. I had

The Sundering of the two moons.

more servants than Selosa ever had, and each covered my every need. After we had eaten, I went to my audience chamber and set to the task of governance. That day, like many other before, I took meetings with the Ilma of my town. Most asked for things damaged in the winter to be repaired so that they may begin seeding the fields. I was shocked when, unbidden, a rider from Cradlin entered. He stood in front of me, wearing a tunic of fine green leathers but I could see from his stature that he was of the Graul.
"I am sorry to disturb you, my lord." He said and he bowed his head, touching his forehead as he did.
I waved him on, and he handed me a note, "Riders have been sent to all of lord Livinor's bannermen."
Before I read the note, I turned to a Graul who stood at the corner of the room. He was young, with short cut hair. A scar ran down his cheek, giving him a vicious snarl. He was young to be my man at arms, but he had been wounded while returning my brother during the battle of the crossroads. He had earnt favour with Aila Cardon, and he seemed a wise choice to lead my guard.
He came to my side while I read the note and then I handed it to him, my stomach tightening as I ran the words through my head again. My eyes turned back to the rider, "Go to my kitchen and find yourself food and water. You may enjoy my hospitality while you need it."
The rider nodded and departed. I stood, trying to understand the consequences of that note. I signalled for Liven to come to my side before looking around the court, "That will do for today. Any urgent business

will be passed to my steward. Please give me the chamber."

There was a murmur as people left. My man at arms remained by my side as Liven approached, "What is it?"

"A message from Selosa to your father." I deadpanned.

"Is she well?" Liven asked, her face creasing with worry.

I held the note in my hand and at once it burst into flame, "She has seen a fleet set sail from Cradsuta. One similar to that which invaded all those years ago." I saw Liven's eyes dilate, and I took her hand, "There have been sightings since from trading ships but there is thick fog in the parting sea right now and their landing point cannot be guessed."

Liven sat on a seat beside me, "What has my father asked?"

"To be ready. He wants us to double our army and gather rations should we need to march."

"Our winter stores are almost depleted."

I ignored her comment and turned to my man at arms, "What will you need?"

He thought for just a second, "I will get the blacksmiths and the armourers to start working. We will take the apprentices and get them to weild shruda and shield. That winter was harsh, and I do not think we will lack for volunteers."

"Find what women you can to work those jobs and the retired. We are a long way from the rest of the realm of Cradlin and I will not see the town grind to a halt."

The Sundering of the two moons.

He nodded and walked away. That was a start, but my head was racing, thinking of all the things that would be required should we need to march to war. The feast for the rising of the mountains would have to be a smaller affair than planned.
"You do not seem concerned." Liven said.
I shrugged obviously, "We have his son. He would be foolish to launch another attack."
"We do not have his son." Liven replied grimly, "And our alliance seems fragile. The Dragor realm sent no troops when Cradlin was sacked or when we launched our war against the Thera-ilma. Maybe Aginor knows that he could ransom Cradlin for his son."
I looked down, sensing the truth in what she was saying but I shook my head, "Our western coast is now secure. We have havens across the north with enough ships to meet them before they landed near Melkamorasuta or Lianosuta. If they are spotted in the north, then they will not make it to the coast. If they move south, to the lands of Minton, they will find a wide plain, surrounded by their enemies."
"Then there is us." Liven said, "And a stretch of land unwatched and unprotected."
My eyes went to the window, to the dark mass of trees just on the edge of sight, "They would not land in Kruntuka. The march through would take to long."
She did not seem convinced, "They will be able to assemble in secret and those trees will provide all the wood they would need for a siege of a city such as this." Her eyes became sad, "And what a pretty prize I would be, now that my father has lost so much."
I stood and yelled for my man at arms. He came

charging back into the room and bowed his head, "Speak to the hunters guild." I said to him, "Tell them to send out all the men who hunt the woodland. I need Kruntuka scouted daily."

"That will take weeks." The Graul said, "Most of our hunters stalk pray from the back of brokin, not in the woods."

"We have many poachers in our jails and in the villages around us. Send them as well. That wood is the biggest threat to our land, and I will know what is happening within."

The man at arms nodded and once again hurried from the room. I turned to see my wife smiling, "Thank you." She whispered.

I sat and mused on all that I had heard that morning until as evening crept closer, two long horn calls sounded. I marched to my balcony and looked out at two lines of marching brokin, their riders dressed in the orange colours of Carano.

Without hesitation I called for my wife and together, with Sand, we waited at the gate for the procession to enter. The gates opened to allow Alia entry. He still looked as regal as I remembered. My time at court had formed a close friendship between us and as he hopped off his brokin, we embraced.

"Welcome my lord." I said, all my worries fading at the sight of my friend.

"I thank you for your hospitality." Aila replied in his sweet musical voice. He bent down to kiss Liven's cheek before presenting Sand with a flower, that she wove into her hair to match the others. As we walked through the streets, music blaring, Aila turned to me,

The Sundering of the two moons.

"Have you received the message?"
"Yes. I have begun preparations."
"Me to." He said grimly, "They found us on the road, and I had to send half my men back to carry my orders."
We walked to the garden behind the fort, where pavilions now stood. Dancing fire wielders and other acts began as the people of Tukanita commenced the festival of rising, marking the date that Crio had risen the dividing mountains. In the wake of the recent conflicts, it had become the most celebrated in our land.
From the land of Minton, great men of the Ilma stood, throwing boulders larger than the fattest gupin in the air and juggling them in intricate patterns. The music played all night and I celebrated with Aila until the sun began to rise.

The next couple of days passed in much the same fashion. We of Tukanita rose late and made merry till the stars passed over head. As the days wore on though, my mood began to sour, and I found my eyes constantly looking towards the west wood. During my times of worry, Aila counselled me. He had little fear for his home. It sat beyond Cradlin, and any enemy would have to fight hard to make it that far inland. He seemed to see sense in Liven's words and before long he sent some of his own men to scout the woods.
As the festival of rising was coming to an end, one of my woodsmen returned, "What have you learnt?" I asked him solemnly.
He scowled, "Some of the poachers have failed to

return."
Aila gave a laugh, "That is hardly surprising, they have probably scarpered. They will appear again in some village jail with birds in their bags."
The Graul bowman bowed his head slightly, "Your pardon my lord but I do not agree. One of my men was with them, one of the Krun-graul from over the sea. He would not have abandoned us. I fear there may be some enemy in the woods."
I took a deep breath. A few missing poachers did not mean that Aginor had landed his forces here, but I would not lose more men in those woods just in case, "recall them." I ordered, "We will have need of good bowmen."
Tukanita was well known for its archers. Many who had founded this town had once lived in Brinsita, where the best archers in Dragor trained. The hunter's guild remained of those traditions, and they trained some fine archers. That was what Tukanita offered the larger Cradlin army. Housed in reservist roles, I had nearly two hundred fully trained archers, but the town offered little else.
As the woodsman left, my man at arms approached. He saluted and I gave my orders, "Talk to the Ilma that arrived from Minton. Tell them that we may soon be under siege, and they should leave now if they can." He nodded and I continued, "Send riders to Cradlin. Tell them that I fear war may be coming here. If this keep falls, Aginor will have a strong footing to continue his invasion." He nodded again.
I took a deep breath. I did not want to give this order and if I gave it without reason, then it would cost

The Sundering of the two moons.

Tukanita greatly in the months to come, "Ready the army." I said finally, my heart heavy.
His eyes widened, extenuating the scar down his cheek but he nodded a final time and left.
That evening the final day of the rising celebration was subdued. The people of my town knew by then of the growing threat and throughout the revelry, my soldiers began inspecting the men. They issued those of healthy body and mind orders of where to assemble in the morning. That night, the stone throwers gave a private performance for my court and afterwards pledged their service to me in the coming battle, honouring their own lord's agreement in the alliance. In the last act of the celebration, a bard sang a song of Crio's power and as he reached his climax, he lifted Sand into the air as Crio lifted the mountains. As my daughter smiled, I suddenly realised what I had to lose. When I fought at the crossroads, I had nothing but my own life. Now I had everything. A city who needed me, a wife who loved me and a child that could one day change the world. My fine coat sat heavy on my shoulders from the responsibility.
That night, sleep would not come. I sat upon my balcony, watching the new recruits gather in ordered lines. They were evaluated and sent to either weild a lucrax, shruda, brinlon or one of the keeps defences.
It was a bright dawn, but mist clung to the fields, creating a haze over the horizon. I stayed upon my balcony until the sun burned away the mist. Aila found me then and his eyes strayed towards the horizon. His white face seemed to pale, "Is it me or do the trees appear to be moving."

I looked up and saw that it was not the trees that were moving but black blocks, lines of infantry marching towards us.

I looked inside myself and searched for the same strength I had shown at the crossroads. Every stone, every pool of water in Tukanita carried my voice as I spoke, "RISE MEN OF TUKANITA, WE ARE UNDER SEIGE. RISE TO THE DEFENCE OF YOUR TOWN!" I released my power and turned back to Aila, "Send out one of your riders. Send him to the lands of Crio and seek my brother in the halls of Cradminton."

He nodded and left quickly. I watched from the keep as the brokin sped off southward. Specks from Aginor's approaching army started to chase but they quickly pulled back into rank. The day seemed to slow. I could not do what Livinor had done at the crossroads and meet my enemy on the battlefield. It would be slaughter for my people. Our walls would have to negate their numbers. We would need to hold until allies could arrive. That night I could see the distant fires of my enemy's camp as I readied to sleep. The next morning the keep began to fill with the women and children, to be hidden away from where the battle would be fought. Liven took care of them while I marched through the streets to stand upon the outer wall. Here the poorest of my town lived and many of their homes had been hurriedly stripped apart to make room for killing. The army of Melk marched on quickly, a huge wall of soldiers who snarled and cried in an attempt to drive fear into my men.

I wore my green bone armour, the same that had seen

The Sundering of the two moons.

me through the battle of the crossroads. I Had grown much since I had worn it last but if fitted me more comfortably now than it ever had then. With a nod from Aila, I retreated to a high tower on the edge of the fort, where I could see all the defences.

Aginor sent no parley or demands. He would not let us leave this place. He needed our stores, he needed me dead and the Graul switched to his side. I did not need to fear a siege, where many of my people would die a slow death from starvation and thirst. Aginor wanted this done quickly, before the armies of Cradlin descended upon him. Stone throwers, made from the wood on my border, fired swiftly. They hurled great boulders over the wall, crashing into buildings, or knocking archers from their perches. Many were hurled back though, like they had hit an invisible shield and I smiled, looking at the Ilma from Minton, who worked with the small amount of Ilma in my retinue to deflect the worst of the assault.

My smile lasted only for a second. Wind riders, hundreds of them, began to soar into the sky, hovering over the town and throwing flaming casks down upon my defenders. Fires broke out everywhere and the Ilma were hard pressed to stop them. This allowed the stone throwers to target our walls again and soon men scrambled from battlements about to crumble. Aila left me then to go and raise the spirits of my men, so I was left alone. I had hidden most of my greatest tool. The archers on the wall were militia. They would hit a few for every ten arrows loosed but my trained archers would be lethal and these I hid in the street beyond my defenders, waiting for the time they could strike.

The infantry soon advanced to the walls edge and my militia archers began to fire but I could not see how many they killed. My hand came up and my trained archers readied themselves. As the first of my enemy mounted the walls, the militia retreated. My hand came down and a volley of arrows fired. The enemy on the wall crumbled while arrows fell like rain beyond the walls onto those who waited. The militia below the walls grabbed lucrax or sword and readied, while my archers fired on the now growing number of men on the walls. My militia could not hold them and there was no point turning the walls into a slaughter ground.

In response to my arrow fire, Aginor's men returned it. They fired without vision and most embedded into buildings. The battle soon became a bombardment of arrow fire. The walls were abandoned for the time but my militia nearly broke with every enemy volley, that seemed to find targets with even greater accuracy. Soon Aila returned to me, "We cannot win this battle this way." He shook his head, "Aginor needs only wait for us to loose all of our arrows and then our advantage is gone. It won't be long until his stone throwers find their mark either."

I could sense the truth in his words. The army of Aginor were beginning to spread out, to surround the town. I could not defend against that. I looked around, eyes instinctively searching for Selosa, but she was not with me, "What should we do?" I asked the more experienced soldier.

Aila turned to my man at arms, the one who would

The Sundering of the two moons.

carry out these orders, "Their archers stand at the front of their lines. Open the gates and engage them with your militia. Then get your archers upon the wall. From that position, every arrow will be a kill. We can press them here and create dis-harmony within their ranks, then us Ilma will ride out in the middle. They will not expect this." Aila pointed to the back of Aginor's line where a small group of cavalry stood, "We may even reach there."

"You want us to take Aginor." I said, surprise coming through my voice.

"Then we can force a surrender." Aila said, his eyes burning like fire.

"Do we have any other choice?"

Aila laughed, like Selosa would of if I had posed such a question, "Maybe." He said, "But if there is, I do not see it."

My eyes darkened, "Give the order." I said to my man at arms before turning to Aila, "Let us ready our mounts."

Bruga was brought for me, his flanks covered in bone armour, and I mounted alongside Aila. Behind us were the Ilma of both of our retinues and the stone throwers who were not fighting fires.

"Thirteen ilma." I said to myself, "Worth a thousand Graul."

A horn call rang out. The gates opened swiftly, and my militia charged out in a disorderly march, bloodlust in their eyes. My archers followed, running up the walls, knocking down the ladders and firing off their first shafts within seconds. I dug my heels into Bruga and charged through the now clear gate. The militia parted for us, and we broke through the first of Aginor's troops.

As we broke through, I felt blue flames tickling on my arms and across from me, orange flames burnt across Aila's. Our auras, the majesty of the Ilma used to kill again, as it was at Fasurasuta.

No Graul could withstand that ride of our Ilma. Many fled before our charge, quivering from the heat of our inner flame. I thought victory may come for us but as we rode through the ranks, the confidence of our enemy returned and they fought harder, trying to gain the walls before the lords of flame returned. Still, we charged on, our mingling auras killing many, our eyes fixed on Aginor's banner.

I did not see the wind rider that knocked me from Bruga, but I fell hard, yelling as I hit the ground. I screamed as my foot caught and the sound of braking bone reached my ears. In a whimper my aura failed, and I looked at the twisted and bent thing that was my right leg. Ahead of me the line of Ilma carried on, unaware of my fall and slowly they faded into the distance, far from being able to aid me. I lifted my hand and screamed out as earth climbed up my leg, creating a cast that set the stricken bone. I stood, grabbing a discarded shruda and prepared to face my death. Graul looked at me in confusion and the ones that moved to strike fell from blasts of water or were scorched by fire. Suddenly a winged shape landed in front of me. I stared into the eyes of Aginor as his wingsuit fell from his body. He wore no armour but a green shirt of soft fabric. The Graul surrounding me cheered, shruda's hitting small wooden shields with a

The Sundering of the two moons.

noise like drums booming across the battlefield. Aginor turned to the Graul, his eyes watching my wounded leg, "Move into the city. The lords have abandoned it."

My eyes strayed to the distant fires of the Ilma. They would arrive at the banner-guard of Aginor, only to find lesser lords, while I died at Aginor's hand.

I threw fire, but it twisted my leg and the flames faltered as I gasped in pain.

"What a pretty thing I have found." Aginor said, his voice full of anger, "What good is your mercy now?"

A shadow spread across the ground as a stone crashed into the back of Aginor, knocking him forward. A brokin reared and from its back, wreathed still in orange flame, Aila stood. The flames came to his hand, all the power of his aura stored within. Aila released it and Aginor met it with his own. Green flame met orange in a battle of wills. I threw my shruda and it grazed Aginor's arm, and he snarled as the rock on my leg began to constrict, earning another wail of pain.

In an explosion, both auras failed. Aila was thrown from his stead, but he stood gingerly. The two men stared at eachother, sweat glistening on white foreheads. From his side, Aila drew a sword made of the bone of a great beast and he smiled at Aginor, "You should have worn armour."

Aginor laughed mirthlessly, "You forget who I come from." He stepped towards a root from a tree that I had long cut down, "The power of Mina runs through me." My eyes widened as the root began to grow, coming up Aginor's leg and thickening as it began to

surround his body.
Aila stepped forward, the bone becoming covered in bright flame, but earth came up and struck at him, blocking every blow. A sudden blast of air knocked Aila away and he stood, staring at Aginor who was now covered from head to toe in roots, moving like they were a part of his body.
"A clever trick." Aila whispered. Fire serpents launched from his hand, but water burst from parts of the root, quelling the flames instantly. In the confusion of the steam, a root grew from Aginor's hand and flames wound around it. Aila ducked and dived with every strike, his arms becoming covered in great gashes as it struck.
The earth around my leg crumbled as I took a stepped forward. Aginor laughed in mirth as he played with Aila, not noticing my approaching footsteps. My arms wrapped around him, and I used my strength to feel for the water inside of him. His blood stopped, held by my power. Aginor gasped and then roots wound around me, crushing me, forcing the air from my lungs. It was now a matter of patience. Who would crumble first? Who would lose control of their power before the other? I knew it was going to be me or it would have been, but Aginor was alone. Aila stood, wincing as he wiped away his own blood. The king of Melk could only stare as Aila drove his bone sword through the gap of two roots. He gasped, as the sword punctured his heart. I felt the roots slacken and I took deep breaths to bring air back into my lungs. I connected to the roots myself, using a power that was weak to me and slowly, with the last of my will, I

The Sundering of the two moons.

forced them to retreat and wind back around Aginor. He gave one whimper before collapsing to the ground, dead at our feet.

I fell to one knee, my power wavering through pain and lack of air. Aila knelt beside me, his face gaunt, "Can you walk?" He asked.

Using him for leverage I stood, and earth once again surrounded my injured leg, "Not well." I looked at the Graul, that slowly began to surround us again now that their lord had been slain, "We should surrender."

Aila stood, his voice being amplified by the ground around us, "Lord Aginor is dead. Surrender and end this war."

Laughter met us, and we stood in the middle of a wide circle of Graul, all of them ready to die to take a couple of the Ilma with them. It became a sudden melee, our powers against the unwavering numbers of Graul soldiers. In their first wave, none came close to striking but neither did we kill many with our power used more for our protection. Eventually I could see both of our powers wavering. The strength of using our aura and our battle with Aginor putting us almost to the point of exhaustion. Then screams began amongst the Graul. Those not immediately attacking us began to charge towards the city, where I hoped my forces still stood.

The ground lifted a confused Aila slightly as the fighting stopped, soldier's heads turning from side to side. Joy filled Aila's eyes, and he pointed to the west, "It appears that the trees are moving."

I used the ground to lift me above the fleeing Graul and my eyes widened. The trees were indeed moving.

The western forest walked upon great roots and in the trees, Krun-ilma commanded them with their words. Where we had brokin, the Krun-ilma had trees and they strode across the battlefield upon great roots. The Krun-graul fired lon's of supple wood into the fleeing enemy.

I stood there, shocked by the sudden change.

A tree stopped by myself and Aila. I looked up and my heart swelled at the sight of Selosa perched upon a great limb, smiling at me, her golden eyes burning. She leapt from the branch and met me upon the earth. She embraced me tightly, causing a wince from my bruised and battered body.

"It is good to see you still alive Bruska." She said with a smile.

Suddenly the tree seemed to bend and standing upon its top branches was one of the Krun-ilma. His hair was like silver and leaves of different sorts grew into it. His white scales had hints of earthy colours and roots seemed to spread from below his eyes, that were a dark green. He was dressed like one of the hunters of Brinsita, in leathers of brown and green.

"Lord Crud, lord Cardon" Selosa said as the man stepped from the tree, "This is lord Alora Bitaran. Cousin to the king of the great wood and descendent of Krun from the line of Gadrika."

"I thank you for your help my lord." I bowed low.

Aila remained standing, back straight, "What is this? You have turned against the sons of Mina, your kin?"

Alora's eyes hardened and when he spoke, his voice carried a musical hint. Like wind through the leaves on a summer's night, "They are foolish and Agral has

The Sundering of the two moons.

marked them. He aims to destroy the house of Mina and darkens their souls. They live with ambitions of ruling as the emperors of Ilmgral. Selosa has told us of your wavering freedom here and it is freedom we seek, for the house of Mina now wants dominion over all the wood and land."

I gave a muffled moan as I listened to Alora's words and Selosa came to my side, "Bruska, your leg."

"Allow me." Alora said as he knelt, examining my stone cast. He flicked his wrist and the stone crumbled but from his pocket he pulled out a small sapling. This he rested against my leg as he began to sing. The words connected to the plant and slowly it began to grow, wrapping itself in many twisting stems, around my injured leg. Once he had finished, the plant worked as a living cast, moving with my leg but keeping the break steady.

With that, we crossed the battlefield back to my home. Trees surrounded all that remained of the forces of Aginor. The dead lay scattered on the ground.

My men, many fewer than had gathered inside the walls, rested, staring nervously at the newcomers. I walked alongside Alora and that seemed to quell their fears.

I looked down at our enemy, broken completely. Without those who walked beside me, any of those could have been sat at my table this night. With Selosa's intervention, I had survived again.

Chapter Eight- A final goodbye.

it took over two weeks for Livinor Cradlin to arrive at Tukanita with a small garrison of soldiers. Rumour of our victory had long reached him, and he had sent home much of his formed army. In the time since the battle, I had ordered the repairs of my town and worked to bury the dead. I held a great funeral for all those killed, attackers and defenders and then we buried them in a mound on the edge of the west wood.
In this time, I also rekindled my friendship with Selosa and learnt much of her travels. She had become a favourite of the king of the Krun-ilma. He had told her of the ever-growing threat of Aginor, who had begun taxing the wood terribly. The wood king knew that the armies of Aginor would need to be weakened and he would need new friends, to stop the suppression of the great wood.
I healed during this time, putting all my strength into the mending of my bones so that I could not even lift water from a bowl during that period. I could stand though, with the plant brace, like I did then in front of Livinor as he marched through our gates.
I bowed low, "My lord."
Liven ran to her father's arms and the pair embraced before the lord tossed Sand in the air and kissed her cheek.
That night we took a grand meal in my meeting hall, with Alora and his Krun-ilma as our guests of honour, "Your help was a last resort and one I did not fully

expect to achieve when I sent Selosa to you." Livinor said.

Selosa sat away from Livinor, clearly still uncomfortable about the past but she smiled at the mention of her clearly successful mission.

Alora nodded, "Our friendship will be well earnt in the future, I am sure."

"What would the family of Bitaran want for our newfound alliance?"

Alora stood and bowed again, "I have no wish to be a lofty lord or to become great in power. Those who came with me, did so for the hope of peace. We in the great wood hold our home by the smallest of margins and it is crazy to have that place as our only refuge." His eyes went from the window to the wood on the edge of sight, "I ask lord, for the forest land on your western border? There, my men, and those who follow, will bring great beauty to that place. Our soldiers shall fight for you and shall defend your borders so it will become a place of dread and fear for your enemies, and a place of beauty for those who carry your banner."

Livinor considered this, and his eyes went down the table to Selosa, "What do you think sir?"

Selosa stood and for the first time I noticed that she wore clothing like the Krun-ilma's. Her shirt was of gentle brown, her trousers green. On her shoulder she wore a broach, fashioned in glass, like the shape of a tree in full bloom. I realised then that rebellion was in her nature. She did not sit here as one of the lords of Cradlin but as a knight of the woodland folk, "My lord." She began confidently, "I have spent years now in the homes of the Krun-ilma. They are a fair people and will only benefit our land by their presence. Never again shall we suffer bad crops if we make this alliance."

"It is said that the children of Mina are also as powerful in this." Livinor said in an offhanded way, "Maybe an alliance with them would be more fitting. They will not like this alliance. It may make them more likely to attack."

Alora shook his head, "No my lord. My cousin has slightly withdrawn his watch over our eastern boundary. Rebels, from the unconquered north, flood through to avoid Camara's winters and they come in search of blood. They still plague our lands, but most have moved through and have taken the fortress of Angralin. The armies of Melk will have a hard time to remove such a force and always more rebels will emerge, especially after this latest disaster reaches home."

Livinor nodded, a light of satisfaction kindled in his eyes, "I can give leave for this, but those woods belong to my son in law, the first marshal of the southern border. I would not place someone on his land without his leave."

I looked towards Alora. I knew his worth and the worth of his people. The thought of that wood transformed into a wood of the Krun-ilma felt to me like some retribution for the events at Fasurasuta, "My lord." I said, turning to Livinor, "Your northern border is secure. The Minton's protect our southern borders, Drage protect our eastern. It would be prudent to have such protection in our forest as well. I

The Sundering of the two moons.

give leave my lord, for this friendship will long protect our people."
Livinor stood, "So be it." A smile widened on his face, "I rise you up to be a protectorate of the realm of Cradlin and I give to you all the land of the western forest, to govern as you will."

With that, the feast ended and Livinor returned to his home. The Krun-ilma settled in the forest and slowly towns grew within it. Great orchids brought fruit that was traded far across our realm and the wood there was like nothing ever seen before in our part of the world.
Selosa lived among the Krun-ilma, in their town of Tukakrunbane, that sat in the heart of the forest, though she often visited me. Aginor's brother did not seek revenge. Being beset by enemies within, he sort peace and offered a trade in spices in reconciliation.
A year after the battle, as a warm summer was reaching its end, Selosa came to Tukanita and played with Sand before the summer celebration. Also in this time, a party of Thera-ilma and Thera-graul came to my town. They were dressed in the typical blue and white, their leader dressed the most regally. He had pearls around his neck and a circlet of shells upon his brow.
Nine there were in total, three of the Thera-ilma and six of the Thera-graul. I welcomed them all to my table, "Welcome my guests." I said as they bowed before me. I made them rise, wanting no lordship over those whose lives we had destroyed, "What brings your party so far south and what can I do to aid you?"

The regal one of the group stepped froward, "My name is Hirgral." He bowed again, "Son of Ingil, who was once a lord of a small town near the city of Amoradrage. We are wanderers now, giving our services to any who need it." He paused, "However, us nine are sent on another mission. My lord we would ask leave to travel freely to the coastal town of Sutakrun in Kruntuka and from there take a boat over the sea to the great continent."
There was an intake of breath from all those who listened. Dark stories from the great continent followed the Thera-ilma.
Selosa sat forward, "What would take you back to the land that you fled so many years ago?"
A tear formed in Hirgral's eyes, "We have heard rumours that some havens of the Thera-ilma remain on the great continent. A remnant of Karomin's people. After the tragic events of the past, we are small in number. We wish to unite with them and maybe find a new life in that land."
I looked down, knowing I could not deny that request. Not if it found these people some form of rest, "I give you my blessing and you shall have lodgings here for the night while I write a letter for Alora. We have a fruitful harvest before us, so I ask you to take whatever provisions you require."
The whole company had smiles upon their faces and Hirgral bowed, "Thank you my lord."

That night the guests dined in my hall, and I spoke with Hirgral about the events after the burning of Fasurasuta. His home had been sacked by Dragor, its

The Sundering of the two moons.

people forced to move or find work under new lords. His father resided now near Dragor as a guest of the high lord but Hirgral and his company, of which this was only a small few, walked the land, taking whatever work they could find. It was a sad plight for those who had descended from one of the vassals. Selosa sat and drank with the party, and I saw that she treated them with more kindness than anyone else I had seen, apart from maybe Sand. As she looked at them, I saw the burden of guilt that still hungover her from her inaction.

The company departed and I found myself alone with Selosa. She looked sad as she played with the last of her food. I stood and she followed me towards the balcony.

"You wish to go with them?" I said as I looked into her eyes.

"With your leave." She replied softly.

I laughed despite the hole that had formed in my stomach, "My leave?" I took her arm, "My dear Selosa. I am and always will be your ward and friend. You go where you please and I will never govern you." Then Selosa kissed me, firmly and passionately but it ended on a subtle edge, showing her frailty and all the feelings she once had held. Then she left me, and I sat on my own in my dark chamber, fumbling with the phial of salt water at my breast and thought back on the events that had led me here.

The next morning, Selosa and the company bid me farewell and in a speechless conversation, I gave Selosa the helm of my brother and she departed with only one look back. It would be the last time I saw her golden eyes beyond the halls of Agraldin.

Six years passed before news of Selosa or the plight of the Thera-ilma came to me. It was a warm summers day, but thunder crackled over the sea when I was summoned to my audience chamber. A smile appeared on my lips as I beheld Hirgral. He was clad again in white and blue, but it was made from a strange fabric that was noticeably light and almost clear. All joy for the sight of him faded when I saw the helm that he held in his hands. It seemed that I would always be presented with it. He handed it to me, and I felt the rough bone sadly, "What happened?"
"We found the havens of the Thera-ilma." Hirgral began, "It took us many months. Once there, we aided the people and Selosa took it upon herself to bring peace to the tribes of marauding Graul. It seemed that Selosa had brokered a peace but there was a slaughter at the tribal ground and the new leader declared the Thera-ilma as a scourge against their gods." His eyes seemed to cloud with tears, "The tribes, now united under a cause, assailed the havens and Selosa led our defence. We do not know of the devices of that land and Selosa was struck by an arrow. The wound was not deep, but it was poisoned and as she battled the poison overcame her. The Graul king was defeated but at a heavy price." He grabbed my arm, "Her sacrifice for the people allowed a new king to take the throne. He is wise and wants peace with our people." He then stepped back, and he looked almost overcome with grief, "Of the ten of us that left your lands and the two sons of Alora who

The Sundering of the two moons.

joined us, only five remain, including only one of Alora's sons. He has found a wooded land beside the sea and some of the Krun-ilma head there now."

This was good. It was a personal heavy price to pay for the freedom of the vassal's people, but it lifted slightly the burden I still felt for Fasurasuta, "Is she buried well?" I asked.

"We buried her in a tomb of stone and prayed for Orna to care for her in the halls of Agraldin. It was a sad loss for we loved eachother deeply, though I fear it was only a small love, compared for that which she bore you." I could see the hurt in Hirgral's eyes, and I was thankful that Selosa had found some love before the end.

"My lord, you have leave to go through my land and all the lands of Cradlin, for as long as your house lasts." I touched the helm, "I thank you for your service and for bringing this token back to me. Where do you go now?"

"Back to my home and to my father. Many shall return with me to the great continent and there hopefully we will find peace." Hirgral said.

I nodded and Hirgral left me to continue his own business. As I sat, looking at the helm, Sand came to me, "Father." She said in a high voice. Her hair now reached mostly down her back and her golden eyes were keen, "Look what I can do." She grabbed a pitcher from my table and held it aloft, then with her right hand, she pulled the water from it.

My dark heart suddenly filled with joy, and I kissed my daughter's cheek, "Your powers have come." I said, "Well done Sand." I looked at the trillon helmet, "I want you to take this as proof that strength comes in all sizes. The greatest warrior of our time once wore this. Look after it well and you shall be as strong as she."

With delight Sand grabbed it and placed it upon her head. I laughed as it fell over her eyes. She giggled with glee as she grabbed a candle from my side and ran from the room, probably in the hope to control the flame. With that I smiled and raised my glass and thought about Selosa. The person who made me who I was and the one who I would never forget.

The Sundering of the two moons.

Thus ended the tale of Selosa Aquitex and Bruska Crud. Though their parts in the events are often overlooked, they left a lasting memory on the tapestry. From the havens of the Thera-ilma of the great continent, the first seers would come to the citadel on Theracali and from Sand would come a union between Minton and Cradlin, that would seal the alliance in blood.
Livinor's surviving son succeeded him as high lord of Cradlin and he lived to an exceptional age. He became one of the most respected lords of his time and was key to the crowing of the first king of the united northern realms.
Cradlin was not again attacked by the armies of Melk, who faced near civil war in this time but the weaknesses of the realms in alliance was becoming clear and swiftly a threat from the south would unite them even closer.

Book Three- The War of the Dividing Mountains.

By Alena Drasig.

The next story takes us east of Cradlin, back to the realm of Dragor in the year four hundred and sixty-one, after the coming of the vassals. Dragor seemed strong in this time, under the leadership of the descendants of Drage Livella. However, the three realms of Cradlin, Minton and Drage were becoming weak due to their unwillingness to unite completely under a king and large nations now surrounded them. This story tells of Suda Drage and his companions as they worked to protect the southern borders of the Dragor realm from the now encroaching armies of the united Scaraden.

The Sundering of the two moons.

I. A Message of Concern

Suda Drage meandered through the Dragor keep, its strong black walls a symbol in the city of Dragor. For six generations now, the family of Drage had ruled. For his sacrifice, Livella had declared that all first-born children of Drage would be male, so that the resemblance of the vassal himself would live on. For Suda that was no different. It was said he resembled the vassal greatly. Auburn hair fell down to his shoulders, held back by a band of leather. His gold eyes seemed to radiate light, and his white face was pure, with only the slightest hint of red scales around his jawline.

Suda smiled as his first-born son, Idris, ran from the courtyard. If Suda resembled Drage greatly, then Idris was like Drage reborn. The young boy had fire in his heart. His hair was as red as the banners that flew in the breeze on top of the keep and his face was almost perfectly clear, like Livella herself.

Suda left the keep and took in the noise and bustle of his town. No town was as large as Dragor in the north of the continent of Aragal. Only in the realm of Scaraden were cities of this size seen. The inner city served as a large market square, where thousands of Ilma resided, working as bankers, merchants, and masters in their crafts. Beyond lay the civilian streets in ordered lines, where the wealthiest of the Graul lived and worked.

Beyond the tall stone walls, the city became a mass of different districts. These were full of jumbled wooden houses built for the Graul that worked in the many different industries of the city. Any Graul could come to Dragor and find work. In truth, Suda knew that Dragor had not yet reached the limit of what the land around would allow it to achieve, and that this city would soon swallow the villages around it, growing larger and larger until it spanned all of Ornadrage. Suda looked beyond the wall to the sprawling worker districts. He had been trained from a young age in governance, but he had never really wished for such a task. These people were his duty though. He could see disease festering in those streets.

Dragor was wealthy, extremely so and Suda knew that once the next winter was done, he would have to see about bringing order to those districts.

Lordship still felt strange to Suda. He was new to it, being risen in the previous year. He had taken over the realm earlier than most of his line. His father had died young due to a troubling wound from his youth.

Suda had been trained in governance, but he did not like it. His youth had been spent leading a company of Ilma as they moved across the country, dealing with brigands and rebels. It was a much more straightforward life.

He turned his gaze back to the inner city. The market square was a hive of activity, with trade coming from all over the world. The market spanned many streets and Suda walked through it, examining all that his city had to offer.

Beside a merchant selling fabrics of different colours, Suda found his wife. She was still beautiful to his eyes. Many lords married for political reasons, but Suda had married for love. Lavia's family were merchants in the city, running the local trade in iron from the mountains. Her hair was of silver gold and red scales gently kissed her bony cheeks. She was slender, garbed in a dress of rich scarlet.

He came to her side and the Ilma merchant bowed to him, as did the young Graul boys who were clearly his apprentices.

"How is the trade Dula?" Suda asked the merchant, who smiled at the use of his name.

"As fair as ever my lord. The summer was not too harsh, and my wagons came laden with silks from the great continent."

"Many of which my dear wife will relieve you of, I'm sure." Suda smiled.

Lavia laughed richly, and the pair left the still bowing merchant.

"How are you, my love?" Lavia asked in a high voice. It was her voice that had first attracted Suda. She had sung at the day he was raised to be a knight in the harvest festival, and he had been enamoured ever since.

"I am well." Suda replied while they walked, his eyes scanning trinkets from Scaraden, "How are the fares?"

"The fruits from the great continent came in this morning. They are still fresh from their voyage to Dragesuta. Your cousins are seeing the wagons brought into the city."

Suda nodded, his mind racing. It was approaching the late harvest festival, where people gave thanks to Gadrika and prayed for a quiet winter. The whole city was preparing for it, with gifts of love appearing on every street corner.

Each day, Suda welcomed singers and bards, and these performed throughout the day at the steps of the keep. This was not the favourite festival of the people of Dragor. That was held at midwinter, as they all lit candles and prayed for the ending of the darkness, which only Livella Remain could bring.

Lavia left him to examine some jewellery and Suda wandered through the streets, out of the market and down the main road to the dragon gate. As he walked, the houses went from dark stone, to brick, to wood. The gate of Dragor was designed in the shape of a great beast, the gate its mouth and big red eyes above. It was built by Crio and designed in the shape of the demon that Drage had defeated.

Beyond the dragon gate, lay the disorderly districts for his working graul. The white stone road became dark grey rock that stretched far into the distance. He could not see much of it though, due to the great train of brokin and wagons that marched in an orderly line into the city. Suda looked beyond them to the fields, where Graul worked like little insects. To his right, Ornadrage's peaks rose high into the sky, their tops glistening with white snow.

As Suda watched, the train of wagons drew close to the gates. It was headed by two Ilma, both riding large white brokin. He smiled as he beheld his cousins. The two riders were twins and at that distance it was hard to tell them apart. They stopped in front of Suda, and the subtle differences became clear. They both had blonde hair, taken from their mother's side who

came from the line of Cambane. Their eyes were the same golden hew, their faces almost mirrors, with red scales both falling from their eyes. The only difference was that Ordin's formed a tear drop.
"Hail lord." Ordin said. To tell themselves apart they wore different coloured, bone plate, armour. Ordin's was a dark, sunset orange, "May we enter your city?" Loxa, whose armour was a dark red, spoke, "Or do you not wish for this lovely fruit?"
"Good sirs." Suda smiled, spreading his arms wide. Both twins had been squires for his late father and the three of them, with Suda's younger brother, had grown up together, "It is my pleasure to welcome you."
The twins kicked their heels into their brokin's flanks, and the train moved passed Suda. He followed behind them at a gentle pace, stopping every now and again to talk to the Graul who walked the streets. He arrived back at the keep as the wagons were being unloaded.
"See that this fruit is stored in darkness." Loxa yelled at one of the stewards, "It will last long into the winter that way."
Suda approached the twins, "How fares your father?"
"He is old." Ordin replied mournfully.
"But our brother keeps him well in check." Loxa smiled. He always was more up-beat than his brother. The lord of Dragesuta, not Suda's uncle but a distant relative, was old now. Friendship between the lords of Dragesuta and Dragor had always been solid, with much of Dragor's trade coming through that port. His first son, and brother of the twins, ran most of the town. He was suited for such a task and had not been

one of Suda's company like the twins. Knowing that the weight of responsibility did not fall on them, they enjoyed themselves as much as they could. Enjoying both the sword and the harp.

"I knew I heard the voices of brigands." Said a new voice that was young and vibrant, with the hint of leaves blowing in the breeze. Another Ilma appeared. He was tall and slender, with slightly earthy white scales and the hint of green in his golden eyes.

"Oh really cousin." Ordin yelled, "Haven't you killed this foreigner yet?"

"Many have tried." The newcomer laughed as he embraced both twins.

"Sirgrin." Suda said to the man who was around ten years his younger, "Have the wind riders arrived?"

Sirgrin nodded. He was a master of the wind, as were many from the realm of Krunmelkin. It was rumoured his great grandfather, Aginor, had been one of the best wind riders ever seen. Sirgrin's grandfather had been taken after the battle of the crossroads and he had resided in Dragor ever after, atoning for Aginor's sins. He had done such a good job, that Sirgrin had become Suda's first squire. He would never be a lord, but he served now as one of Suda's stewards.

The twins and Sirgrin began jesting with eachother and Suda left them to it. He entered the keep, the guards of Dragor bowing with fingers to their hearts as he did. He marched up flights of wooden stairs and corridors covered with rich tapestries, to reach his bed chamber. He stripped off, flexing his muscular frame before grabbing a tunic of soft fabric. It was richly made, with golden flowers embroided onto its

The Sundering of the two moons.

sleeves. His trousers were thick and of the same red hew. He grabbed a sword from his side and stared at its majesty. This was his most treasured heirloom. It was made of a black rock that seemed to shine at night with a hidden flame. No Ilma could connect to the black stone from Amoradrage, and it seemed to give strength to his gift over fire.
He sat in his chamber until night fell and music began, and fires danced in the sky. He turned as his door opened.
"I hate it." Idris said as he walked in, pulling at his own red shirt. His red hair was combed backwards, held there by a band of leather.
"Behave." Lavia said as she came in behind him. She now wore a gown of white, beautifully framing her body.
"Father." Idris said, standing in front of Suda, hands on his hips, "Why do I have to wear this?"
A girl followed him in. She was also dressed in white, and she had a silver ribbon in her red hair. Alina, Suda's oldest daughter, smiled at him. Finally, a toddler stumbled into the room. Belia was Suda's youngest child, and she also pulled at the dress she was wearing.
Suda knelt in front of his son, "Now Idris." His voice was stern, "Tonight we celebrate Gadrika and the food that he blessed us with. We must dress for such an occasion." A smile appeared on Suda's face, and he whispered, "And if you are good, I will let you stay up late to watch the fire dancers."
A smile grew on Idris's face, and he bounced on the balls of his feet.

Lavia coughed, "Have you forgotten Suda?"
"No I have not." He replied as he stood and walked to his dresser. He pulled from it a small scabbard, which held a short metal knife. He turned, smiling at the young boy who watched the knife curiously, "Now Idris." Suda knelt before his son, "Today you are six harvest festivals away from becoming a ward. For this reason, you shall receive your first blade, as I did at your age." Idris smiled gleefully as Suda fastened the blade to the boy's belt, "Look after it well. My father had it made for me."
Idris nodded and charged out of the room, most likely to show his friends. Alina and Belia ran up to Suda expectantly.
"I have not forgotten you both." He said and walking back to his dresser, he pulled out two bright red flowers. Kneeling beside them, he wove the stems into both of the girls silver bands, "These grow only in the soil around Amoradrage, or upon lands where the Drage family have lived. They are a gift from Livella, showing our connection to her. Wear them tonight and the vassal of light will bless this house."
The two girls left, both standing taller, like grace personified.
Suda stood and kissed his wife upon her lips. From his desk he took up another cutting of livora and handed it to Lavia, "For the one who holds my heart." He whispered.
She smiled and wove the flower into a loop at her breast. Together they left for the grand reception hall. Musicians played and Ilma from the merchant families danced, drank, and ate.

The Sundering of the two moons.

At their entrance there was silence and Suda stood, arm in arm with his wife and addressed the crowd, "Happy harvest to you all." His voice echoed in the hall, "Bless Gadrika for the life that he has given to us. May the tapestry that he weaves continue to bring you all and the realm of Dragor prosperity. Today we shall celebrate the gift that Gadrika has given us and celebrate the gift of eachother. May the stars guide you all."
A cheer went up in the hall and then the guests went back to their feasting and dancing. Suda stepped towards an old woman. Her hair was white, and her face wrinkled. She knelt by Alina and entertained the girl with a trick that made the fire the old woman produced, change colours. It was rare for a woman of the Ilma to be able to still use her power at that age. With every child of the Ilma born, the mother diminished, part of her own power going into the child. That was the reason twins were rare, or it was unusual for women to have more than three children. Lavia could barely produce a flame now but what she lost in power; motherhood gave back in beauty.
"Mother." Suda smiled as he approached the old woman. Alina looked fondly at her father before running off to follow Idris. The old woman turned towards Suda.
"You look regal my son." His mother said, her gaze fell downwards as she examined the sword at his belt.
"It suited father better." He replied. His gaze swept across the party goers. He had spent many harvest festivals with his men, staying in inns where no one cared that he was the heir apparent to Dragor.

"Your father never liked the harvest festival."
"He never liked celebrating."
His mother gave a hearty laugh, "He was a pious man. He believed in celebrating the gods every day, but you are not cut from his cloth."
Suda nodded as his mother left him in search of food. His father had not been a ward for any lord or learned much of fighting. Unlike all the other first born of the house of Dragor, his father had spent the years between his coming of age and his rise to lordship, studying in the church of Brinsita. Suda believed that was why, when need for battle came, that he had been wounded so badly.
Lavia came and kissed her husband before taking the children out to enjoy the festival. As he sat, Ordin and Loxa grabbed harps and began to sing for the hall. Their voices were sweet, and they sang songs of Gadrika, just as well as they sang songs of debauchery in small village taverns. As they sang, Sirgrin came and sat next to him, "My lord." He whispered, "You should go to the square and be amongst your people."
Suda's heart warmed at the thought, but he shook his head, "My father never went out to the festival grounds."
"Your father believed he must rule from inside these walls." Sirgrin said, "But you are not your father, and you are well loved by the people. You can be a different lord than he."
Others would not have spoken to him so, but Suda had helped raise Sirgrin and he trusted his counsel above most others.

The Sundering of the two moons.

Suda nodded and stood, his shirt feeling a bit lighter as he stepped out into the cool autumn air. Two Graul soldiers followed him, there red shirts shining, a black dragon embroided on their chests. People cheered at the sight of their lord and Suda walked through the streets, smiling at Graul and Ilma who danced and sang under the stars.
Suda danced with his wife and his children and watched as wind riders with great torches performed elaborate routines in the sky. He walked amongst the stalls and paid handsomely for all that was offered to him. The last of the stalls he came to was watched over by a Graul woman, who was slender and red scales covered most of her face. She bowed her head at his presence.
"Inderil." Suda said, causing her to lift her eyes, "I am sorry for your loss." Her husband had died earlier in the year, when a mine shaft had collapsed.
Her eyes glistened with tears, "Thank you my lord."
"I did not know you had a stall." Suda said as he examined the many sweet treats. There were fruit cakes, jams, and tarts, all made from different fruits. Her sons worked in one of the orchid farms just outside of the city. This would have been most of what they were paid with, "Very full it is also. Are your sons stealing from the orchid?" Suda added levity to his voice, showing his jest.
"No lord." She said, still startled, "But we are on lean times. I hoped to sell some of my goods to pay for winter grain."
Suda looked down. Inderil lived beyond the walls and the cold winters would be hard in the wooden shacks

that was her home. Suda hated that he could not cater to them all. They earnt what they could, and the city tried to provide them all a ration of grain but every year more people would come to the city and more would need to share that grain.

"What food will you eat all winter?" Suda asked.

"The bread that the lord supplies." She replied, smiling. Not everywhere would that grain be given. Suda grabbed a tart and paid twice the asking price for it. He bit into it and his face lit up.

"Inderil." He smiled as he savoured the flavour, "You have grown in your skill since I was a child, stealing from your mothers' shop." He thought for a minute. He could not help everyone, but he could help one who had always treated him with kindness, "My children would love these."

"Take some then my lord. It would make me happy knowing your children enjoyed my treats."

Suda laughed, "You mistake me. These should be eaten fresh. Inderil, I call you into my service. I shall tell my stewards to prepare rooms inside the keep for you and your sons. I would like you to prepare these treats for my children's lunch."

Inderil stared at him in disbelief, "But my lord already has cooks."

"I do but why should I give gold to those of foreign lands, when my home boasts cooks just as good."

Inderil had tears in her eyes, "Thank you my lord."

"Report to my steward in the morning. If you have any cakes left over, you should bring them with you." He nodded at her and walked away. The festival was reaching its conclusion, but Suda walked back to the

The Sundering of the two moons.

keep. He found the steward and gave his orders before returning to the hall. Then he relaxed and drank merrily with his cousins and danced with his wife well into the night.

The next morning came dark and damp, with autumnal rains blowing in on a southern wind. Suda felt tired as he went to his study and began the task of governing his vast realm. Messages arrived throughout the day from all the townships. They reported on their harvest and whatever surplus they might have for Suda to acquisition, to distribute where it was needed. The coastal towns as always had more food than they needed, with fertile farms and fresh fish. He brought thirty percent on their surplus, removing it from next year's taxes. He would send this to lesser lords in the small townships. Merchants would buy the rest of the surplus, but they would sell it across all the six realms, where the fish here were treated as a delicacy.

Most of his large towns had enough to feed themselves but not enough for Suda to take a surplus. He would let them sell it on their own. Langorn Langeline was short though. Reports had reached him a month ago of a wildfire that had spread to quickly for the Ilma to quell and it had ravished much of their crop. From Grinlavine he purchased much grain and dried fruits, with orders for one of his merchants to see it sent there.

It was worth doing this, keeping all his realm fed. Langorn bred the best brokin this side of the ocean and supplied a tribute of these to Suda's army. All the major towns served a purpose, and it was why the realm flourished as it did.

"My lord." Suda's steward said as he walked into the room, "The woman Inderil and her family have been settled. She has brought some cakes with her."

"Pay her for them but send them down to the order of Gadrika. They have many ill with the flu and the cakes will ease that burden."

Suda then began his plans for spring. They mined most in the winter months, when workers from the farms could be spared. Quarries would bring a huge store of stone, and ores of iron and gold would be smelted at twice the capacity at this time. He would sell some of that to raise money to improve one of the outer districts but that would take time and more importantly, Ilma. There were always too few Ilma. He wondered why the chosen people were always too few. The strain on the women was a clear reason. There were reports of Graul marrying Ilma. He had seen it in his own city, but he did not like the idea. The children would be powerless, lessening the blood of the Ilma. Suda stopped his musing as his steward entered again, followed by a rider in dark blue. He was of the Graul, short and very thin. He breathed heavily.

"Be calm." Suda said. He lifted his arm and a pitcher of water rose and travelled to the Graul, who took it gratefully but did not drink.

"My lord. I have ridden for two weeks to reach you." He took a deep breath, "Fighting has broken out at the southern end of Sikaorna. Brigands have pushed back the forces and the mines are abandoned beyond the high pass."

The Sundering of the two moons.

"Why ride here? Lerou and Langorn would have enough men to repel some Graul brigands."
The Graul's face grew tight, "It is not the brigands that trouble us. They have some Ilma with them, strong Ilma. They have collapsed several passages and sent flame through the tunnels to burn miners alive. There are few Ilma in the south capable of stopping them."
Suda was troubled. Rebels from Scaraden had tried to assail Sikaorna before. The mountains were rich in gold and other ores. Many kings of the southern realm felt they should share in the spoils. They did, since they held the town of Karmaorna, where many mines worked. Suda knew that kings were never satisfied though. Every next king had to one up his predecessor and the last king of Scaraden had conquered islands between Aragal and the great continent.
Suda looked at the Graul rider, "Got to my stables and find fresh brokin. Then ride back to your lord and tell him that help will soon come."
The rider departed but he was followed in by Loxa, his determined eyes showed that he had heard. Suda addressed him, "Send out birds. Call the knights to me. Our company must set out again to aid those of the high pass."
Loxa smiled broadly and moved with an air of delight to carry out Suda's orders.
Suda sat back down but he could not think of anything but this new threat. He hoped that this was just some brigands and not an attempt to steal the southern mines of Sikaorna. They had been gifted to his family by Crio when he raised the dividing

mountains. They belonged to Dragor.
Soon Lavia appeared, "The birds have been sent out?" She asked, concern in her eyes.
Suda took her hand, "Sikaorna is under attack by Ilma rebels. An army of Graul cannot help."
Lavia rubbed at Suda's cheek with a warm hand, "Will your ride with them?"
"I have not decided yet."
"Your heart is troubled." She whispered, "Inderil has prepared some fresh cakes. Come and see the children's delight."

Over the next couple of weeks, the lords of Suda's company arrived and prepared. With Sirgrin, Loxa and Ordin already in Dragor, they prepared pack horses and gathered supplies. Suda's brother, Linya, arrived a week after the orders were given. He resembled Suda a lot, with the same red hair and minute red scales but he was shorter and better built. He was fiercer of a warrior than Suda also and he wielded fire like Drage himself.
Then came Dusan Ridon, priest of the church of Brinsita and brother to the lord of that town. His hair was blonde, pulled back into a ponytail and he had red scales on his forehead. He wore clothes like the rangers of that enchanted wood. His shirt and trousers were made of brown leather, and he was covered in a green cloak, clasped at the shoulder by the star of Livella.
Lastly Ogra Langorn arrived. He was tall and proud, with dark black hair and tilted eyes. Red scales clung to his jaw that was square and pronounced. On his

The Sundering of the two moons.

back he carried a large metal lucrax, that he wielded with deadly precision.
in the audience chamber, where the other five lords had gathered, Ogra knelt before Suda, "My lord." He said, bowing his head low, "I fear I come with grim tidings. Things are worse than you were first told." Suda nodded for him to continue, "Karmain fly between the towers of Karmaorna and Lerou. The bannerman are being called southward in preparation for war. The king of Scaraden has declared himself as king of the world and has asked that all bow down to him, including the lords of Sikaorna. He has declared these for himself, speaking of the tribute those of the middle lands once paid in the years before Crio. His brigands are only an attempt to steal the southern halls so that his army can move through with stealth." Suda felt his jaw lock and had to restrain himself from gritting his teeth, "Fools who take a king only create a tyrant to rule them." He said as he slowly stood, "Kings always seek more power and now he aims to take from me the gift of Crio." He felt his anger rising, "Far has his arm reached and further it will stretch before this king is satisfied with his hold. His men will take Sikaorna. Then they will strip it for its ores and use our own resources to launch his campaign across our lands and across the sea." He lifted his head high, "I will ride with you my bannermen and see that this would be god is sent packing back to his four towered church."
Dusan placed his fingers to his heart, "My lord, the light of Livella shall shine upon our journey, yet we travel to the land of death and Agral's curse still sits

heavy upon them. Beware if you do war in his domain."

Suda nodded. The curse of Agral was seen most amongst those of Scaraden or of Mina's house. It was said that since the unification of Scaraden, the king's chief advisors had all been children of Agral's line and their taint was heavy, "I do not go to do war. I go to secure our freedom. Still, plans should be set in motion should our mission go ill. Dusan, how well stocked are the lands of Brinsita?"

"They shall nourish all who you send." Dusan grinned eagerly.

"I will send all that I can spare with them, but I do not know how long the assembly will last." Suda then turned to his brother, commander of the Dragor army, "What do you reckon to our forces?"

"A full army can assemble within a couple of weeks." Linya replied, "but we do not have the arms for a large militia force."

"I intend not to need one." Suda smiled, "The militia shall form separately and long shall be their preparation. Instead call the banners. Have them bring all their trained soldiers. They will assemble in Brinsita, where they can come together in secret before they march to Sikaorna."

"Wise council Brother." Linya smiled.

Loxa tapped on the table where he sat with his twin and both had their feet upon it, "What of our Alliance?"

Ordin laughed, "The alliance all but died when we went to war against the Thera-ilma."

"The children of Crio are still loyal." Dusan said.

The Sundering of the two moons.

Suda nodded, "So are most of the Cradlins." His hand came to rub at his tired eyes, "Send birds to Minton and Cradlin. Ask them to join in our mustering."

Suda's lords left him to sit in his chamber and think about his course. Soon Lavia came to him wearing a flowing red gown, "I have heard your commanders discussing a mustering."
Suda took his wife's hand in his own, "I thought to have at least a year before I had to worry about war. My father never once had to worry about it."
Lavia's free hand rubbed at his cheek and Suda closed his eyes, savouring her touch, "That was because he had you. You and your company wandered the countryside, rallying all who you came across, but you are a high lord now and your company is disbanded."
"Our enemies think us weakened in my rule." Suda deadpanned, his eyes opening as his frustration overcame her touch.
"They think you are not yet a lord."
"I will ride with my men."
Her hand stiffened, and her eyes became sharp, "Then you will prove them correct. You will show that you are only a warrior, who would abandon his duty for the rush of war. You belong here, you are lord of Dragor."
"That is not all that I am lord of." Suda said, unwanted anger creeping into his voice, "I am not just the lord of Dragor. I am lord of this realm and Sikaorna sits within it. If I cannot defend my lands, then how can my lords rally to me?"
Lavia's hand continued to work upon his cheek but

there was desperation in her touch, "Send your lords but command from here. Oversee the mustering of your forces. Be more than just a hunter of brigands and show your son what it means to be the high lord." Suda thought about the lord's long past. Lords who did exactly as she said. He thought they were cowards, hiding behind rows of men who were doomed to die just because they were not born into the lord's luxury, "I am going with my lord's and when I stop this king of Scaraden, I can send the soldiers home to their families."
Lavia's eyes met his and there was desperation in them, "Make sure you return to yours."

The Sundering of the two moons.

II. The Road South.

The next morning came warm and bright as the company prepared to set out. Suda stood beside a tall chestnut brokin, its horns a dark grey. He wore bone plate armour, rapped in crimson leather. He also wore the obsidian sword at his side and felt the fire within. Dusan stood beside him. He wore still his green cloak and brown leather tunic, but he wore no armour like the twins Loxa and Ordin, who were busy checking over the companies supplies. Sirgrin was dressed in green armour, the colour of his home but the bone it was made from was light and the wing suit spread from his arms.

Ogra was already sat upon a beautiful white brokin, with horns that curled twice. His armour was dark grey and light for riding, but he carried still his large metal lucrax. The last of the company, Linya, wore armour of the same hew as Suda's and embroided on the chest was the black Dragon of the house of Drage. Stood to attention nearby, also dressed for riding, were several of Suda's personal bodyguards. They were all Graul, but they were also the best riders from the city, and they would prove useful against the Graul brigands.

"My lord." Lavia said as she approached the company. Idris was at her heels, and he looked in awe at the assembled soldiers, arrayed as they were.

Suda smiled at his wife but knelt in front of Idris, "I ride now to battle." He said solemnly and the boy seemed confused, "I do this for your safety and the safety of this realm. These are tough decisions that you will one day have to make." He leant forward and kissed the young boy's forehead, "Be good for your mother and watch out for your sisters. They will need you while I am away."

Idris smiled and kneeling before Suda, he presented his knife. Suda laughed and pulled his son into a warm embrace.

As he rose, his eyes met his wife's. His heart broke at the pain within them, "Do not cry my love." He said as he kissed her cheek, "I shall return."

The well of pain that was her eyes, looked deeply into his, "I prayed to Livella last night and she came to me. If you go now, then we shall never again share a bed or dine in this keep together."

Suda's breath caught but he tried to stand taller. He took her hands in his, "Livella can be wrong, and the stars do not foretell my death. Nor do they foretell the fall of Drage. I shall return."

Her gaze fell to the floor and regretfully, he released her hand. He mounted his brokin and nodded at his company and slowly they departed. He looked back at his wife only once as they marched down the paved street. She never looked up though and a weight seemed to have fallen onto her shoulders. Solemn Graul watched them from the streets, bowing their heads in respect to their lord, but many went to hidden places and found armour and weapons long abandoned, wondering when the doom that called their lord forth, would also call them.

They passed through the dragon gate and down through the districts of wooden houses until they left the town completely. Then they entered wide and flat fields, all stubble now after the harvest.

"What a merry bunch of fools we all look, riding together again after so many years." Linya said cheerfully.

"Some of us have never stopped riding." Ordin mocked, "But lord Suda here looks like he has forgotten how to sit his saddle."

Suda laughed, "A jester as always cousin but I have only been out of the saddle for a year."

"Yes my lord." Loxa joined in, "But that is a year of luxury and servants. Do you even remember how to set up a camp or hunt for game."

"Luckily he has all these fools to look after him." Ordin said as he gestured to the company.

"Arodo." Suda yelled to the commander of his guard. A short and gruff looking Graul, who was missing one of his eyes, "During camp tonight, make sure my cousin never wakes."

"As you wish my lord." Arodo laughed grimly.

They jested long into their march, reminiscing on their past deeds when they had roamed the countryside together. In the afternoon, the road passed through the woods on the edge of Dragor's farms. On its northern side the road was well used, and the sound of nearby lumber camps filled their ears. Slowly though the forest grew thicker and the road roughened. The company became silent now, for even this close to Dragor, bands of brigands were known to roam.

in the woods, Sirgrin and Dusan took charge. Both had

spent much time in the woods of Brinsita, where the best woodsmen in all of Aragal trained. This was an example of why they had survived so long together. Sirgrin and Dusan were the survivalists, the hunters and if they were in your camp, you never knew hunger. The twins were the jesters, they would find you food or shelter in any town or city and they were little matched in their powers. Lidya and Ogra were fighters to their core. Few would best either of them in single combat or command large armies better. Then there was Suda, a cut above the rest. He was not as skilled as a hunter as Sirgrin, not as powerful as Lidya but he was a leader who inspired, a leader who made people want to be better and he brought the best out of every man in the company.

They saw nothing but the flight of birds as they marched. The sun set early, but they continued to march by the light of fire balls that the Ilma hung in the air around them. Late in the evening, with the setting of the moons, they set up their camp.

They were riding again as the first rays of sun caught the edge of Ornadrage, which this wood skirted. The road soon took them back out of the woods, and they marched through days of untilled land, coming across the occasional farmstead or small village but they stopped at none. On the eighth day of their march, they came to a land of rolling hills. Upon one rise, that looked down across distant valleys, Suda stopped and smiled, "We have made good progress. We approach the Langorn valley."

Ogra looked down on the valley of his home, "We

The Sundering of the two moons.

shall have no need to camp among the stars this night my lord."
Villages became more frequent as they marched to the town of Langorn and everywhere brokin grazed in huge flocks. As they approached the town, Arodo unfurled the banner of Dragor. It showed a black dragon upon a scarlet field.
Soon the devastation of the field fire became obvious. Rising hills were covered in black stubble, the ground cracked and dry. The road again became paved as they reached the town. It sat in the cover of a great valley and many of the homes were built into the hills. A keep sat in its centre, made of wood. A precession waited on the main road through the town and Suda was approached by a rider in grey. His eyes went to Ogra though and he bowed before the heir of the Langorn valley, "Lord Ogra." The Graul man said, "Your father has ordered the mustering of our riders."
"How many?" Suda asked before Ogra could. The Graul's eyes fell to Suda and then shot to the banner that swayed in a gentle breeze. Suddenly the man bowed and placed two fingers upon his heart, "Your forgiveness my lord, I had not seen you. Welcome to Langorn Langeline."
"Ruca." Ogra said sternly, "Answer the question of lord Drage."
"Two hundred riders my lord." He said quickly, "We set out for Brinsita tomorrow."
"Thank you." Suda said quickly. His eyes went to some of the riders. They learnt to ride at an early age but for many that looked like it had not been long ago. He hoped he would be able to soon send them home.

"My lord Drage." Ruca said in a stuttering voice, "I must let the lord know that you have come."
The Graul rider sped off towards the keep and the company followed at a slower pace. The street was lined with inns. The town was a great spot to rest if you were travelling with goods from Scaraden and it was never short of foreigners. The twins, who were not well loved by lord Langorn, disappeared into one of these, their instruments in their hands.
The rest of the company continued to the keep. It was a long building and not tall. Inside a great fire burnt in the centre, making the room extremely warm. Suda walked to a large table at the end and bowed his head to an Ilma with grey hair. He was still tall, but he seemed bent over and he showed none of the strength of his youth, where he may have bested his son.
The old man regarded Suda with hard eyes, "Lord Suda, you look tired."
"And you look old."
"That's because you have summoned my people and my son to war." He replied tartly, his eyes falling to his son, "He should be settled down by now, producing me an heir."
"I promise I will not keep him long." Suda said and finally the old lord bowed to him, "You will want food and lodgings I suppose."
"Just for one night father." Ogra replied.

Seats were brought for the company and Suda sat in a tall chair, opposite the old lord. It was not the position fit for the high lord of the realm but Suda respected

The Sundering of the two moons.

lord Langorn and would not demote him without need.
"I will not refuse you of course." The old man replied, "The food you are sending to us, has stopped my people from starving. I can spare some for yourself."
Suda sat at the lord's table as they ate dried fish with summer root vegetables, "You have mustered well my lord." Suda said as the food was taken away and replaced by a fermented bitter drink.
"I am just sad I do not ride with them. I was but a child when my father rode away with our knights to walls of Cradlin. We have not marched in force since."
"It is hoped I will not send them now." Suda said sadly. His own grandfather and great grandfather had ridden in the host to the walls of Cradlin and had returned with Sirgrin's grandfather.
Lidya spoke from the far end of the table, "We do not wish to be heading south with winter approaching but we fear this may be a prelude to an all-out invasion."
"More than just a prelude." The old lord said, "Riders have arrived from Lerou. They have taken the pass through Karmaorna with messages from the king of Scaraden."
Suda's eyes widened, and he could feel the tension forming in his lords. It was rare to kill someone in your homestead but evil stories, from the great continent, of guests welcomed only to be slaughtered, gave them all a pause.
"Have no fear." The old lord said, almost sensing their nerves, "I did not welcome them here and they saw nothing of our mustering."
Dusan leant forward, "What did they ask?"

"They asked if we took a king. I said of course not but they offered us peace if we swore ourselves to their king and supported their claims to the dividing mountains."

"And your reply?" Lidya's voice was cold.

"What do you think boy?" Anger bristled on the lord's brow, "Since the coming of powers, my family have ruled in this town and since that time, we have sworn allegiance to the house of Drage. Ever have my family been treated as one of their kin. If I had my way, that boy there" His finger pointed at Suda, "would be wearing a crown. That is the only king I would ever follow."

Suda felt heat flush in his cheeks as several of his lords and members of Langorn's court, nodded in agreement.

"We want no such thing." Suda said sternly.

"Why not boy?" The old lord leant forward, "That will be only way to fight this king in the south. The alliance will fall under the banner of Dragor if you ask it."

"I do not ask it. Kings are tyrants, and I will take no such title. Not even if the Gods and their vassals wove it into tapestry that I was to do so."

The old lord seemed disappointed, "So be it but be wary lord Drage. A high lord may not be strong enough to hold back this storm and it may be that lesser men take that title in the years to come."

Suda stood and bowed to the old Lord, "I thank you for your hospitality and for your counsel. Do not trouble to wake for us. We shall leave early but I hope to see you at the mustering."

The old lord shrugged, "I do not expect to ride again."

The Sundering of the two moons.

He seemed to sag in his chair, "And I do not expect to see you again, though I hope it is just a darkness upon my heart. Go with the light of Livella guiding you lord Drage."

They slept in the hall of Langorn and rose again before the night had passed. Lit by torchlight, the Graul guards watched them depart over the hills and out of sight of that hidden valley. Dawn rose over the blackened fields and brokin watched the company. The day of that march ended on the edges of Ornadrage, that finished on two high peaks. Suda looked towards it, seeing the true boundary line of his home. Here the land fell downwards as the edges of Orna Drage met with the rising hills at the edge of the dividing mountains.
On the second day they came across a company of soldiers who had marched from the tower of Lerou towards Suda's mustering. They had close ties to the south, but it seemed that they would hold true to their oaths to the house of Drage.
As they marched southward, the dividing mountains became a wall that dominated their view east and west. They rose higher and higher, snow-capped peaks glistening in the sun. Steadily the ground began to rise towards the town of Sikaorna. The edges of a tall mountain formed a semi-circle in front of them, its face sheer. Over three days the walls of Sikaorna grew closer and as night fell on the fifth day from Langorn, torch light showed from the city of Sikaorna. They slept only a short while that night and as dawn crept into the sky, they found the wall of the city, built

between the edges of the crescent. The vast mountain loomed over them, its sheer walls bathed in the red light of dawn.

The gates crept open and one of the Graul stepped out, clad in bone armour, his hands relaxed on his lucrax, "Hail lords." He said with a smile. The threat was from the south and never from the north.

Sirgrin stepped forward as Arodo unfurled the banner beside him, "Open your gate, for here stands Suda, realm lord of Dragor and protector of the dividing mountains."

At Sirgrin's voice, a great cheer went up inside of the walls. Suda and his company stepped in. A great archway loomed in front of them built into the sheer wall and beyond that, lit by many fires, the great hall of Sikaorna sat inside the mountain. The streets of the city were full of stone buildings but anywhere that had once been green lawn, tents now sat. The outer city was cramped, full of Graul whose pale red scales showed that they spent much of their lives doing shifts in the mines. The company carried on through the town, eyes of the Graul watching them, cheers ringing out, echoed by the vast chasm beyond the archway.

The company passed through that vast arch, that stood at least fifty feet above their heads. The halls roof sat even higher, creating a great hall spanning far into the distance. Great pillars of rock held it aloft and everywhere buildings carved of rock stood. The hall was lit by great fires, but natural light came though many windows and shafts, invisible from the outside wall face. This hall had not been built by many Graul or

The Sundering of the two moons.

even many Ilma. It had been crafted, nearly as it stood then, by the vassal Crio. In his battle against Camara and the rising of the dividing mountains, he formed this city and many more cities in like fashion across the range. Sikaorna was the jewel though. The city stretched across the width of the range, with a southern and northern city, joined by the great bridge of Crio, where the vassal was buried. From every wall, passages led off to other parts of the city and the many mines brought great wealth to the Dragor realm. Suda marched to the southern edge of the hall, where a great high church sat in reverence to Orna and there the lord's chamber stood.

The lord of Sikaorna was the same age as Suda. He was a large man, with grey in his eyes from his mother's relation to those of Crio's kin. His main power was over fire though and in his youth, he had been a member of this company. Suda embraced his old friend and they sat as that, and not as lords.

"I thank you for coming." Rivon said quickly, "I have few Ilma here who know anything more than finding metals and quarrying rock. They would be outmatched by the Ilma the king of Scaraden has sent."

"What news do you have?" Ordin asked as he accepted a large glass of wine from one of the serving Graul.

"Nothing good. We have abandoned the southern city and now every mine beyond the high pass. Some of my men hold the bridge now and they fight skirmishes often. I fear though that they are using the southern hall as a mustering ground."

Ordin shook his head, "Marching an army across the high pass would leave them weakened. They would lose many of their men in the attempt."

"Indeed." Rivon nodded, "But it is these Ilma that come with the army that worry me. The winds without the power of the Ilma are treacherous on the high pass. Enough of the Ilma would clear my forces away easily."

"That is why we have come." Suda said sternly.

Rivon leant forward, "Some believe this is a ruse. Something to steal our attention while the armies of Scaraden really move through Besuda."

"That would be a long march." Ogra said. In learning his mastery over metal, he had spent many years with Crio's people, defending the arm, "And one that would gather us ample time to strike back."

"Seaward would suit him better." Sirgrin replied.

"It matters not." Suda said grimly, "We can only deal with the threat in front of us."

Rivon nodded, "What do you need of me?"

"Nothing." Suda said to all their surprise. Ordin put down his wine cup, "We shall move at once." Suda continued, "It is a four-day march to the other side, and I do not wish to delay."

"Very well." Rivon replied. He pointed to a figure who charged across the room. His hair was a light brown, and his red scales, that moved in a line from his ears, mirrored Rivon's, "This is my son, Brid." The lord said, "He shall lead you to the high pass and make sure none of my guards hinder your passage."

"I thank you my friend." Suda smiled, "We shall return to your halls when this threat is dealt with but the

people within your courtyard cannot stay there. They must make for Brinsita. There they shall be protected."
After a quick breakfast with Rivon, the company departed by the large southern door. This was the main road that joined the northern and southern cities. It had been designed by Crio to support the large caravan of Bring Drage's refugees. They walked almost in a line through that wide hall. Great shafts of light came through huge tunnels and lamps of different colours added a live almost fresh feeling to the underground tunnel. All around, roads lead off to different living quarters and the sound of mines continued unceasingly.
Soon they passed out of the habitable areas, where only mine shafts and guard posts stood. At one they stopped with a company of Graul who were marching back from the high pass. They welcomed the company and that night they sang and ate their rations in joy.
The next morning the company were solemn though. Slowly the sound of mining ceased, and the occupied areas became less. The road was climbing steadily upwards.
Suddenly the stuffiness of the underground tunnels gave way to a fresh brisk breeze. As the light fell from a distant opening to the outside world, Suda called Brid to him, "Return back to the halls of your father." He said sternly, "We pass now into danger and the only guards that will halt us, will be our enemies."
The young man nodded and left. Night was falling in the world beyond when they stopped at the last garrison of Rivon's people. Beyond their resting place,

the door to the high pass stood. In a guard house, the company rested but there was no singing that night. The soldiers were on duty, and they listened for any call of the approaching rebels.

Suda woke up feeling cold and the company ate just a small part of their provisions. They forbid the soldiers from following them as they made their way out of the door to the high pass. The air was cold, and a wind howled across the open valley. Above them lay the peak of the northern mountain, in front of them the peak of the southern mountain. Between them a great bridge spanned. Its arched supports reached down into a mist covered valley below. They stood in the heart of the dividing mountains and clouds hung about them. In the middle of the bridge, a jut of rock sprang up. Suda marched towards this. The four graul took the lead, with Lidya and Sirgin at their backs. The twins flanked Suda, with Ogra and Dusan taking up the rear.

They were all cold upon that march but at times, almost like it was designed as so, the mountains blocked out the breeze and warm autumn sunshine fell onto the company. Soon they came to the rock outcrop and there they bowed their heads. A hall stood there and guarding the hall was the image of Crio, holding up the stone roof. There may have been a door once, when Suda's forebears had buried Crio within but now it was just a wall of flat rock. Dusan knelt beside it and said a whispered prayer, asking for Crio and Orna's protection as they crossed into the southern portion of the pass.

The Sundering of the two moons.

They came to the door into the southern mountain and at once the pathway began to fall. There was no sound of mining or signs of life. Litter was scattered across the floor, with the possessions of those that had been forced to flee. They slept in one of the old guard rooms, three of them keeping watch at any one time. They continued as dawn crept through the door to the high pass. Now they were cautious. It seemed that their footsteps echoed in the nearly empty halls, like an army was marching behind them. Arodo walked at their head, a shruda in his hand.
Suda did not see the glint of bone that flew from one of the side passages, but he heard the desperate scream from Arodo as it pierced his leather armour. The Ilma of the company brought fire into their hands as shouts came from all around them. Graul burst from side passages and the lord's sent fire into them. Graul continued to flood in, stepping over the bodies of the dead and swinging shruda's and long steel swords at anyone they could reach. The graul soldiers fought valiantly, slaying any that broke the ring of the Ilma. Though, soon all the company could do, was surround themselves in flame.
"Sirgin, Dusan, come we will need use of your wind." Suda yelled as he dodged thrown shruda's that appeared through the flames.
Sirgrin and Dusan ducked to the centre, and they brought wind from the high pass to swallow the thrown shruda's. Ogra laughed in delight, and he grabbed his lucrax, launching it into the Graul and swiping many of them aside as though he was in a dance.

Arrows began to be fired into the company. So many so, that Sirgrin and Dusan were hard pressed to stop them. One caught Suda's arm, bringing with it a fresh trickle of blood. Then he noticed a change. The arrows ceased firing and there came an uneasy calm. They were all flung backwards as a great wall of water collided with their fire barricade. Boiling steam filled the tunnels, scalding the Graul and making them step back but with the company on their knees, they charged again. Suda drew his sword and black flames spread across the obsidian and this he drew through many of the Graul.

They all fought desperately now, using their powers to carve through the seemingly endless horde of Graul. Suda lifted his arm and one of the walls broke apart, crushing the approaching soldiers and blocking one the of the side tunnels. His eyes sort for their Ilma commander but away from them Lidya screamed. He had been flung by the wall of water and he had found himself far from the company. Graul surrounded him while he danced, a snake of flame following him to keep his enemy at bay.

A great rumble came from the southern hall and the Graul jumped backwards. Suda watched, stuck to the spot, as a great chunk of stone fell from the roof, crashing down upon Lidya's head. He fell to the floor, his skull crushed and shruda's were driven deeply into him.

Suda yelled as he charged towards his fallen brother. The flame from his sword, shot off in many directions, setting the Graul aflame where they stood. The Ilma lord, that had delivered Lidya's death blow, stared at

The Sundering of the two moons.

Suda. On his chest was painted the four towered church of Scaraden. More rock fell but a great wall of wind from Dusan kept the walls from collapsing. The Ilma lord brought a great jet of water, but Suda lifted his arm and a shield of rock knocked it back down the southern pass. With the force of a thousand punches, Suda launched his shield. The Ilma lords arm came up but not quickly enough and the sound of shattered bone filled the passageway. Suda struck with the sword but a shruda deflected it. He changed stance, driving the still burning sword through the Graul before sparks arced in Suda's left hand. The Ilma lord forced Suda away with a last desperate wall of air, but he could not retreat before Sirgin loosed an arrow. The tip took Suda's flame from his sword and with the power of Drage, it broke through the shield of wind and crashed into the eye socket of the Ilma lord. The Graul that remained, fled into passages and many were hunted and killed by the company in their blood lust, but Suda collapsed by his brothers' body and wept tears upon the path of Sikaorna.

III. The Kings plan

"My lord Suda." Came Sirgrin's voice to Suda's ears, "My lord Suda, we cannot stay here."
Suda looked up from the dead eyes of his brother. He did not know long he had been sat there, his mind stricken by grief, but he was sure it must have been some time.
All the company had returned, most of their clothes stained with blood. The bodies of two of his guards, Arodo and Lindi, were placed upon pedestals of stone, ready to be moved. Suda stood slowly, feeling pains in his body from the fight.
"Ordin, Loxa, what news do you have?" He asked slowly.
Ordin stepped forward, "The Graul fled before us, but they could not withstand our powers. They led us to a small township, abandoned apart from a company of brigands. We drove them out and those we did not kill, fled through newly made passages."
"They had one of the Ilma with them." Loxa said, "He fled as well. We believe these passages lead back to the southern hall."
That told Suda that he had indeed spent long in his grief.
Ordin placed a hand on Suda's shoulder, "The high pass is now secure. The Graul are scattered, fleeing back now to the southern hall. We have them on the run."
"Randew." Suda called to his new commander of the guard. The Graul came near and bowed, "Go back

The Sundering of the two moons.

across the bridge. Tell the men there to push forward and to hold the southern entrance. Then return to lord Rivon and tell him what has occurred."

Randew nodded, two fingers pressed to his heart. He went to leave but Dusan's voice stopped him, "Go and tell him yourself. We have done what we came here to do, and we have paid a heavy fee for it."

"I have not done what I set out to do." Suda said, fire burning in his eyes, "I set out to make sure that none of our lands are ever governed by a tyrant king and I stand by that pledge by any dark road that Livella cannot light for me. I shall go into the southern realm and end this would be God's rule."

The company were speechless, and they stared at Suda as though seeing him for the first time. He seemed tall in his grief, a fire burning in his red hair like Drage of old. To them he was the vision of a king, with a crown of red flames upon his head.

Randew left and Suda stepped towards Lidya's body, "Your idols Dusan." He called behind him.

The priest nodded and from his back he pulled out four disks, each as large as his palm. One was of silver, with an image of a star. The second held the image of a mountain and it was made from a mix of many metals. The third disk held a glass phial and clear water from the rivers of Brinsita sat within. The last bore mirrored glass, so that one could truly admire Gadrika's work. Dusan placed these upon Lidya's body. The mirror atop his head, the phial of water at his mouth, the star upon his chest and the disk of Orna on his midriff, "Son of Dragor, descendant of Livella, let your soul go now to rest within her halls.

Soon we shall find a ship and Thera shall carry you beneath the stars, where Drage will claim you."
They prayed together but when Dusan went to retrieve the tokens, Suda stayed him with his hand, "On these four tokens I lay a pledge." An eerie silence grew in the cavern as everyone seemed to hold their breaths, "I, Suda of house Drage, pledge that I shall not return to my home. Nor shall I find simple rest until the king of Scaraden is laid utterly to ruin and his four towered church is destroyed and in its place a star of Livella built. If I should fail, then my house shall ever be laid in enemy of Scaraden, and I swear not to go to the halls of Livella until this pledge is fulfilled." He lifted his sword from the floor and ran his hand along it. He winced as blood dripped towards Livella's token. From the chamber below a wind rose and the blood fell not onto the star but the mirror of Gadrika. As it touched, there was a blinding flash of green flame, and the blood became a pungent sickly smoke. An eerie calm fell over the tunnel and doom weighed heavy upon the company.

"Livella is ill pleased with that pledge." Ogra said, staring at Suda in amazement, "She did not accept it." Dusan had tears in his eyes as he stared at the mirror, "No but Agral has. The green flame was his. He will hold you to that pledge Suda and turn it against you and your kin. Beware, for we enter his land now and it is still tainted from his touch."

Suda was unmoved, "Whether Livella, Agral or any other of the vassals accept my plea, I stand by it." Suda picked up the token of Livella and it was hot to the touch. Suddenly it began to glow, and he gritted

The Sundering of the two moons.

his teeth as the wound to his hand was seared. As it cooled, he passed it to the distraught Dusan. The tokens of Orna and Thera held no change, but the mirror was blackened by the fire. Suda stared into it. His golden eyes seemed dull and lingering behind him he saw a ghostly figure, garbed in black, a broken sword hilt at his side.
As Dusan took it, he wiped at the mirror, but the stains remained. Saddened, he placed the tokens away. Together they continued their march southward, carrying their dead upon pedestals of stone.

After another day of marching, they came to the southern hall of the pass. It mirrored the northern city, just on a smaller scale, with a lesser grand hall and a smaller arch. It seemed that Rivon's fears were well placed. Provisions were stacked high, and it seemed a great force had once rested here. Nearby came the sound of stone being worked, but the small company of Graul were easily driven out. Then the company set to work destroying the provisions and a great smoke billowed out from the archway.
Suda led them out of the arch. Here a small town lay and around it stood a collection of farmsteads. The town had been burnt, pillaged for all they had collected for winter. On a hill of broken stones, the standard of Karmaorna lay, fluttering in the warm summers breeze.
Thatched roofs seemed to move and then Suda noticed shapes upon them. Graul appeared, dressed in browns and greens, brinlon in their hands. At the

urging of Sirgrin, Suda stepped back and bowed his head. Appearing from behind a stable, one of the Ilma appeared. He was a noble sort, tall and clear of red scales. His nose had been broken but the rest of his face appeared as though it was carved from stone.
"Hail lords." He said, his voice thick with a southern accent that made him pronounce every word clearly, "What brings you into the realm of king Harda."
Suda wanted to step forward, but Sirgrin shook his head again and Suda nodded, his rage boiling still inside of him.
Ogra stood forward, hand holding his lucrax in a non-threatening way, "I am Ogra Langorn, from Langorn Langeline beyond the mountains. I have come at the urging of my lord to drive brigands from Sikaorna. A land protected by the line of Drage."
The lord nodded, "Ogra." He said in a familiar way. Suda felt he knew him as well. One of the king's favourites, he was sure, who may have even been welcomed to Dragor in years past, "I had not heard that you now commanded this company." The Ilma continued, "Where is lord Drage? My king greatly wishes to treat with him."
"The lands of the north are free." Loxa said and he smiled as brinlons were drawn, "They hold no king and treat with no king."
"Free for now." The lord whispered, his eyes seemingly wanting to burn into Loxa, "These were not brigands that you drove from these halls but soldiers of the king. Sent to share in the great fortune that the Dragor family have horded for so many years."
"They were given." Dusan said, his hand gesturing to

The Sundering of the two moons.

the star clasping his cloak, "To lord Bring Drage, by the vassal Crio. Would the king deny the power of the vassals."

"Speak more softly of the king in his own land." The lord whispered, hands twitching as though he was preparing to strike. The others moved also, placing the pedestals carrying the dead on the floor, allowing them the use of their powers.

"You have dead." The lord declared, "Take them back to their homes and tell lord Rivon and that fool Suda, that all the mines south of the high pass now belong to the king of Scaraden."

That was the final word spoken. The twins launched from the earth and landed with a flurry of water and flame onto many waiting archers. A great wind rose up and Sirgrin lifted on his wingsuit and from above, he rained fire down upon the waiting Graul. Dusan found cover and from there he fired his metal tipped arrows into any Graul that fled from Sirgrin's and the twin's onslaught.

Suda stood back, still afraid to reveal himself, so it was Ogra who attacked the southern lord. A great many metal knives Ogra threw, all of them tossed aside and from the sky, the lord brought lightening that crashed into the ground with a tremendous bang. Ogra whipped his lucrax forward, causing the Ilma lord to backtrack, hurling pieces of stone and water to deflect the spinning blade. More lightning strikes landed, causing Dusan and Loxa to take cover but Ogra ignored it all, constantly forcing back his enemy. There was another flash in the sky and a bolt of lightning charged towards Ogra, but he knew not who he faced. The lucrax, made of a special metal, that channelled the power of the user, shot towards the heavens and the bolt of lightning soared into it. It glowed a violent red and with that increased power, Ogra drove it through the Ilma lord's chest. His eyes dilated and a venomous curse fell from his lips as he collapsed at the feet of Ogra. The remainder of the Graul fell swiftly to their barrage and calm silence filled the near lifeless town.

"Well then." Loxa said happily, "They now know that we have arrived."

Suda stepped towards his friends, "And still my presence remains unknown. That may stop king Harda from sending all his might against us."

Dusan crept from the shadows as he filled his quiver with bloodied arrows, "But the armies of Karmaorna will not be far away and when they learn what has happened here, that will only hasten their march."

"There are many inns." Ordin said, "A few miles down the road if this mess has not disrupted them."

Suda stopped him, "We may not yet be in open war with the realm of Scaraden, but we will not find any welcome in any inns in this land. We must find shelter in the wild and learn what we can of the king of Scaraden."

They retrieved their dead and made off for a nearby woodland. Passing through it they soon came to a fast-flowing river out of the mountains. Ogra studied it, "I believe this flows down to Elmsatomen and then follows the river there to the sea. This may be the chance to send your brother to the starlight shores."

Suda nodded and together they grew the limbs of the

The Sundering of the two moons.

trees into straight branches, that once felled, fit together to form a raft large enough to bare the three bodies. From a stone, Ogra fashioned a lamp and Suda filled it with a bright flame. Dusan and Sirgrin then sang to the raft and great branches grew and leafed, concealing the three bodies from unfriendly eyes.
"Go brother." Suda said, "And if Thera has any mercy, nothing will hinder you on your final voyage."
The raft lazily began its voyage downstream, and Thera did show mercy and he picked up his current, so that Lidya passed through the inland sea of Elmsatomen and came through a wide river to the sea under the stars. Coming to the place where Theracali would one day rise, Livella lifted his body to the halls of Livinden. The last of the house of Drage to be allowed entry.

The company camped in a thicket of nearby trees. The next day Suda set to his plan and sent the company to scout the lands. Loxa and Ordin he sent to the west, to scout the coastline and to check on the safety of Besuda. Ogra, he sent back along hidden mountain paths towards Karmaorna, to learn of their mustering and Dusan he sent into the greatest danger. The priest of Brinsita went south, to scout the lands near to Elmsatomen, deep in the heart of the kingdom of Scaraden.
Sirgrin and Suda stayed in the thicket, drawing maps, and gathering what supplies they could. During that time, Suda's mood darkened and Sirgrin watched as the dark pledge began to take hold. Suda began to speak less of treating or of holding back the king's

advance and his mind turned to an invasion of Scaraden. He thought of fortifying and what great battles would be fought on his conquest southward. Weeks passed before the twins returned. They had marched to the coast before splitting, one going north to the arm and the other south.

"The army at Besuda has not marched to the mustering." Loxa said, "But they have taken their own counsel and are forming a militia and have scouts on all the main roads. I have spoken to some, and they talk of watch fires that spread to Cradminton and Brinsita. They will be lit at the first signs that the king marches that way."

Suda nodded as he listened and his eyes turned to Ordin, "I do not believe they will march that way." Ordin replied, "Signs indicate that provisions are being sent southward from the coast. You would not do that if you meant to march that way."

"You heard his lord." Suda grumbled, "The king does not want the arm, he wants the dividing mountains and the riches in their hearts."

It took another week for Ogra to return, and he was grim, "I have spent a week trying to flee from pursuit." He said as he sat, finally taking rest by the fire, "The whole area of Karmaorna is on alert. Armies have gathered there and from the town, wagons of stone are heading south but the stone is not being kept, it is being dumped a mile out of the town. I believe they are widening the tunnels between Sikaorna and Karmaorna."

Sirgrin examined a small map that had been crudely drawn. Suda's eyes went to it as well and he saw there

The Sundering of the two moons.

a rough drawing of the passes of both Sikaorna and Karmaorna. They were joined by several tunnels, many north of the high pass. Sirgrin ran his finger along one, "They can attack on two fronts." He said, "A main host could move through Sikaorna, while others went in secret across the frozen chasm."
"And then surround any defence of the high pass we hoped to hold." Suda agreed, "A smart move."
In the next few days that followed before Dusan returned, Suda drew up new plans, recalling all he could of the town of Karmaorna.
When Dusan did return, his news was dire, "Two vast hosts are assembled." His face paled as he spoke, "Some march eastward to the sea, another is camped just south of the tower of Krim. Every able soldier must have been gathered for such a force."
Suda looked down, "Then it is an invasion. While he feints his conquering of the dividing mountains, another army will strike at our homelands." His hands balled into fists, "Are kings ever satisfied to hold the lands they do?"
"How long do we have till that army reaches the coast?" Sirgrin asked.
Dusan shrugged, "The force moves slowly. Winter will not be an issue for them as it is in the north. I suspect they will gather by the sea and strike at springtime, when we are all a little bit weaker."
"Time to do something then." Ogra smiled.
Loxa agreed, "Our navy sits ready, surely we boast the better fleet. We could sink their ships in the sea and scatter their armies before they reach our coast."
"We do not boast a better navy." Ogra replied, "Not

without the Cradlin's and the woodland folk but they cannot reach the eastern coast this side of winter. The north is impassable this time of year. We cannot defend both from the land and sea. We have not the soldiers."

"Ogra is right." Suda said. He did not have the soldiers. His realm was too divided, too reliant on old ways to assemble a worthy enough force to match that of Scaraden's, "We must beat them somewhere and must act in a way that they do not expect." Suda looked towards the map of Karmaorna, "If we can delay them, even for a short time, then I shall return to my mustering."

Sirgrin watched him closely, "What is your plan?"

"The key to this invasion." Suda began, "Is the king needs to secure the highpass before winter comes. He will use his force at Karmaorna to do that. If we can delay that force, then we delay his whole invasion." He pointed to the passageways between Karmaorna and Sikaorna, "We need to gain access to their tunnels and collapse as many as we can, like the brigands did in the southern pass."

"That is like going into a den of grignin with meat strapped to your back." Ordin smiled and then he laughed gayly

"It may be like that but me and Ogra have travelled the passes of the mountains more than any Ilma beside the Minton's. We know paths that foreign lords do not. With them, we shall disrupt this kings' plans."

They took rest for the day and marched again as night

The Sundering of the two moons.

fell, traveling by the waxing light of the two moons. They reached Karmaorna on a moonless night and stared down into the great many fires of camps that surrounded the town. The tower of Karmaorna rose high into the sky, its white walls reflecting the light of the campfires below. The town itself seemed quiet but there was a great amount of movement at the sheer wall of the mountain where a similar hall to Sikaorna, led into the mines there.

"Dusan." Suda called the ranger of Brinsita forward, "Find us some clothes and a secure way in."

Dusan smiled and nodded and left them on silent feet. In his green and brown cloak, he disappeared quickly into the darkness. He returned an hour later, carrying a bundle of cloaks and hoods but he did not explain how he had come by them. They dressed quickly, all in the grey colours of the armies of Scaraden and then they crept towards the camp closest to the mountain hall. They looked, in the dim light, like a returning scouting group but they kept themselves away from campfires and the main bulk of the town. Instead, they marched towards a nearby quarry and from there they found a service entrance to one of the many mines. Two guards stood at its front. They were leaning on their lucrax and were singing to themselves, unthreatened within this camp in their homeland. Suda nodded to Ogra, who pulled out two iron darts and stood.

He approached the guards casually and one held out a hand to stop him, "What do you need guardsman?" The Graul asked, his face a mass of red scales.

"Death and glory." Ogra whispered and the darts

flew, piercing each Graul in their windpipes. Their screams were muffled from a wind Ogra created and he held it there until the two guards fell motionless. Suda and the rest of the company joined him and they opened the door into the mine. Torches lit the paths in front of them. The twins concealed the bodies while Suda and the others entered.

They marched, using the torches for light, wearily checking for signs of their enemy. The paths began to turn back towards Karmaorna, climbing as they did. Nearby passages were full of the clink of tools, where men hacked at the rock face. The mountain seemed to shake as great horn calls went up and echoing down passages, came the shouts of guards as they searched.

"The bodies have been found." Suda said grimly, "We must hurry."

A quick turn took them into a wide passageway. It led off into darkness and Suda guessed that its path led to the frozen chasm and beyond that to the high pass. Its walls were roughly hewn and many of the scratches were fresh. A group of soldiers stared at them as they entered the passageway, and seeing in the clear light, the groups original armours, they charged, heedless that they faced Ilma.

A flaming brand appeared in Suda's hand, and such power was in it from his grief that the Graul could not withstand him. He moved like a snake, his brand felling Graul or throwing them to the company, where they were quickly broken.

Suda stopped as the last Graul fell. The passage was filled with the smell of burned flesh. Shouts could be

The Sundering of the two moons.

heard all around now. Choosing the eastward way, Suda led the company down the passage. Ordin charged past him as they came to a large hall, the sound of soldiers coming from within. He charged into it, heedless of any threat and there he was caught. Stone grabbed at his foot and as he lunged, a sickening crack echoed through the hall. As it incapacitated him, the stone continued to climb up his body. The others entered more slowly, and they saw there one of the Ilma, his hand outstretched, calling the stone up Ordin's body. Suda charged at the Ilma and his hold on Ordin was broken. Ogra cracked the stone and dragged Ordin to safety while Suda launched fire into the waiting Ilma. Loxa and Dusan followed on from Suda's barrage and a great wind lifted Sirgrin into the air. Loxa and Dusan launched fire, merging with Suda's but a great slab of stone burst upwards to block it.
Sirgrin ducked thrown rock as he soared through the chasm. He threw water down upon the Ilma but bolts from nearby archers sent him off course. Water met with the companies flame and steam filled the chamber. Dusan charged through it, mirroring the movements of the Ilma, whose arms became crusted in stone. Wind balled around Dusan's fist and air met rock with a tremendous crash, but the stone proved the stronger and Dusan flew backwards, landing into the wall with a dull thud.
Suda ducked out the way, launching water from a nearby well, distracting the Ilma lord. Regaining his wingsuit, Sirgrin threw flame to Loxa, who added to it and it span around his arms. It flew, fire forming a

spear point that crashed through the distracted Ilma's chest and he fell to the floor at Suda's feet, just as the stone was about to envelope him.

For only a second, they revelled in their victory but stopped as the first wave of arrows flew from the far end of the hall. They all created a shield of wind and the arrows fell weakly to the floor but Graul in great number were approaching and some of the soldiers held flame within their hands.

"We must go." Loxa yelled from the passageway.

"No." Suda said through gritted teeth, "We must collapse this hall."

"They will overwhelm us." Ogra agreed as he pulled Dusan towards the tunnel.

Sirgrin landed beside Suda, his eyes watching Ordin who winced as he tried to straighten his broken leg, "Our cousin cannot move swiftly." He said in Suda's ear, "We cannot defeat them all."

Suda's teeth gritted, "Go then and I will collapse this tunnel."

"No." Ordin said, his voice breaking with the pain, "This passage is just one of many. It will slow them, but we must collapse more. I will hold them here; you move through and collapse the others while they try to free those trapped."

Loxa looked horrified, "We leave no one behind."

"With me like this, it is only a matter of time till a shruda takes me and I will not have one of you die getting in the way." Ordin's eyes were like fire and tears streaked down his face, but he tried to stand resolute. Another barrage of arrows were fired and again Sirgrin kept them back. Ordin took a step

The Sundering of the two moons.

forward and lifted his hand to the rubble on the floor and the rock formed around him, "Now who will move me from this place."
He created fire that made the approaching Graul retreat but sweat glistened on his forehead and Suda knew he could not hold it for long. Arrows were being knocked again and the Ilma were approaching, "Go now." Ordin ordered.
Suda nodded. They could all die here, or they could achieve something. As Suda departed, so did Sirgrin, Ogra and Dusan, all with tears in their eyes. Loxa looked at his brother, desperate to stay but Ordin's eyes were full of confidence, and he signalled for him to go. Regretfully, Loxa followed.

They ran as fast as they could and five minutes into their march, there came a great rumble. The whole mountain vibrated as great chunks of rock began to fall in front of them. Dusan lifted his hand and wind came from the frozen chasm beyond. It swept passed the company and charged at the funnel of dust and rock, that crashed through the passageway. Dust and rubble bounced against Dusan's shield, and his face contorted in his effort to control the blast. The rest of the company joined in and soon the power of the collapse was spent, and the dust settled beyond their shield of air. Sirgrin gave a grunt and forced the dust and rubble back down the chamber.
All was silent for a second, apart from the distant sound of screams. Dusan knelt, facing the grand hall, "Here shall Ordin sleep beneath the mountains of Karma. Never again will they hear him sing by the sea,

but the halls of Agraldin will be sweeter for it." He stood and walked over to Loxa, who cried silent tears, "Orna has delivered him and now he will weave our victories into the tapestry."

Nothing seemed to ease Loxa's grief, but Suda saw a fire in his eyes, most likely the same fire that was seen within his own. Suda turned to Ogra, "Take Loxa and Dusan. Take the northern way and collapse all the passages from there to the frozen chasm, then meet us back at Sikaorna."

The company parted, Dusan and Loxa followed Ogra, while Suda went with Sirgrin. They worked tirelessly during their two-day march, collapsing any passage large enough for men to walk three abreast. As peace came, Suda began to brood, conscious of the fact that he had lost two friends on this march. More than he had ever lost when he led the company before. They came to the passageway where Lidya had died. Men guarded it now and a cool breeze came from the highpass.

They stepped onto the bridge between the mountains and Sirgrin called a wind from the direction of Karmaorna. He listened to it and smiled, "It worked, they are trying to clear the passages, but this wind has travelled far, and I believe they are still working to free those trapped by Ordin."

Suda nodded, "Then we have gained time for us to strike back."

The sun beat down upon them both but a shadow lingered on Suda that could not be broken. Below the bridge, the green fertile valley was visible. He wished he could find a passage down there, where he could

The Sundering of the two moons.

build a house and forget his responsibility, but his pledge had begun to darken his heart.
"My lord." Sirgrin said, "Your mind is clouded by grief, do not let it overcome you."
"We cannot wait in Sikaorna until we are surrounded." Suda replied angrily.
"No, my lord, but in Brinsita we could long hold."
Suda laughed mirthlessly, "And in that time, king Harda would feast within the halls of Dragor, scour the fields of Grinlavine and strip the dividing mountains. What sort of lord would I be then?"
Sirgrin's head dropped, "What then will you do?"
Suda felt a cold and stale breath fall against his neck and he shuddered, remembering the image of Agral within the mirror, "I shall return to the lands of my home and pray to Livella for her guidance."

They returned to Sikaorna the next evening and there they were greeted by guards. The hall seemed empty. The usual merchants had moved on and the lord himself had moved to a pavilion beyond the wall. As Suda and Sirgrin passed the archway, they were met by Ogra, who rushed over and embraced them both.
"How fared your mission?" Suda asked with no joy to his voice.
"We have collapsed many passages. Our enemy will have to work hard to reach north of the highpass from Karmaorna." His face seemed to grow sullen, "I fear Loxa's grief is maddening."
"What did he do?" Sirgrin asked.
"We came across a party of Graul. Scouts I think." Ogra shook his head in his regret, "Loxa burnt them in

his aura."
Suda's jaw tightened. Graul might have been the servant race, but it did not mean they were trillon to be used and slaughtered, even if some of the Ilma believed it so, "Where is he now?"
"In one of the inns, drowning his sorrows." Ogra spat on the floor, showing what he thought of that, "Dusan is with Rivon in his pavilion."
Suda turned to Sirgrin and placed a hand on his shoulder, "Bring Loxa, we shall not rest in Sikaorna. We shall find plenty of it once we return to Brinsita."
Sirgrin nodded and charged down a street, where the buildings held signs out front. Suda followed Ogra, who signalled to some of the tents along the roadway. Most were filled with male Graul in hastily made armour, "He has armed his militia, if armed you can call it. Most weild mining equipment. They will not hold off a long assault."
"I hope they will not need to." Suda replied.
They entered a large tent where Dusan and Rivon were talking. They smiled at the pairs entrance and Rivon beckoned them to sit. Loxa and Sirgrin soon followed, and food was brought for all of them.
"You are less than when you first left my halls." Rivon said and Suda's eyes went to Loxa, who sat hunched over his food, his scales dull and his hair unwashed.
"We lost my brother just south of the highpass, two of my guard also, and Ordin gave his life to collapse the hall of Karmaorna."
Rivon looked down, "Tonight I shall pray for them beneath the stars."
Sirgrin told the story of their travels in the southern

The Sundering of the two moons.

lands and what they had learnt there, disquieted lord Rivon. He left out only Suda's pledge, of which none of them would speak.

"We will stay here." Rivon said as he finished his meal, "We will hold the pass in case they attack again. What of your plan Suda? We could use you here."

"I am weary." Suda replied and he finally felt it. The weight of all that had gone wrong, fell on his shoulders. He would sleep for a week but knew he could not, "And my heart his heavy for the loss of my family. I must return to Brinsita and take counsel there."

"Then we will hold the pass for you." Rivon smiled, "Go now to your beds and try and find some peace."

Suda stood and bowed to his friend, "Thank you. Keep the pass open to us."

IV. The Council of Brinsita

Suda tossed and turned in his sleep, locked within his own dark dream. He was wandering the outer city of Dragor, but it was not how he had left it. Decay filled the dirt streets. The buildings toppled, wooden frames burning as they hit the ground. The sky above was dark with swirling clouds, that seemed like flame of orange and green battled within them. The mountains of Ornadrage loomed high above him and they were a dark grey, like teeth of a great beast protruding from the ground and no snow topped them.

He continued down the main street but stopped as he saw the dragon gate. Smoke lifted from the beast's nose and its eyes were a deep, glowing red. The bottom of its portcullis dripped blood and Suda was unsure whether the beast would allow him to pass. All his will told him to turn away and run but he stepped into the city of his birth. As he passed, the portcullis fell and the dragon's head crumbled, consumed by a fire within. It seemed fire had destroyed most of Dragor. The brick buildings were in heaps on the floor, burned by a sweeping fire.

He continued through the market, moving to the only building that still stood untouched. The keep of Dragor. As he did, he heard the footsteps of something large. A figure appeared above the keep. Its eyes were gold with a long, reptilian like face that burned from an inner fire. Great wings spread over the keep and its talons ripped into the hard stone.

The Sundering of the two moons.

The dragon lifted into the air and Suda cowered behind some rubble and as he looked, he saw Agral upon the dragon and at its words, the beast torched more of the city. Suda knelt and wept as screams surrounded him.

The city was back to how it should be, or almost. The keep was gone and, in its place, stood a grand building of pure white stone. At its centre was a great dome and from each of its corners, four towers rose. The church of eternity, the centre of power in Scaraden.
He saw his family, bowed down in front of the church, collars round their necks as they served king Harda, but he saw also, a ringlet of flames upon Idris's head. King Harda lifted his hand and Suda could only scream as that fire consumed the small boy.

Suda woke with a start, fire balling in his hands. His eyes softened as he spotted Sirgrin in the entrance to his tent, "Day breaks my lord." He said as he bowed his head and ducked from the tent.
Suda could feel the cold morning breeze against his sweat soaked skin. It would be a cold day. He dressed in warm furs and stepped out into Rivon's camp. As they nearly always did, the remaining company left before many had begun their morning tasks.
They marched more swiftly on their brokin, taking little rest for meals and sleep. They marched over many hills, crowned with short grass, burnt by frost, or ripped up by grazing trillon. Days after leaving Sikaorna, they came to a forest and Dusan led the way

through it. Slowly as the day darkened, they noticed that the trees seemed to glow, emitting a small amount of light to guide them.

Suda had travelled these woods before. He had spent much of his youth at Brinsita, and he had travelled there most recently for his father's funeral. His eyes went to the trees above them, where he was sure grey and brown sentinels would be watching. Soon the trees began to thin and the sound of running water greeted them and Suda heard another noise. The sound of many people.

The island between the three rivers was usually an empty place. The town of Brinsita sat at the northern edge of the island, where a canal had been built in years gone by to join Sitalin and Sitaliv earlier in their course. This was originally done to prevent flooding, now it acted as a natural protection for the most precious Ilma built church in all of Dragor.

They came to a bridge which crossed Sitaliv, which was fast and flowing at this time of year. Two Graul soldiers guarded the bridge, but they simply bowed their heads as Suda passed.

He gasped as the trees broke, and he looked across the flat, nearly treeless island. The usual farms were now occupied by many sprawling camps, each erected in a different segment off the main road. The company marched down the long white paved road and Suda saw many camps, under the banners of his lords. There was the dragon boat of Dragesuta, the high white tower of Lerou, the leaping brokin of Langorn and the lighthouse of Amoradrage. There were many banners from lesser lords of his realm also.

The Sundering of the two moons.

A grain of wheat on a green background for Grinlavine and a towered hut for the small town of Linsita. There were many others from the lords of the other kingdoms. From Cradlin came those of Tukakrunbane, their banner a tree in the shape of a tower. The wooden keep of Tukanita was present and the violent rose of house Aquitex. There were less of those of the Minton's. A boat with a burning torch for the town of Livsita and a large hammer for the Cradminton's.
As they approached the town of Brinsita, the tents grew in size and so did the number of banners, but they all showed only three things. The three peaks of the Minton's, the two towers of Cradlin or the dragon banner of his own line.
Suda came quickly to his own camp and found a tent laid out for him by his steward. He rested and washed before wearing a shirt of deep red with black trousers, the obsidian sword strapped to his side.
He walked into the town proper, down the white slabbed road that went in a straight line towards the church. It was a sight to see. Its walls of red brick were polished so that they shone in the light and a great domed roof rose above it, but the dome was made of glass so that the stars could be seen from the chamber below. It was a jewel of the northern kingdom, built in the place where Livella had first walked upon Ilmgral and where she had met Gadrika, with flowers at his feet.
An Ilma approached him. He looked much like his brother Dusan, only his hair was cropped, and a circlet sat upon his brow, bearing a white gem.
"Welcome my lord." He said, his arms spreading to

embrace Suda, "Livella has guided you here. Find counsel in her church."
"Thank you Drixan." Suda nodded.
The lord of Brinsita was not like his brother. He dedicated his life to the church and went very rarely from its borders. He was a scholar, a writer of the book of the holy quadrant and pious to his core, "I ask permission to pray in your church." Suda continued, "I will take my meal within and rest. In the morning, a council will be summoned, and we must decide on the future."
"Your words have darkness behind them." Drixan seemed concerned as his golden eyes watched Suda's, "I will make sure you are not disturbed. You will need to be alone with Livella this night."
Suda nodded his thanks and entered the church. The door opened into a wide hall, lit by many magnificent lamps.
At the far end of the room rose a statue of Livella, carved from marble. Her skin was beautifully, almost wrongly, perfect. Her left hand was outstretched, bearing a lamp. The right, just a stump, covered by a gown.
This was a place for ceremony but also for the Graul. Many huddled within, receiving their evening meal from the kitchens. To his right, a door to the library sat guarded. Word of his coming must have spread for the door was opened for him and was closed and locked after he had entered. He climbed the staircase and stepped out into the library of Brinsita. The heavens spread above him, made more beautiful by the glass dome. Suda approached a candelabra that

sat by a smaller statue of Livella. He knelt before her and touched two fingers to his heart, "Livella my foremother, forgive me for the trouble I have brought upon your people. I need your guidance, now more than ever in my life."

Silence came to the church and Suda gasped. His eyes went upwards and the sky that had only just reached dusk, was now as black as midnight. In a blink, stars began to appear. First came the stars of creation as great constellations in the shape of the four gods. Then many stars and many constellations swirled in front of him. He saw the star of the warrior, the stars of gift and betrayal, the stars of separation and finally the red mountain star rose, the other stars of the vassals falling beneath it.

The red mountains star, the star of Drage Livella, began to glow violently and then it grew in size. Suda ducked as it seemed to charge towards the church. A faint thud echoed beside him and suddenly he was lit by a strange light. He looked up and at once fell to his knees again.

"Rise child." A man said in a voice that crackled like fire in a hearth.

Suda did as commanded, and he lifted his eyes to look at the figure. His prayers had been answered. Drage had returned to the mortal world. The vassal's eyes were like bright lamps and his hair was fire that spread far down his back. He wore still the scarlet armour that he had worn on his northward march and at his side, he had a blade of fire.

"Forgive me." Suda whispered, "I am humbled by your presence Drage Livella, vassal of fire."

"There is nothing to be forgiven." Drage's voice was full of warmth and Suda felt courage rise inside of him, "Long have I watched over my house and guided those lords who came before you, though none have ever been so troubled I fear."

"No lord has faced such a war as we face now, and it has come so swiftly and un-looked for. Now I wish that I had stayed in my keep."

"Had you done so, you would not have learnt of the king's plans." Drage replied, "Agral works in their hearts, and he hates me and my kin. He brings the darkness, but we are the light that guides the Ilma."

"So, the land of Scaraden is cursed." Suda looked down, remembering the image in the mirror. He was cursed now as well, "It was folly for me to enter that land and to expect good to come of it."

Drage's eyes softened, "Not all that land is dark, for Krim once lived there and he is of light as am I. Child, you cursed yourself before you entered his land. You made a pledge with Agral against his own people."

"That pledge was made for Livella." Suda said, the shame tearing at him.

"Livella accepts no such pledge. She wishes you to be pure of heart so you can rule steadfast and true to yourself." Drage's flames seemed to grow and Suda felt the heat of them, "It was a dark pledge, made worse when you killed as soon as you entered Scaraden. I do not fully know what evil this pledge may bring but I know that until it is fulfilled, Livinden is closed to you. Agral owns you after death and he owns the souls of all your line. They will come to his dark chambers in Agraldin, far from the land Livella

The Sundering of the two moons.

promised my kin."
Guilt now overcame Suda, and he collapsed to the floor, crying at the feet of the vassal, "Oh please, father of my house, is there nothing I can do to undo this pain. Is there no way of saving our house?"
Drage lifted Suda, and his eyes went to the heavens. New stars flickered into the sky, and they formed a shape like a ringlet of flame, "In the stars lie a crown. It resides only over this land. This is her sign Suda. There is no way you can take back your pledge, you must complete your goal. Ride to war in the lands of Agral but go for light and not vengeance or conquest. Go as a king and treat with a king."
Suda paused, thinking of the glory he could achieve. His breath caught for a second before he could speak, "We take no king." He deadpanned and he felt a cold hand upon his shoulder, "We never shall."
Drage's eyes became sad, and his flame faded slightly, "If you do not take yourself to be king now, then the curse shall follow you and your family, till the universe is consumed."
Suda's head dropped and the flame of Drage faded. Birds sang outside of the church and the night sky was replaced by the dusky light of the real world. Suda felt drained and the words of Drage circled through his head, battling with the thoughts put there by Agral. He started as there came a knock at the door. It opened and someone dressed in gold-coloured robes entered. The young Ilma male, placed the plate of food on the table before bowing and leaving.
Suda ate slowly and sat beneath the domed roof until the stars came out. They were the normal stars for

this time of year. The constellation of Livella sat on the low horizon, It would come to prominence in late winter. Gadrika's was proud in the sky, sat beside the blue stars of the Thera-ilma, that were always present in the north. He saw no sign of a crown in the stars though.

Throughout the night he welcomed many people, and he took counsel with them. He spoke to the members of his company, to the high lords and lords from his realm. To none did he tell of his vision or Drage's dark words. He listened to all their advice and began to form some plan in his mind. As the red mountain star skirted over the western hills, Suda left and went to his tent to sleep.

The next morning, Suda took council in a large pavilion beyond the town. Every lord and high-ranking member was present, but the three realm lords sat at the centre of the pavilion, their entourage spreading outward from them. Suda sat there, next to Andorgrin Minton and Adan Cradlin, who was very old now. He had lived long and seen much. He had escaped with his father when the Thera-ilma had sacked Cradlin. That had been the beginning of the end for those children of Camara.

Suda welcomed all the lords and began the council by recounting the company's journey through the pass of Sikaorna and what they had learnt in the lands of Scaraden.

"So." Callano Cardon began, "You believe that the collapse at Karmaorna has hindered them?"

"Yes." Suda replied, "If only to give us enough time to

act. I ask lords, what would you have us do?"
"The arm at Besuda is well defended." Andorgrin said. He was a squat man, with grey eyes and long grey hair. He carried a great war hammer at his side, that the sons of Crio used to better direct their power, "They will not pass that way without great loss."
"They do not seek Besuda." Sirgrin said but his eyes went downward. He was not there to speak. He was not a lord.
Ogra saved his graces, "Their army passed eastward, away from the arm."
"That was before you interrupted their plans. Who knows now what path they seek?" Andorgrin said.
Suda looked at the other realm lord, "A fair point. What army holds Besuda?"
"I brought much of my forces here, but I assembled my militia in early spring, when rumours of king Harda calling his banners reached me. I have left enough trained men to guide them. Their forces will find a difficult task breaking through the arm."
"That would mean waiting for them to try and come into our land." Ogra said defiantly, "While we did that, they could ravage our eastern lands."
Andorgrin gave a mirthless laugh, "This could happen wherever you chose to make your stand, lord Langorn. We cannot hope to spread our forces across all our border."
Ogra smiled, looking at Suda, "I do not suggest that we do such a thing. We cannot win this fight through strength of arms. We must do something that the king will not expect."
Adan Cradlin, who had seemed almost asleep, looked

up, "That would mean going into their land and doing war upon their people. Never has one of our armies marched into a foreign land in force."

Suda nodded at Adan, "And then that is what we must do. The king expects us to be passive as we have done many times before, thinking us above the other Ilma due to the vassal's blood that runs through our leaders." He stood, "We must move into the southern land and do war in his townships, in his fields, so their people know what it is like when a king asks them to do war upon a godly people."

"We could march through the arm." Andorgrin said with a rare smile, "Regroup with my militia."

Suda shook his head, "No. King Harda will expect that. We must take the path he wanted. We still hold the high pass. There will be no battle upon that bridge, no force trying to delay us in the mining passages. If we did not take this road, then Sikaorna will fall, and our lands will soon follow."

"Our armies cannot all go through Sikaorna." Adan said, "Such a journey would take just as long as a march down Besuda."

"I do not believe our army should travel as one. We must do as our enemy intended and hope to trap the armies of Scaraden. Does your fleet still lay hidden by the Krun-ilma?"

Adan laughed, "It cannot be secret if you know of it."

Suda turned to the Ilma of Crio's people, "Andorgrin will send one battalion back to the arm but send riders first to your militia. They are to push to the very border of the land of Scaraden. Send them on a path to Elmsatomen. My lord Cradlin, take your forces back

The Sundering of the two moons.

to the havens in the west wood. Have them take to the sea and come up the wide river to the lake's shores. My forces will take the pass of Sikaorna and move to strike at the tower of Krim. He will fear me holding that castle and he will send out a force to meet us long before we can reach it."
There were murmurs of agreement but the lords of Cradlin looked uncomfortable. Many still did not like taking long sea voyages, where the power of Camara was still strong.
"if we go to war." Adan said slowly, his voice full of age and wisdom, "We must not go as realms divided. We must go under one banner, one lord, one king."
There was a sound of many deep intakes of breath. Again, Sirgrin spoke out of turn, "We take no king."
Suda panicked, worried that he had brought the curse from Scaraden back to his home and the words of Agral now poisoned the old lord, making him yearn for glory.
"No but maybe it is time that we did." Adan lifted his hand and with an old, wrinkled finger, he pointed at Suda, "There is the king we all follow."
For a moment, a flash of jealousy filled Andorgrin's eyes, but he eventually stood, "I owe everything to the house of Drage. I would happily follow you and your kin as my king."
Suda felt the cold hand of Agral upon his shoulder. Power, greed, visions of an empire filled his mind, but he quelled them, thinking of quiet nights with his wife, "I will not accept that charge while I live. We are a free people, without king or tyrant." Adan and Andorgrin looked down, hearing the resolve in his

voice. Murmurings of dissent arose that Suda would need to quell quickly, "Under one banner we shall go though. Two towers built upon three peaks, with a dragon guarding their gates. Ever has our realm worked as such." A few cheers grew at that remark, "Have these banners made, so that king Harda knows who rides to defeat him in battle."

A cheer grew, cries of "The three realms." Echoing to those outside.

Slowly the council faded, as the lords left to relay their instructions. Suda's company remained as did Adan and one more of his house. The old realm lord approached Suda on weak legs, "You should take the mantle. Our realms are ready for it."

Suda shook his head, "They never will be. To crown me will only invite challenge. I will speak no more of it."

Dusan stood forward, "It is decreed." He said in a soft voice, "That the holy quadrant view a king only just below the vassals."

"Blasphemy." Suda barked, "Spread most likely by the sons of Agral as they whispered into lord Lidon's ear. Why should the people of Carano or Tukanita follow me as their king?"

Adan's voice was level, "Because their lords told them to."

"Then a tyrant I would be."

Adan looked down, doubt creasing his forehead, "If we sail south, we will need to pass through the flow of Camara. She hates my people. Under a king, maybe we would be allowed passage. I fear for my ships."

Suda looked down, again feeling that pull from Agral,

The Sundering of the two moons.

"No." He said at last, "I will hear no more of it."
Adan lowered his eyes and beckoned for the Ilma behind him to approach. His hair was shaved, his nose had been broken and red scales sat under his eyes but there was no hiding that he was close kin of Adan.
"My middle child." The old lord said, "Buskino will lead the fleet southward."
Suda nodded to him, "I will pray for safe winds on your journey."
Buskino bowed, two fingers pressed to his heart.
"I will not live another winter." Adan whispered sadly, "But if my last act is to send my men to defend their homes and bring an end to tyranny, then I could rest easily in the halls of Agraldin."
"I will see that you have that privilege my lord." Suda placed two fingers upon his heart and bowed his head to Adan.
The council ended like that and quickly the armies were readied for the march. The next day, those of Cradlin and Minton departed to begin their long journey. On a bright and cold morning, Suda led the combined host of Minton and Drage, out of Brinsita and they crossed the wide lands to the passes of Sikaorna.
Rangers of Brinsita went before them, and taking the mountain passes, they scouted the lands of Scaraden and halted any of the enemy they encountered.
Suda sat at the front of a vanguard of cavalry from Drage and Langorn. Following him came trained soldiers from all his realm. He put aside all the doubt from his dark pledge as he led this army to do war in Agral's land.

V. The Battle of Elmsatomen.

The armies of the united realms marched through fields on their way to Sikaorna. They made no real camps, sleeping under the stars with great bonfires dug into the earth to warm them.
A great cheer went up as the vanguard entered the walled city. The militia there cheered, hands upon their core in the fashion of the Minton's.
The march through the halls of Sikaorna was strange for Suda. He led his vanguard, with the steady and in sync footfalls of the brokin behind. The sound that followed the united army was a deep boom, that rattled the foundations of the mountain and frightened those who still worked in Karmaorna.
On the second day, Suda stopped on the southern edge of the high pass. He looked out across the bridge, seeing the split in his army. It would be foolish to have soldiers spend the night on that high place.
"You are nervous lord." Sirgrin said as he stood beside Suda.
The mood in the camp was low. Many had never been in Sikaorna before and were unaccustomed to the stone tunnels they walked in. The brokin were skittish, held only to their will by the soldiers who cared for them.
Suda smiled at his friend, "I wish we went straight to war, when summer was still lingering." The cold chilled his bare arms, "We go beyond our borders in winter, and I feel like I am losing control."

The Sundering of the two moons.

Ogra came forward, "We would have been trapped if we had. This was wise counsel, or our people would have suffered in their own lands."
"What difference does it make what land you suffer in." Suda deadpanned, "Mothers will lose sons, wives their husbands and I have set a dangerous precedent for my son. Will he spend all his reign as high lord in bitter wars in foreign lands? A king that would make him indeed." Visions of the flame crown consuming Idris filled his mind. He would find no sleep this night.

It took another two days to reach the burnt-out town beyond Sikaorna and a further two days for the army to emerge in its fullness. Other than a few skirmishes with those of Karmaorna, Suda found no trouble.
As the army readied to march towards the tower of Krim, Dusan and the rangers of Brinsita, returned to the camp, "Karmaorna is emptied." Dusan said as he approached Suda, "The signs show that they moved southward, likely to join the southern army. We believe their main body lies by Amoraorna."
Suda nodded his head, "Harda will know that we are here by now. He will not risk an invasion with us ready to ravage his lands. He will choose to make a stand somewhere and then we will have him caught between our two forces."
Sirgrin smiled, "That will mean we need to pick our battlefield."
"I will continue to move towards the tower of Krim. Our two forces should then meet upon the southern border of Elmsatomen."
"A wise plan." Ogra said and he moved away to relay

the orders to the other lords.

Suda had given Ogra command of the infantry of the united army, while Suda would hold the vanguard and the cavalry from Langorn. Sirgrin would be at his side, but Dusan would march with the rangers of Brinsita and would command the archers. Loxa, still locked in his grief, had been left in Brinsita.

The army went on, slowly marching southward, the weather growing warmer with every step. For some parts of Scaraden, winter was a mild affair, with only the occasional snow flurry. Here it seemed that autumn lingered just a bit longer and only a mild dew rested on the ground when they woke.

On their eastward side, the horizon shimmered. Elmsatomen, one of the great lakes of the world, sat there and Suda watched it hopefully, praying for the force that would soon navigate its wide river to reach them. Southward, the mountains Ornamora rose. There, in years past, lord Lidon had defeated his final enemy and had taken the mantle of king. Now Suda would go to end a king's rule in the shadow of the fortress in the mountains.

Slowly they could begin to see their enemies' defences. A great line of tents covered a hilltop on the edge of the mountains and stakes had been driven into the ground. Ogra began the erecting of their own defences and Suda, flanked by Dusan and Sirgrin, surveyed what would be the battlefield, "Assemble the archers here." Suda said, "The kill zone will be the valley between our two peaks. They should be able to fire into the soldiers moving down the hill."

From the other camp, came the sound of many voices

The Sundering of the two moons.

and Suda heard Sirgrin mutter a prayer. He looked up, eyes staring towards the enemy, "I can hear many voices on the wind. King Harda has with him a large force."

"Then let us hope our luck holds." Suda deadpanned, "Get the armies into rank. They must rest where they are needed. A parley may come before night settles, and I will not have our army caught unaware. Hide the cavalry below the rise, they can flank across the plain to our right."

They returned to camp, passing soldiers that moved in ordered ranks to the places Suda had commanded. For most it would likely be their grave. As they came towards the main host, riders from the army of Scaraden approached. They carried a long streaming banner, a sign of peace and parley.

"What do you reckon he will demand or offer?" Sirgrin asked as he stood taller in front of the three dismounting Ilma lords.

"Neither." Suda whispered in reply, "He will only threaten. That is the way of kings."

"My lord." The three Ilma bowed, their hands pressed against their foreheads. One stood out among the rest. His white skin seemed slightly sickly, and his irises were wide.

"*One of Agral's brood.*" Suda thought to himself, and a cold wind rustled around him, and he heard within them, the words of his pledge.

"What is this?" The kin of Agral looked around, clearly looking for Suda's pavilion, "Why are we kept like beggars at the door? Is it not custom to welcome guests in your land?"

"You will forgive my discourtesy." Suda smiled grimly as he spoke and the Ilma lord's eyes narrowed, "I am weary of conversing with the lords of Scaraden. All they have brought me are the deaths of my brother and kin."

Eyes flashed between the emissaries and fingers twitched as though they were readying their powers. The leader, the one who would bare doom as his last name, spoke, "Well maybe that is the fate you bring, when you do war in someone else's lands."

"We did not start this war." Sirgrin said, anger filling his voice, but Suda lifted his hand to silence him.

"What would king Harda ask of us?" He replied, "I am impatient of talk. The tower of Krim awaits me. Rumours are it is a pleasant place to stay during the winter months."

"Krim?" One of the lords whispered, "What business would bring you to that tower with such a force?"

"It is a prize, is it not?" Suda said, "The tower the vassal built. It would be a fitting place for one such as myself. One who has not forsaken the light like the king of Scaraden. A king whose closest advisor's hail from the vassal that nearly destroyed the world."

"And what right do you have, son of Drage, a lord in name only, to claim that tower?" It was the kin of Agral who spoke, his words full of venom.

"The same right that a king has in claiming dominion over the mountains that were given to my family by the vassal Crio." Suda seemed to grow larger as he spoke, and the two lesser lords stepped backwards but the son of Amora stood resolutely

"Run back to your king." Suda continued, "Tell him

The Sundering of the two moons.

that if he wishes to hold the tower of Krim, then he should run there, like the fool he is and pray for the mercy of Gadrika."
The lord spat at Suda's feet, "Enjoy your rest now lord, for in the morning your doom shall come."
Suda watched as the lords remounted and disappeared into the night. He suddenly felt extremely tired. There had been a battle of wills in that discussion. Two children of vassals matching eachother. Still, he was pleased with the exchange.
"Was it wise to anger them so?" Sirgrin asked.
"Yes. We learnt part of their mind." Suda said, "This move of ours was unexpected. They knew less of our plans and strength than I had thought. We also know when they will strike. He was not clever enough to leave that parting remark as a feint. His soldiers are ready for war as the sun rises and so we must be the same." He turned to Ogra and Dusan, "Sadly the men can rest only a little this night. Keep sentries ready and have drums to wake the men. We will have need for shruda's as the sun rises."
Ogra and Dusan nodded and strode away. Near them was a small rise that sat above most of the soldiers. Suda walked up to it. The stars were out and Suda thought that to be a good omen but over Elmsatomen and the sea beyond that, lightening lit up the sky.

Lord Buskino woke as the ship lurched. The lantern above his head had been extinguished by the movement of the lamp as the boat swayed. He lifted his hand and flame darted into the air, illuminating a Graul who looked into the cabin, "My lord Buskino,

we need you on deck."
Buskino stood, his body lurching as another wave crashed into the prow. He had sailed much in his youth, but he still struggled to stand in these strong waves, "What is the matter?" He asked gruffly.
"We have lost our way my lord." The Graul's eyes were panicked. Both nearly toppled over as the boat rose and fell rapidly.
"USE THE STARS YOU SILLY FOOL!" Buskino yelled.
"But my lord there are no stars." The Graul made his way up the ladder and Buskino followed. Sounds of the ship hands reached him and most were panicked. Soldiers, most of which were unused to the sea, were huddled against the walls, head in their hands to fight off sickness. Buskino followed the soldier up to the deck. His view over the prow was obscured by a large wave. He was facing the heavens, but dark clouds covered the sky. Lightening ripped across the clouds, illuminating the rising crest of the wave as the ship broke over it. He had not heard the thunder over the driving wind and the crash of waves. Panic filled him at once. This was no ordinary storm. To each side he could see the edge of the storm that boiled over them. Camara held the seas, and she was vicious in her use of them.
"MOVE TO PORT! FIND LAND!" Buskino yelled as he grabbed hold of a rope that whipped violently across the deck. It had fallen from the mast and one of his sails was ripped down the middle. His power carried his voice, but it was still barely heard over the driving winds. A shape seemed to appear in the cloud. It seemed like a great roaring figure and lightening was

The Sundering of the two moons.

hurled from its hand.
"May Thera bless us." He said slowly and then his heart sunk, "CAMARA HAS COME! HARD TO PORT, HARD TO PORT! WE MUST REACH THE SHALLOWS!" He gathered several of the Ilma and charged to the prow. He looked up. The violent wind had turned his sails, pushing them further out to sea, "Bring down the sails." He felt forward and with the other Ilma, he began to fight against the storm.
It gained him a small rest bite, but his eyes could see the rest of the fleet being pummelled. Masts were thrown down in her anger, ships toppled, and crew cast overboard.
"ROW! ROW!" He yelled, "WE MUST GET TO SHORE!" A great bolt of lightning lit up the sky, revealing another ship. Buskino held the rail as its prow collided with their starboard side. Crew fell, some toppling over the rail. In those waves, there would be no saving them.
"TURN US AROUND!" He yelled. His ship whined but the damage was minimal, "TURN US AROUND!" Slowly the wind changed direction and his ship did begin to turn but it was not by their power. Camara heaved them back and the storm followed them northward, until as dawn fell, they passed Besuda and came back to the seas of their home. Then the storm abated but the ships were ruined, some lost to the depths. Buskino had no choice but to abandon Suda.

The morning came with a thick mist. It was cold and dew lay heavy over the fields. Suda walked with Ogra as he examined the troops, offering many words of encouragement. Their eyes seemed to brighten as he spoke but as he passed, a shadow crept back over them.

As they rounded a hill, Sirgrin approached. The mist was lifting and the edge of Elmsatomen came into view.

Sirgrin pointed, "Does that look like ships upon the lake?" There was cheer to his voice and Suda felt his own heart lightening.

"The armies of Cradlin have arrived in time then. Go Ogra. May Orna harden your blade."

Ogra bowed, two fingers upon his heart as he mounted a brokin and rode to command the large amount of lucraxia and shruda infantry.

Suda mounted his own brokin and rode to the front of his troops, "MEN OF THE NORTH!" He yelled, his power carrying his voice, "You have sworn oaths to defend your land and I ask you not to fight for conquest today but to fight for those lands and the loved ones who remain. This tyrant king would see them all in chains. NOW FIGHT, FIGHT FOR YOUR HOME! FIGHT FOR LIVELLA!!"

Cheers went up as Suda passed his long line of archers on the hill, headed by Dusan and made his way to his hidden cavalry. Ogra would handle the command of the battle while Suda would ride, bringing Drage's wrath down upon his enemy.

Great trumpets blew and the greater force of Scaraden moved forward. Dusan loosed his first volley and arrows fell like rain against the marching Graul, but many survived that first attack. Of all the armies of the four nations, only Scaraden wore armour in open

The Sundering of the two moons.

battle. It was viewed as a sign of the Graul's subservience, and a sign of their lord's supposed might.

Another wave of arrows fell, mirrored by less from Scaraden. The infantries met and the metal superiority of the armies of Scaraden broke through the first wave, but arrows poured into their back line, held now by the melee in front.

"HOLD!" Suda heard Ogra yell.

War brokin danced about behind him, eager for the battle and his men were to. Most of his Ilma rode with him here, though some preferred to be in the thick of it. Indeed, earth erupted on both sides, swallowing Graul as two sets of Ilma battled.

A horn call rang out and Suda's infantry gave way slightly, pulling the armies of Scaraden forward in an unorganised blob. The brinlons fired into the killing zone, slaying many. Suda watched his infantry line hold as, with every volley, soldiers of Scaraden fell. Still more were pouring through, their armour glinting in the midday sun. The archers of Scaraden broke off and a line of cavalry moved to the front of the opposite rise, ready for their chance to strike.

Sirgrin rode up beside him, "If we do not press our advantage now, our infantry will be overrun."

"Not yet." Suda said, eyes moving to look back towards Elmsatomen. The armies of the Cradlin's would join them soon. Arrows launched into the sky from Scaraden's side and Suda heard Ogra yell, "SHIELDS!"

His army disappeared under painted shields. One volley landed and as soon as it did the earth began to

crumble. Scaraden's infantry poured forward, using the confusion to smash into Suda's lines.
"Blow the horn." Suda ordered.
Sirgrin let out a long call on his horn and immediately the cavalry charged. All around him war brokin from Langorn Langeline, created a thunder across the earth. Bone sheeting covered them, their long and menacing horns directed towards the enemy.
Suda drew his sword as he charged, and flames danced upon it. Flames grew around the brokin's horns, so they charged together like flaming icons from legends of old. Beside him, Sirgrin smiled, the wind blowing through his hair. They crashed into the back line of the army of Scaraden with an almighty boom. A wall of fire went before Suda, splitting Scaraden's forces like a knife through butter. Many brokin were cast down, their riders slain as they fell but the mass pressed onwards, straight into the throng of the battle. Ilma battled there and Suda charged his brokin towards them. He wheeled about as earth crashed upwards. Brokin and rider launched into the air as the ground itself heaved.
From behind came more horn calls and Suda smiled broadly, his sword channelling lightening from the sky as it crashed into more of Scaraden's infantry. "The armies of Minton and Cradlin must have arrived." He said joyfully to no one as he continued to charge with his quickly diminishing cavalry.
Panic suddenly came from behind his ranks. Desperate shouts grew and all Suda's joy faded. He signalled and the cavalry turned. They charged away, back towards their line while arrow fire from Scaraden fired after

The Sundering of the two moons.

them. He came back to the front line, who had reformed in the rest bite his charge had given them. There Dusan and Ogra held council. Suda ordered his cavalry to reform as the two charged towards him.
"We are betrayed." Dusan said. His eyes were wide, and blood covered his tunic. He had lost his cloak, the star of Livella on his shoulder broken, "The army of Scaraden lies behind us."
Suda turned to Ogra, "Hold them here."
Ogra nodded but Suda could see the despair in his eyes.
"What will you do?" Dusan asked as Ogra charged into the fray, his lucrax wielded with flame upon its blade.
"I must unite our forces. Something has delayed the Cradlin's." Suda moved back to his cavalry and sent them before him. They charged passed their archers but stopped dead. A mass of soldiers stood in their path, infantry, and cavalry. Banners flew in the breeze, all bearing the four towered church.
Suda nodded, and the cavalry moved. Earth erupted in front of them and many brokin fell. Then a violent wind roared up, unseating riders but Suda pressed on. He was staring at the line of cavalry. At least thirty Ilma lords sat upon brokin, causing the devastation that buried his men.
"The Cradlin's have betrayed us." Suda growled, feeling the pull of Agral's curse and hatred for the folly of his war. He stopped and the cavalry pulled up, many still being torn to pieces by the Ilma.
He was trapped between two armies; this would be a massacre. He turned and stared at the dividing mountains. That way still lay secure, but it would not

be for long, "RETREAT!" He cried, "RETREAT! FALL BACK TO THE MOUNTAINS!"

Cavalry scattered, and his call was repeated. Soldiers began running in an orderly march back northward. Then the cavalry of Scaraden moved, cutting down ranks as they could. At every charge, Iucraxia, led by Ogra, held the cavalry back from the other forces but every charge saw more fall.

"Ride with the cavalry Sirgrin." Suda ordered, "Have them support our retreat."

Sirgrin nodded and began gathering the cavalry. Ilma lords stayed with Suda though, holding back the Ilma of Scaraden's attacks. Suddenly a flash appeared by Suda, and he stared at Drage, the vassal of fire, garbed for war.

"Ride." Drage said. He was covered in flame from head to toe and his eyes were like a tempest of fire. Suda nodded and heeled his brokin forward. The Ilma lords followed and with the vassal they charged into the line of Ilma. Drage gave his fire to Suda and Suda wielded it like a man possessed. His red hair became flame, his eyes burnt and that heavenly fire he placed before him. Ground settled in front of it and wind faltered. Suda slew the first Ilma he approached and as the others scattered Drage followed them, not to kill but to protect the retreating soldiers. Suda pressed onwards, his own aura knocking many aside. He found, fighting still, the armies of Minton. They were broken and bloodied, many already fleeing. Suda rallied them and as his lords protected them, he sent them northward. Then with one despairing glance towards where Scaraden lay, Suda fled into the north,

The Sundering of the two moons.

utterly defeated.

They were pursued long into their escape and even with Drage's intervention, many were ridden down and slain. As night began to fall, Suda stopped, and his company followed.
"Our forces will not make it back to Sikaorna without time being given to them." He said as their host moved about them, stumbling away from the still approaching army of Scaraden
"No." Ogra agreed, "We must get you to the front of the train my lord. Your people will hold the pass for you."
Suda looked down. He thought about the decisions he had made to this point, the dark pledge, and the folly of his march to war. Did he deserve to flee more than the soldiers that followed him, "I seek that not." He replied.
"I see your mind." Sirgrin said, eyes locked on Suda's, "Your life for that of your people."
Ogra drew himself up, "You cannot."
"It did not work for the Cradlin's when they took my grandfather hostage." Suda felt the nerves in Sirgrin as he gripped Suda's arm tightly.
"I do not wish to be a hostage."
It was then that Dusan stood forward, "Then you wish to die. You think that will rid you of the curse. That this sacrifice will free you in the eyes of Livella, but she does not hold your bonds, Agral does."
Suda looked at his friends. They had served him well, now he would serve them, "My friends. Long have you tried to sacrifice yourself for me. I have one

chance to buy us freedom. A challenge of single combat."

"He would not go for it." Ogra deadpanned.

"He might." Suda retorted, "Kings are vain, and they must show their strength to hold their power." He looked at Dusan and Sirgrin, "Keep the armies moving. Set all the Ilma to the rear guard. Have them hold the pass until our men have all journeyed through. They will see spring in their own lands."

Sirgrin had a tear in his eye as he nodded, "Yes my lord."

"Your will." Dusan replied, "May Livella give you strength."

Suda embraced them both and then they left.

He turned to Ogra, "I would order you to leave but I know you would not."

"I cannot. The king may just kill you and claim you lost in combat. He must be held to witness." Ogra turned away from Suda and his eyes examined the fleeing soldiers, "Wait here." He left and mounted his brokin. He began riding between the fleeing soldiers and soon some were riding back towards Suda.

Suda rested there with an ever-growing number of guards of Drage and Minton. It was dawn when Ogra returned. He looked exhausted but, in his ride, he had gathered a force that would be able to defend Suda. As the morning progressed, the armies of Scaraden marched towards them and Suda's troops became an island in a sea of metal garbed soldiers. Eventually a procession of soldiers rode towards them. At their head stood king Harda.

He looked regal upon a white brokin, long brown hair

The Sundering of the two moons.

in a ponytail, a circlet of silver upon his head. Suda had to admire his arrogance. King Harda wore gleaming metal armour, decorated with gold. It was rare for one of the Ilma to wear metal, but Suda guessed he was well trained in his control over it.
At king Harda's side, the kin of Agral rode. He had a terrible sneer on his face and a triumphant air to his posture.
"Lord Suda." King Harda said in a very musical voice, "What has stopped you in your flight? Have you come to swear fealty after your foolish war?"
"Maybe it was foolish." Suda said, his mind wandering to all those who lay dead upon the battlefield, "But I will not stand idly by while a tyrant tries to take our land."
King Harda's smile faded, and his eyes became like stone, "Bow down to me and give up your control of the dividing mountains and you can go back to your home in peace."
"I will do no such thing." Suda replied. He stared into the king's eyes and pulled what resolve he could.
"Then you will die." The kin of Agral said.
Suda laughed and several of his guard joined in. Ogra just looked troubled, "You must earn the right to be king." Suda drew his obsidian sword, "I challenge you to single combat. Show your people that you are truly powerful enough to hold such a foolish title."
Suda had expected laughter but many of the king's retinue looked troubled as they looked between Suda and king Harda.
"Why would I risk such a thing?" King Harda asked, "I have a vast army. I could kill you and take the pass by

force and leave nothing to individual chance."
"Because king." Suda said the title with clear disdain to his voice, "Our soldiers hold the high pass. You would lose thousands trying to take it. On this day, you may have spared your men that. What will they think of you then king, when your cowardice sent them to their deaths?"
King Harda considered Suda, "At noon then, we fight in single combat for the dividing mountains and an end to this war."
Suda bowed his head, his fingers pressed to his heart. King Harda only shook his head as he turned his brokin around and headed back through his line.
Suda rested in the time before noon, while his soldiers formed a ring around him. Small skirmishes between the forces broke out but Ogra was able to keep the men calm. They could not give the numerous forces of Scaraden an excuse to slaughter them.
Soon king Harda re-appeared. He was now dressed in a simple leather tunic and wool trousers. A mix of both armies formed a circle around them and Suda undressed also. He handed the obsidian sword to Ogra, who held it like it was something precious.
The two rulers approached eachother and they gave half-hearted bows. A horn call blew and Suda was knocked backwards by the first of the king's barrages. Water pummelled Suda and he called all of his strength to deflect it.
Suda moved the earth, earning him some rest bite and between his hands, fire spread. He launched it at king Harda, who pulled the earth up to defend himself. The battle became that then, both men evenly

The Sundering of the two moons.

matched, trading blows equally. Just as Suda stopped a barrage of stone, he felt a static charge between his fingers. As Harda charged towards him, brandishing a metal shruda that he had called from somewhere within his army, Suda let the bolt fly. It crashed hard into the king, who flew several feet backwards, but a great mound of earth came up to defend him. His tunic was marred by Suda's attack, but the king seemed barely to have felt it. In fact, king Harda smiled with childish delight. His golden eyes were burning, and a flash of blue electricity arced between the king's hand and his chest. The ground launched the king upwards and as he fell a bolt came from the skies above. Harda's fist and the bolt, caught Suda at the same time and he fell to his knees, blinded, his head spinning. Another punch came and Suda fell to the ground. He was being pummelled into it, all of king Harda's punches, magnified by power.
"NOOO!" Suda heard someone yell. His vision returned in time to see king Harda stumble, a shruda still quivering in his shoulder. Suda's eyes filled with tears as he looked into the stunned face of Ogra, his hand still outstretched from where he had thrown. A great swirl of water from many sources suddenly surrounded Ogra, pinning him in place.
King Harda stumbled backwards. He withdrew the blade as blood poured down his arm. The king gave a cry as he sealed the wound with a white flame from his hand. "Fool." He cursed, eyes burning into Ogra, "You are a cheat. The fight is forfeit, as is your life." Suspended by the water, Ogra could do nothing as Harda took Suda's sword and placed it squarely

between two of his ribs. It shattered as Ogra gave a yell, but he was dead before the water allowed him to fall.

Suda screamed and the earth lifted him to face the king. He could not lift his head, but he would look his enemy in the eye.

"I am not done." He whispered, blood leaking from his mouth.

"No." King Harda held no triumph in his eyes, "but I am. I am wounded by one of your men. The challenge is done."

Suda lifted his arm and earth weakly sped towards the king, but a flick of his hand sent it back towards the ground, "You never stood a chance." King Harda spat, "Now go to your rest lord Suda and think upon your failure for the rest of time."

The ground rumbled and Suda was pierced by many spikes of the earth. As Suda felt death reaching out for him, he watched the army of Scaraden slaughter his men. A tear fell from his eye as darkness took him. There passed Suda, taken by a curse and the treachery of the vassals and the line of Drage was darkened ever after.

The Sundering of the two moons.

VI. A coronet of flames.

Sirgrin walked at the head of the long train of northern soldiers. He was bent over, grief stricken, and he could feel the point of the shruda as it pressed against his neck. They had not reached the pass before the armies of Scaraden had surrounded them, bearing the body of their lord and Ogra. They had all surrendered then, less they be slaughtered where they stood.
They had been marched endlessly through the passes of Sikaorna. The Ilma lords were bound, their bodies on the brink of being torn apart by well rested lords of Scaraden.
They were approaching the halls of Sikaorna. That was good. Sirgrin had been forced to rest upon the highpass, huddled together with the Graul to try and survive the night. Many had not.
Sirgrin must have been feared. During the final march, king Harda himself had been in charge of holding him, making sure he did not use his powers. The body of Suda moved next to him. He seemed peaceful in death. The order of Gadrika had cared for him well. At least Suda would get the chance to sail to the sea. Not many would, left behind on the edge of Amoraorna. They rested with many who had died in those fields in battles of the past.
"A question." Sirgrin said as he walked, "Can I ask a question?"
King Harda nodded his head.
Sirgrin's head turned to where he could see Ogra's

body, also being tended, "Why did both lords die, when they went for single combat?"

The king was silent for a second and Sirgrin was sure he caught a sense of pain in his golden eyes, "It seems lord Drage was well loved. Ogra would not see him beaten or humiliated. He foolishly attacked."

Sirgrin looked down, sensing the curse of Agral in that action.

"I would like to have met him in different times." The king said to Sirgrin's shock. There was compassion in the king's voice, "I would like to learn how he earnt so much love from his friends and from his people. I was born into my role, as was he, yet I am not loved so."

"That is because he was not a king." Sirgrin said solemnly, "You cannot hold such a title and yet be one of the people. Have you ever graced a village inn or seen the festival of life beyond the walls of Scaraden?"

"I have not." Harda deadpanned, "That would not befit one such as myself."

"Then there is your answer your grace." Sirgrin deadpanned, "Now my question has been answered and I thank you king, for answering it with grace and speaking with kind words on one who I loved. Now I must march again in silence and overcome my grief."

They marched into the grand hall of Sikaorna. There was a great intake of breath from those of Scaraden as the vastness and majesty of that hall came into view.

Forces of lord Rivon stood guard. Dusan had ordered those who guarded the highpass to surrender and this meagre force could not overcome Scaraden's might.

The Sundering of the two moons.

Tears filled Sirgrin's eyes. Stood beside lord Rivon was Lavia, Suda's widow. She looked proud and stern, but he could see she was grief stricken. Her three kids clung to her dress. Seeing their fathers' body, they charged towards him and the order of Gadrika allowed it.

King Harda dismounted and stared at Lavia, "Where are the other lords of your united realms?" He asked.

Lavia stepped forward, "Andorgrin is dead beside the waters of Elmsatomen, and lord Cradlin is too old to ride. I speak for them."

Harda nodded and stepped towards her. He showed none of his compassion now, "I have here four thousand soldiers and many Ilma, including those who were dear to your husband. Agree to my terms and they will go free."

"State your terms and end this." Lavia said through gritted teeth.

"You shall give over to me the right of the dividing mountains and they shall be governed by a high seat in the southern hall. Lord Rivon may keep his position, but he must send tribute to the southern hall every season." Harda looked at the lord of Sikaorna who seemed to shrink, "No force may go in numbers across the highpass and Drage must also end all tariffs on Scaraden's goods." His eyes locked back onto Lavia's, "With that, our armies will depart."

Sirgrin watched her eyes fall towards Idris and she finally shed a tear, "You will want a guarantee." She knew there was no counter they could offer.

She beckoned for the boy, "This is Idris, heir to the line of Drage."

King Harda seemed stunned and Sirgrin thought that he was battling something inside himself, "NO!" He said finally, "A son would serve me ill and the line of the vassal's must be maintained. I shall take a daughter and she shall wed into my line."
"No!" Lavia yelled. She went to move forward but stopped as many lons were strung.
A lord came out and grabbed Alina while she still clung to the arm of her father. No one, of either army, could lift their heads as Lavia and Alina called for eachother. The girl's calls lasted long until she was out of sight, carried beyond the borders of the great city.
Sirgrin dropped his head. This was and would remain, the only way to keep Dragor free. Sirgrin felt the pressure in his body release. It felt weird to be fully in control of his own skin. He walked over to Lavia as a lord came to discuss the terms with lord Rivon. A battalion, king Harda left behind but the king and most of his forces departed.
"My lady." Sirgrin said, completely lost for words. Her skin looked dull, her golden eyes bloodshot but a fire was burning inside of them, "Call the lords. We must do something."

Brinsita seemed empty after the great host that once occupied it had departed. The armies had returned to their homes, ready to begin the process of planting the spring crops. Many lords did not come to the assembly, only those with great influence and power. They brought Suda to the water and laid him to rest upon a boat that had been readied. In the waters, Drixan gave a sermon that ended with, "Under the

The Sundering of the two moons.

light of the stars, in the sea of the universe, you shall rest lord Drage.
Then Lavia came forward and she placed a weak flame within the lamp. The waters rose and Suda was carried downstream but those of the company were sad as they watched it, knowing what the pledge meant. Suda did pass to the sea, but his soul went not to Livinden and went instead to decorate Agral's realm and none of Drage's line rested where they should for many generations.

After the lamp had pulled far out of sight, Lavia called the lords to the church of Brinsita and beneath the great glass dome they held counsel.
"I ask lord Cradlin." Lavia said with a vicious undertone to her voice, "Where was your fleet? What treachery left my husband surrounded?"
The old Lord looked down, "Only treachery that we have long had to contend with. Camara would not open up the seas to us and we were pushed back. If I could have changed it, I would. Suda was in everything but title, a king."
Lavia looked down, "Then our war angered the vassals and for that, we have paid the heaviest of prices." She turned to look at old lord Langorn, whose head was bowed in grief, "You have paid heavily for this."
He nodded, "Suda took my son away and he dies without an heir to carry my name. The Langorn's will fall from Langorn Langeline."
Lavia's eyes fell towards Sirgrin, Suda's most faithful servant, "My lord Langorn, perhaps we could keep

your name alive." She beckoned to Sirgrin, and he knelt before her, "Long you served my husband and long have you been faithful. Yet you bear no last name due to the crimes of your sires."

"That is correct my lady." Sirgrin whispered.

Lavia looked back at the old lord, "Lord Langorn, will you take Sirgrin to wed your daughter, if he vows to take your name?"

For a moment the old Lord was silent and then he smiled, "I have known Sirgrin since he was boy." An old finger pointed at Sirgrin, "Child, you were loved like a brother by both Ogra and Suda. I would be happy for you to take my name."

Sirgrin stood, his face a mess of pain and wonder. He had a name now; his line had been forgiven.

"What do we do now then?" The lord of Carano asked as Sirgrin seated himself again, "Do we dare fight against the might of Scaraden?"

"We cannot." Lavia replied, stilling many voices who called for conflict, "They have my daughter, and I could not bear anymore grief."

"We must suffer this bitter defeat." Adan Cradlin said, "But we must learn from it. We lost this war for one reason. We were not united. The crown in the heavens has not yet been taken."

Lavia nodded her head towards him, "If you would stake such a claim my lord, then the line of Drage would follow."

The old man laughed, "I speak not for myself. Where is the boy?"

Lavia turned to one of her servants and in a confused voice, asked for Idris to be brought to them. The boy

The Sundering of the two moons.

came in, dressed in black, his red hair unbrushed, his eyes bloodshot, yet he held his sword proudly at his waist.
Adan turned to Buskino and then the pair stood and knelt before Idris. Adan could not conjure a flame, so Buskino did it for him."
"Lord Drage, I swear unto you my power and fealty, for as long as you reign as my king." He said, his voice hoarse but proud.
Lavia was shocked but before she could offer argument, Dusan, Sirgrin and Loxa knelt before Idris, "For the love we bare your father and your family." Sirgrin said before they all spoke together, "I swear unto you my power and fealty, for as long as you reign my king."
Suddenly all the lords of Dragor and Cradlin were on their knees, fire outstretched towards the boy, and they all repeated the line. Then the lords of Minton knelt, showing tokens of gold, "The mountains were bestowed to the line of Drage for all of time and the mountains fight for you as our king." The new realm lord of Minton declared.
Drixan stood above Idris and between his hands a coronet of flames burst into life. He placed it upon the boys red hair, and It did not burn or leave a mark, "Rise king Idris of house Drage." Drixan said loudly, "First king of our northern realm. May Livella light your path, Orna keep your people in good earth, Thera keep your lands watered and Gadrika keep you pure in heart."
Then it was done, and the three realms became united under a king, but Lavia was nervous, and she wept

openly.

"War will come if king Harda learns of this." She whispered.

"Let it be decreed." Drixan said to them all, "By a pledge of Livella. All first born of house Drage shall be crowned king, but the coronation should be secret and none beyond our families shall know of it until a time of war. We are all bound to secrecy and should any of us break that oath, then our houses will be laid utterly in ruin. Here in this church only will the name king Drage be spoken and here shall Idris and those who follow be crowned."

Then the council stood and with their flaming hands raised, they cried, "ALL HAIL KING IDRIS!"

The Sundering of the two moons.

So, Idris became the first king of the northern realm and after him kings were crowned in secret, but they could not escape the curse Suda laid upon them. The pledge that Suda made, lasted long, and affected many of the events in Ilmgral, including the coming of the kingless times and the great wars following the enlightenment. I believe that the dark pledge, that soon affected all those of the Dragor realm, was in part what brought Earth into this wide tapestry. In years gone by the church in Scaraden would be moved to Abgdon and not destroyed. Enemies of Dragor were placed on Earth, until one from the Dragor realm released them and did war upon them just as Suda did long ago.

Book Four. The Sundering of the Two Moons
By Andira Belarn

The Sundering of the Two Moons is probably the most beloved story of the early years of Ilmgral. It shows one of the true tragedies of the age while also highlighting the power the Ilma could reach, and the growing strangle hold Agral had upon the chosen people.

Of Morelin, Anglin and Lucarnia.

Though Morelin and Anglin called themselves cousins, they were not connected closely. They both descended from the line of Mina, but Morelin was more closely related to Sirgrin, who at this time ruled as the lord of Langorn Langeline. Both Sirgrin and Morelin had Aginor as a great grandfather. Anglin's great grandfather had taken the thrown after his brother's death and through greater power, was able to hold onto it.

Lucarnia came from the family of the great wood. Her father, Nargir Bitaran, was the current wood king, who could trace his heritage back to Krun Bitaran. Lucarnia was an evergreen of her people and powerful in control of the wood and from her womb, the lineage of the saviours of Ilmgral would come.

The Sundering of the two moons.

1. A meeting under the moons.

The two moons illuminated Morelin Diactra in their beautiful mingling light, as he walked through the clearing at the edge of Elmkrun. The great wood was a marvellous sight, that covered most of their northern realm. It was said to carry a sense of magic from Krun's time and standing there he could believe it.

Morelin's footsteps were light and did not overcome the music of the wind blowing through the silver autumn leaves.

Morelin looked up to the heavens, where Umoria shone with silver light, that mingled with his own silver hair, while the dusky red light of Aradtoria gave its hue to his white face, falling away to nothing on the red scales that gently kissed the underside of his eyes. Morelin turned from the great wood, his gaze going southward. There, behind the distant hills of Angralangeline, sat his home. The home that the vassal Mina had built.

As he turned, he caught the sound of a crackling fire and the murmur of his companions. He strode towards his friends, the unlucky ones who had come on this mission at the behest of king Anglin. Morelin was chief warden of the wood this year, a title bestowed upon a member of the Ilma who went to the court of the wood king, to protect his land as the people of the wood fell into their winter slumber.

A life of defending his home from brigands had turned Morelin into a fierce warrior and he was the most trusted general of his cousin, the king of Melkin. Morelin had always been happy to help the forest dwellers. They were kindred in a way, though it was many generations since Mina and Krun had been born to the vassal Krim.

His heart was heavy though. Since Aginor's foolish war across the sea, the two kindred had become sundered. Anglin believed that the rebel force at Angralin were being allowed reinforcement from the northern waste because of king Nargir. He had tasked Morelin with a secondary task. To find proof of this.

"Come Morelin." Said one of his companions. The pair were sat by the fire, warming themselves like common Graul, "The fire is warm, sit with us." The one who spoke had hair as dark as the night. Red scales covered a nose that had been broken in a fight and a scar split his chin.

Morelin laughed, "Tell me Langia, what sort of Ilma would I be, if I needed a fire to keep warm?"

"One like us." The other said. He was broad and short for one of the Ilma, as were all from his people who had once commanded the nomadic tribes of northern Kuratex. His hair was cropped short in their style, and he carried a long spear, used mostly for hunting the great beasts of that land, "Who does not wish to use up all their strength to keep warm."

"Dorel." Morelin shook his head, "This is the great wood and the spell of Krun lies upon it. I would not sit upon its border when Umoria is full and Aradtoria is not far behind."

"Then go." Dorel bellowed "But do not get lost or fall into some spell meant for brigands."

The Sundering of the two moons.

"If I get lost." Morelin bowed to them, "Then you shall find me in Linkrun just within the wood and likely the only spell I will be under, is that of drink and music."
Morelin turned from his companions and walked towards the great wood. The air of Elmkrun was not as stuffy as he had expected. The woods around his home were usually a mess, full of debris and tangling brambles. There was an order to this wood. Nothing fought for the space it occupied. The forest was in harmony, from tall tree to shadowed shrub. Morelin took a deep breath. There was a scent to the air, full of life even though winter was approaching. The smell of fallen leaves and dampness had never seemed so comforting.
He stood in those woods for a time, listening to the wind that seemed to carry words between the trees. He listened more carefully, there were words on the wind. Morelin walked towards the sound and the words grew in their clarity. He stepped towards a clearing and gasped. Beneath the dusk moon, a woman sat, singing to the ground, as vibrant blood red flowers bloomed at her words. Morelin, like all the Ilma, could speak to plants and command them to grow. It was the only part of his power that had been bestowed by Gadrika when the gift of the Ilma had been forged, yet he used it little. Morelin was a warrior, he needed his powers to be a weapon.
He stood in the shadow of the trees, watching her as she worked.
From that moment the doom of Morelin was locked and the greatest tragedy of the Ilma's youth was set

in motion. He had heard rumours of Lucarnia and had seen her once as a child but in her womanhood, no story could convey her beauty. Her skin absorbed the red light of the moon and gave it back in greater beauty. Un-like Morelin, she had no red scales but instead lines like roots came down from her eyes and clung delicately all the way down her cheeks. She was slender like a flower in spring, but Morelin could feel the strength of the trees in her.

A wind rose around Morelin and seemed to flutter around Lucarnia. He watched as a smile crept onto her lips. She sang again and a beautiful red flower bloomed. Her gaze fell suddenly towards him, "Come out fair lord and bask in the light. Umoria will soon come across the glade and their light will mix. Come and see the flowers, you are upsetting the trees."

Nervously Morelin stepped into the glade. He bowed slightly; his hand pressed against his forehead. She did the same, "Hail lord of the Ilma." Her eyes went to the silver flower pin on his shoulder, "You are of the house of Mina?"

Morelin stared into her piercing green eyes that seemed so strange from the golden irises he was used to, "I am Morelin Diactra." He said in a shaking voice, "From the town of Minagrin."

"It is a pleasure." She said as she turned back towards the flowers.

"You must be Lucarnia Bitaran, daughter of the wood king."

She nodded and Morelin stepped closer to her and as he did, Umoria moved across the sky and gave its silver light to the clearing and it mingled, as she had

said, with the light of Aradtoria.
"Tell me wood daughter, how did you know I was here?" He asked.
"You said it in the name you give me. We who live in the wood, hear the trees and many do not like the hearts of the Ilma, who chop them down for their machines of war." She laughed like it was some joke, but Morelin hesitantly looked towards the trees, his power reaching out to silence the wind that blew through them. His eyes then went down to the flower, "This is livora." He said, "That grows only on the lands where the kin of Drage have lived."
She looked up at him, taking in the lines of his face, "It was sent over by my family who reside over the ocean. It does not like our soil so I must force it to grow." She pulled a seed from the top of one of the flowers and placed it in Morelin's hand, "Perhaps you could grow them in your garden my lord."
Morelin shook his head, "I have not the power."
She seemed confused, "But you are a child of Mina." She took the seed and placed it in the soil in front of him.
"I never learnt her gifts." Morelin could not help but falter under her gaze.
"Close your eyes."
Morelin did as she commanded and suddenly everything, but the sound of the trees was cut out.
"What do you feel?" She asked.
Morelin sensed through his powers, "I can feel the water in the soil. There is a stream southward. I can feel the wind, it comes from the south, carrying a late autumn warmth."

"Feel beyond." Lucarnia ordered. Her hand grasped his and forced it towards the seed.

Morelin gasped. He felt it, the small nugget of energy locked within the ground, "I can feel it." He whispered.

Her hand released his, "Now spread it. Imagine the flower to grow, give it your strength to grow."

Words came un-bidden from Morelin's mouth, and he did as commanded, giving his strength to the flower so that it could grow. He had the image in his head, the image of the flowers Lucarnia had formed, and he focused on the that.

His connection broke as Lucarnia laughed beside him. His eyes shot open, and he sighed. It might have been a flower. There were some petals hanging onto a stem that was too thick to be supported.

"You will need practise." She stood, her smile widening, moving the roots upon her cheeks. She sang and a seed grew on the flower. She handed it to Morelin who tucked it in his pocket, "Can I ask a question now lord?"

"Of course."

"Why are you here? You are far from Linkrun if you are making your way there." She considered him as she spoke.

He stood as well, "I am the guardian Anglin has sent to watch over your people during winter."

A full smile grew on her face, "I do not wither over winter. Though there are few of us who do not. It will be a pleasure to speak more with you in my home." The smile stole Morelin's heart, and he felt heat rise inside of him, "And I shall feel warmer for your

The Sundering of the two moons.

company." Words suddenly seemed to come unbidden to his lips, "For nothing that I have seen in this world is more beautiful than Lucarnia Bitaran as she sings beneath the dusk moon."
Her eyes fell towards the ground, and she suddenly seemed to withdraw into herself, "Speak only of the beauty of the earth Morelin." She looked up as the dusk moon passed from the clearing, "You should go now to your rest, for the night grows late and you are far from Elmlin."
"What about you? You are far from home as well; would you like to rest in our camp?"
She laughed, and it again warmed his heart. He watched in awe as she stepped towards a tree. She sang and it bent towards her, "I have the wood to rest in and it will take me home." She bowed to him, fingers pressed to her head and at the command of her song, the tree lifted on its roots and disappeared into the forest.
Morelin walked back through the wood, and it seemed to him that he was waking up from a beautiful dream. The magic of the wood seemed to diminish as he came again to his camp. The sound of Dorel and Langia singing sounded coarse after the sweet voice of Lucarnia.
Dorel spotted him first, "Ah, he has not fallen down a hole."
"No." Langia agreed, "But he looks as though he has been hit by a spell."
"That I have friends." He said dreamily, "But it was a spell that I did not expect, for I saw a beauty that has long been hidden in these woods and it is not of leaf,

stem, tree or flower but one of all these things."
"A woman." Dorel said, laughing with delight as he did, "Now your absence makes sense. Our lord was falling in love beneath the moons."
"Her name?" Langia asked, being as ever the more reserved of the trio.
"Lucarnia Bitaran." He whispered in reply, savouring the sound of her name.
His two companions stared at him in shock until Dorel laughed heartily again, "Then it was a curse indeed, for pursuing that thread with our mission, will surely cost you your head."
Morelin laughed with them as he laid his head down upon the bed role. He turned to face the wood and he wondered where she was now in that vast labyrinth of trees. He fell asleep, hearing her song in his mind.

Morelin woke as the sun was rising. His eyes went towards the woods, but it held none of the majesty that it had under the two moons. There was a menace to it now and the trees seemed to swallow the light of the morning sun. The three companions crossed its border with a heavy heart and eventually found a path that would take them to Elmlin.
They camped under great trees, on a bed of silver leaves, hiding from the autumnal rains.
The next day they began to climb towards Elmlin, on an ancient roadway, with steps crumbling to nothing.
"Why do they need us when they have such strength as they do in these woods." Langia said, "I do not believe any threat could penetrate these trees."
"They are already threatened." Dorel replied, "Rebels

The Sundering of the two moons.

hold their northern borders and winter is a time of death for them."
Morelin nodded in agreement, "In the winter the people of the wood wither in strength like the trees themselves. Most slumber until the new leaves bud in spring. They cannot defend their borders in this time, even with the evergreen's and the Krun-graul who avoid the slumber. They need some of us to keep their realm in order."
Langia looked down as he walked, "It would be a fair charge, if that was all we were asked to accomplish."
"That task is mine alone." Morelin said sternly, "You have no need to feel guilt for it."

As they marched along the road, the aroral trees, full of thick foliage, swapped for tall lintran's, their tops shaped like great bells. It was at this time that Morelin began to feel like they were being watched and as they approached a large thicket of evergreen's, a Krun-graul emerged from the shadows. He was smaller than all three of the company and he seemed to sag as though he was exhausted. Roots crawled down from his eyes, but they looked as though they were receding, "Hail lords." He said, "The main road to town is south of here."
"Apologies." Morelin said as he stood forward, "We lost our way yesterday, but we are expected." He handed over a sealed letter, "I am Morelin Diactra and shall be the guardian of winter."
The man smiled, his eyes going from the letter, marked with a karma bird flying over the wood for the king of Melk, to the flower pin on Morelin's shoulder.

He gave a whistle and the hedgerow parted, revealing a road into the town of Elmlin.

It was not named for its size. The town was small for a king's capital and was one of the smallest towns of the great wood. It was named for the lintran trees that grew there. None grew taller in all the world and its tallest reached higher than the towers of Lerou and Karmaorna over the sea. It was said that Krun was buried under the central tree, and it was his strength that made the trees grow so tall. The buildings were built around the trees, the commercial hub on the ground, the residence above, built into and around the tree's vast trunks. Meaning the town did not grow outward but upward.

They walked to the central lintran tree. On the ground around it, built between its huge roots, were the buildings of most importance and there, in times of peace, king Nargir held his court. The guard took them inside the hall. Great fires burned within and at a high table, king Nargir sat.

"May I present lord Morelin Diactra, the guardian of winter and his two companions." Their escort said. The king beckoned them forward. He was regal though he looked tired. Silver leaves sat in his hair, but some had fallen to the ground behind him. Roots climbed far down his cheeks, and he wore a robe of fine green silk with gold embroidery. Morelin's eyes went to Lucarnia, who wore a gown of subtle blue, but she did not look up at him.

Morelin bowed to the king and in return he took Morelin's hands in his, "I thank you for your service." Morelin kissed Nargir's hand and then stepped

The Sundering of the two moons.

backwards. He gestured to his companions, "With me is Dorel Matronas and Langia Sulkas. They will assist me in my mission."
Nargir nodded his head to them both, "Your thanks."
"Dorel will head to Linkrun and Langia to Tirakrun. We should be able to watch the whole realm from there." Morelin continued. The pairs assignments were well chosen. They provided the best chance, being close to rebel smuggling roots, to learn if there was any truth to the rumours of king Nargir's treachery.
"Lucarnia." Nargir said, gesturing behind him. She stepped forward, a small smile spreading on her lips for Morelin, "My daughter has the strength of the evergreen's and does not wither like myself. She shall act as my steward." He took her hand, "Daughter, show lord Diactra to his lodgings."
Lucarnia did not speak as she beckoned the trio from the room and Morelin was shocked by her coldness. She showed none of the warmth she had in that clearing.
"Are you well my lady?" He asked as they stepped back into the town.
"I am lord."
Morelin turned to his companions who both smiled sympathetically at him. She led them to a small house that stood below one of the lintran trees. Morelin was happy that they were not climbing one, "Your companions may stay this night, but they will have to leave tomorrow if they wish to reach their charges before winter comes." She did not look at him as she said, "You should dine with myself and the king this night."

Then she left and Morelin's heart grew cold at her reserve. It did not improve as autumn stretched towards winter. He did his duties, gathering the forces of ordinary Ilma and Graul and mixing them with the evergreens of this wood. Lucarnia was gone often and Morelin yearned to talk with her.

With the falling of the leaves, Nargir's people began to wither. Men, who a week before could have worked a day, tired after one hour of labour and soon most of the streets of Elmlin were silent.

One day, after a harsh frost, Nargir took Morelin's hand, "Today is the time that I must go to my sleep. My realm is in your care."

In this moment, Lucarnia returned. Morelin was startled that she looked no different, when most of her people could barely stand. She kissed her father and from the Lintran tree, a stand was lowered. Nargir lay upon it, and it was hoisted upwards and finally the last silver leaf fell from the tree's upper branches.

"My lady." Morelin said as he approached Lucarnia, "You look radiant."

She smiled fully, like she had in the clearing, "Now your charge begins."

"Why is it you do not wither?"

"The evergreens live in me." She seemed to flush, and the roots grew slightly on her cheeks, "My mother came from the tower to the east, that is now held by rebels. Krun grew tall trees that did not shed leaf there, as a refuge should Agral's wrath come upon his people. The power in those trees lived in those that resided there, so that while the rest of the forest slept, wardens would be ready to fight. Now that

The Sundering of the two moons.

tower is lost, the power wanes in us."
Morelin smiled. For the first time since that clearing, she spoke to him as a person and not as a lord, "I am glad, for I shall not be alone during winter. Your company shall make spring come quickly."
Her eyes dropped to the floor again and Morelin was sure that he saw a wall, blocking her off from him, "That will be good." She murmured.
He approached her, "Why do you slip into this veil of sadness." He asked as his hand gently touched hers, "At times you are like a flower, eager to show your beauty and colours but then I say something, and you hide your petals, becoming as cold as winter."
"It is no fault of yours Morelin." She whispered.
The use of his name made his heart catch in his throat, "Then whose fault is it?"
"You are just a leaf in the year." She said, looking him in the eyes, "Here for just a short space of time before you move to your next mission."
He saw the pain in her eyes, the pain of loss, "Now I understand it. You have been in love before, with one on this mission."
"I have." A tear formed in her eyes, and it fell down one of the roots, clinging to it, "I have, and it was a bitter parting. My father would not allow me to marry beneath me and I could not go with him. He left and returned to his home, and he died beside the shores of Elmsatomen in Drage's war."
Morelin felt his heart break, "I am sorry my lady."
"I never got to say goodbye." A smile touched her lips, but it was mirthless, "Every year since a hero has come to our land, and he has always been both bold

and brave. Like a foolish child those feelings awoke in me again."

Morelin knelt before her and she laughed, "Then I ask to be just your friend and companion, to end some of that hurt." Morelin held in his hand a livora seed, the same one she had given him at their parting, and he sang to it. The flower grew, beautiful in shape and strong in stem. Lucarnia smiled as she beheld it.

"You have been practising." She laughed, "I am impressed."

"I had a good teacher." Morelin smiled and beckoning her to join him, he scouted the town.

They conversed much on that first winter month and their friendship grew rapidly, along with Morelin's love for her. She exuded so much power that he was often left in awe of her and yet she was kind to all things that grew or walked on legs. He thought of her much like Mina, even though she came from the line of Krun, because of her compassion.

Their winter peace would not last though. On a cold morning, close to midwinter, an evergreen scout came and found them out.

"My lord Morelin." He exclaimed before bowing to them both, "A fire burns north of here. A rebel sacking party has attacked. They are after the seeds for the spring groves."

"How large a force?" Morelin asked as he quickly pulled his winter cloak from his back.

"Not large sir but the people are un-armed. I fear they will burn the wood there to cover their escape."

"Lead the way." Morelin said, "Feeling power soar

The Sundering of the two moons.

through him." He turned to Lucarnia and smiled, "If I could spend winter just talking to you, then I would but this is reason I am here."

"Do not go alone lord." Lucarnia said and she sang to a tree, small in comparison to the lintrans and it moved towards her. She climbed upon it and beckoned Morelin to follow. He did reluctantly. She laughed at his shocked gaze, "What? I am a woman with the strength of the trees, and this is my forest. I will defend it."

He nodded, and the tree began to wind around Lucarnia, forming a thick armour. With that the tree began to move, following the scout as they went to defeat the rebels.

2. A conspiracy revealed.

Morelin felt uncomfortable as the tree heaved underneath him, moved by the words of Lucarnia next to him. He watched her as they moved through the forest. Now he saw a different side to her. She seemed like a warrior, her eyes burning, living armour surrounding her. The tree suddenly stopped and on great lifting roots, it climbed above the forest canopy. Morelin relished the feeling of the fresh breeze that he had forgotten in that covered forest. Ahead of him a great plume of white smoke rose towards the sky.
"It was as we feared." Lucarnia said through gritted teeth, "They are burning the wood."
"What do the trees say?" He asked.
Lucarnia closed her eyes and the song changed. A great wind rose and surrounded them. When it faded, she seemed to sag, "They have chopped down the new-borns and are burning them green without care."
"Are there any Ilma there?" Morelin asked but Lucarnia shook her head.
"The trees know not the difference between the Graul and Ilma."
The tree lowered again and in long strides it marched towards the burning. Soon they heard the sound of fires, and the wood became full of smoke. Morelin pulled the wind to shift it and they stepped into a clearing. It was a small village, full of houses and groves of fruit trees, all leafless in winter. Graul ran about in rough clothing, chopping down trees and fighting others who defended a large store house.

The Sundering of the two moons.

"I will do something about those flames." Lucarnia said as she leapt from the tree. She moved towards the burning groves and using the power of the Ilma that still flowed through her, she began to divert the flames away from the young trees. Rebels turned their attention onto her so Morelin leapt to the ground. He pulled at the flames also and he wielded them like brand. A boulder he launched at the first two and as they dived away, he sent them to the halls of Agraldin.

Quickly the rebels regrouped and charged towards the pair of them. They wielded bone shrudas and Morelin smiled. He held no pity for rebels. His home had been raided countless times by rebels and he had sent many to serve Agral. Morelin dived aside as bone shruda's were launched at him. He came back up with the moisture from the ground, creating a swirl of water that sent two to the floor. The others rushed into him. A stone shield formed in front of Morelin, blocking the blows of his enemies.

He moved, shifting the ground, knocking several to the floor. Fire soon surrounded them from Lucarnia and one by one Morelin began to swallow them with the earth.

"FLEE NOW!" He yelled, "AND DO NOT ATTACK THIS LAND AGAIN!"

The flames parted and one by one Morelin let the Graul flee into the trees. Those that continued to fight on, were quickly dispatched. As one remained, still pinned by the earth, Morelin turned to Lucarnia, "Make sure the others flee and do no more damage." She smiled at him and moved off, trees following her

as she ran. Morelin approached the still trapped Graul. He clenched his fist and the Graul yelled, his stone surround crushing him, "I will release you, my friend." He said menacingly, "But you must tell me something."
"Agral curse you." The Graul said through gritted teeth.
Morelin unclenched his fist and the rock loosened slightly, allowing the Graul to breathe.
"What brought you here?" Morelin asked and the Graul stared at his outstretched hand.
He was shaking with fear and finally he answered, "It is our job."
"Who orders it?"
"I cannot say." The man looked close to tears as Morelin clenched his fist again. The man wailed and then in a pained voice yelled, "KING NARGIR!"
Morelin's heart sank and so did his arm. The rock loosened and the man scrambled, desperate to work himself free.
"What do you mean?" Morelin asked.
"Nargir orders these raids." The Graul said, just as his legs emerged from the earth.
Fire sped from Morelin's hand and hovered just in front of the Graul's eyes, "You lie." He said maliciously.
"He needs to maintain the rouse." The Graul's eyes reflected the fire that could kill him in an instant, "The wood must appear to be weak. King Anglin must always have the forest as his concern."
Morelin released his flames and beckoned for the Graul to flee. He did gratefully and he pushed passed

The Sundering of the two moons.

Lucarnia who smiled at him, "The rebels are running, and evergreen sentinels will make sure they return to the rebel tower."
Morelin heard what she said but was not truly listening as the Graul's words circulated through his head. She stared into his eyes, her brow furrowing, "What troubles you?"
He looked into her dark green eyes, his mind muddled by his love for her and his duties to king Anglin, "These rebels concern me. I did not believe the true extent of your plight."
Lucarnia took his hand, and he relished the warmth in it, "Let us help these people and then we can celebrate the night of stars together."
Morelin smiled and together they removed the flames and helped restore some of the village to order.
During that time the words of the Graul went through his head. It was as they had long expected. The raids were organised by king Nargir. Always enough to grab attention but never enough to bring any real price upon his people. He knew that he would have to tell king Anglin, but he wanted no trouble to come to this beautiful wood, or to the forest daughter, whom he loved with all his heart.
A moonless night came as they set back out for Elmlin, but they did not return to the town, instead they stopped in a clearing and watched the stars of Livella climb far into the sky. For that night, alone with her, he forgot what he had learned from the rebel.
"I love the festival of stars." Morelin smiled.
Lucarnia watched him, "Surely the festival of life is your favourite, being a child of Mina?"

"I celebrate all things." He replied, "I spent many years travelling in my youth. I have seen the cursed tower of Agral and have taken the harvest meal in the tower of Krim. I have blessed Orna on the high pass in early spring before it was lost to the southern realms." He smiled, his eyes locked on hers, his mind back in all those amazing places and far from the troubles he had learnt, "But no place was more beautiful than the celebration of the stars in the church of Brinsita." He touched her cheek and the roots seemed to caress his fingers, "Whether it be by some magic of Livella or some ancient craft, it seemed like you could touch the stars on that day. In no celebration had I ever felt so close to the Gods. It seemed like Livella was among us."

Lucarnia looked down, allowing Morelin's hand to fall from her face, "I have never visited that blessed wood, but my cousins have, and they speak of its beauty often."

He nodded, "I think it just exemplifies the beauty already in the world. Like the moons did in that clearing when we first met."

Suddenly she was beside him, eyes staring into his. Morelin laid back against the ground and looked up at the stars. He was looking for a sign of what his next course of action should be. Prayer had never found him many answers, but he needed one now. He was in the company of one he loved, one who he would need to betray. He looked at the stars of separation, Livella's foretelling of the biggest betrayal yet to come for the Ilma. On the edge of the horizon, the red mountain star loomed. He stared at it and whispered,

The Sundering of the two moons.

"Mother Livella guide me for I am lost and am on a desperate mission, afraid of what I must do. Give me strength and guide me in this dark winter."
Lucarnia laid down beside him and placed her head against his chest. Her hand coming to her scaled cheeks, "Your mission is just, and you shall do well with it."
Morelin pointed back up at the stars, "Somewhere within that tapestry, the stories of the heroes gone or yet to be born are written. I often wondered as a child, whether I would be one of those heroes."
"You are." She said, green eyes locking his gaze, "Even if it is not written in the stars."
Morelin stared into her eyes and was lost. He kissed her then and as the stars of separation passed over the clearing, Morelin and Lucarnia became one and their doom was wrought.

As winter began to pass, the love between Morelin and Lucarnia flourished as they walked the orchids and fields of Elmlin. Frequent skirmishes with rebels revealed more of Nargir's deceit and as his love for the wood daughter grew, his hatred for his mission followed. He wandered the woods, outside of Elmlin, alone as the time for his meeting with Dorel approached. Doubt plagued him constantly, his mind thinking of the betrayal he would be forced to commit. There she found him in his musing and his eyes betrayed his worry.
"You are fitful lord." She said, her delicate hand brushing his cheeks.
"Dorel sends me troublesome news. I must go and

meet him." His voice was level and that seemed more likely to betray him. Her brow furrowed, searching his face.

"Shall I go with you?" She asked.

His hand took hers, "No." What remained of her smile faded, "I need you to watch Elmlin for the days that I am away."

He kissed her and before she could offer argument, he strode from the woods, but Lucarnia sang and the trees hearkened to her and ever the wind passed their branches, following his steps.

Morelin marched back through the old paths, down the crumbling stair that was now like a waterfall with the melting snow from the hilltops. Silver leaves dotted the floor but around him the trees were bare, and he was thankful for this, knowing no spy of Nargir could conceal himself within them.

Under a canopy of tall trees, that in summer would be home to many songbirds, Morelin found Dorel. The short man seemed to have taken well to his charge, he was broader than before, and his hair had grown long.

"Hail lord." He said with a bow.

"Dorel." Morelin embraced his friend, "How fares your mission?"

"A few skirmishes." He said, "But traffic is frequent between the rebels of the north and those of Angralin."

Morelin nodded, "Evil tidings I have learnt, and my heart is broken to even think of it."

"Speak then and lessen the burden. I have messengers that could reach Anglin swiftly." Dorel explained.

"The rebels are under orders from Nargir. As the king before opened the wood to allow the conquest of Angralin, now does he allow passage and grain to the north. These attacks are a feint to hide that lie."

Dorel's face hardened, "For what gain?" He asked.

"So we come here. While the southern lords worry of the rebels march southward, king Nargir sits safe in his halls, knowing that his lands are secure and ours weakened by the guardian's absence."

"King Anglin will not like this." Dorel exclaimed, "He is un-hinged as it is. They say Agral touches the line of kings of Mina. He is vain and vengeful and would not like to be played so."

"I do not like being played so. I know of king Anglin's mood but how do we not know that Agral also touches those of Krun's children? Helping keep this division between the children of his brother." Morelin shook his head. These questions were beyond him, "It is easy to blame all the faults of the Ilma on Agral's touch but maybe greed and violence are just traits of ours."

"What do we do?" Dorel asked, his face troubled.

"Send word to Langia and to Anglin. We must be vigilant, if the wood folk learn of our mission, then we must be prepared to flee."

Dorel bowed, hand to his forehead and left for the trees. Morelin stayed for a time, listening to the wind that seemed to move around him before rushing back towards Elmlin, carrying his words upon them but to Lucarnia that wind did not go. Instead, it climbed to the tallest branches of the Lintran tree and came to the evergreen guardians there, pulled by the power of Krun

Morelin walked long on his journey back to Elmlin, resting by hidden lakes and glades where late winter flowers bloomed, foretelling the coming spring. He was restless though. The forest seemed more awake than it had all winter, and the trees were watchful. His suspicions were proved true as he stepped back within the city of Elmlin. He was met by drawn lons and he stared into the eyes of Nargir. The king looked weary, bent over with exhaustion, roots around his eyes only slightly visible.
"You should not be awake your grace." Morelin said, arms outstretched in peace. He took a step forward and an arrow loosed, brushing his shoulder and landing in the wooden gate. He froze in place.
"I thought of you as a friend." Nargir said weakly, "Someone to be trusted and yet I am betrayed."
"I do not know what you mean my king." Morelin replied.
Footsteps charged towards them and Morelin's heart broke as he watched Lucarnia run towards him. She stared in shock, first at the archers, their lons pointing at Morelin and then at her father, who should not have woken for months yet.
"What is this?" She screamed.
Nargir looked hard at his daughter and Lucarnia's eyes flickered towards Morelin. He sighed but his eyes seemed to burn. He turned back to regard Morelin closely, "Not only do you spy upon me and my people, but you have also stolen the heart of my daughter."

The Sundering of the two moons.

Lucarnia gripped her father's shoulder, "He has only ever served you faithfully."
Nargir's smile was vicious as he stared at Morelin, "Should you tell her, or should I?"
"Be careful your grace." Morelin replied, arms still outstretched in peace, "For what you say may bring more hurt upon yourself, than on me."
"So, I shall be the stronger." Nargir shook his head and he turned back towards his daughter, "Why is it that your heart always goes to fools. Lord Morelin here is a spy for king Anglin as I expect have all the guardians of winter been."
Rage filled all of Morelin's mind. He connected to the wind, ready to strike. The people were weak, he could stop them in a second, but his eyes fell onto Lucarnia's. They were wet with tears. She was staring at him, looking for the truth in her father's words and Morelin could not stop the shame of it from falling onto his face. Her head bowed and tears fell freely as she read it in his eyes. He released his power.
Nargir stared at Morelin as though he was waiting for the lord to reveal what he had learnt. He was expecting Morelin to pit Lucarnia against them both, but he loved her dearly and would not do that here.
"Killing me now king." Morelin whispered, his broken heart like a searing pain in his chest, "Would only bring war upon your borders."
"I will not kill you." His voice grew haggard, "Morelin Diactra, you shall remain here in Elmlin, only free to leave once Anglin has paid your ransom and admitted to his crimes."
Two of the Krun-graul rushed forward and took hold

of Morelin. He did not fight them, and he allowed himself to be led to the base of the lintran tree. A platform was lowered and Morelin stepped upon it. His heart became dust as Lucarnia turned away, not even sparing a glance as he was slowly lifted into the branches.

The climb was long, and a harsh northern wind blew everything about him, until he came between the limbs of the lintran's highest branches. Here a great house was built between the limbs and Morelin was led to its lowest section, where there was a prison made of the tree itself. Great branches twisted into the cell, meaning Morelin could look down to the ground below. He was placed inside, where bedding had already been arranged. The tree closed in around him and Morelin rested, the image of Lucarnia's hurt stuck inside his mind.

As the weeks passed, Morelin's isolation soon began to become un-endurable. He had no contact, apart from the occasional guard who passed him food through the twisting tree. He was exhausted as he used his power to warm himself on the cold winter nights. The first few days he had feared that king Nargir would create an accident for his demise. He feared that the limbs would open enough for him to fall to his tragic, but not unsort after end. That fear had lessened as the exhaustion and solitude grew. In truth, at times of mass desperation, he wished for it. No part was worse for him though than the hurt he had caused Lucarnia. He craved to see her, to explain his actions to her.

The Sundering of the two moons.

He was shocked then, when twenty-one days into his imprisonment, he woke to see her standing at the entrance to his cell. She seemed timid; her eyes full of pity for him.
"Lucarnia?" He whispered, desperate to clear the sleep from his eyes, "Can it be that my dream has become reality? Or have I finally gone mad in my loneliness? How can you be standing there, like an angel clad in green?"
"I am no dream." Her voice was still full of pain and anger, "But I am no angel, and I cannot take away your pain."
Morelin crawled to the edge of the cell, "Why then have you come? If it is to show me your hatred, then appeal to your forebear and have his power open this cell so I can fall, for I cannot bear it."
Anger seemed to slip from her eyes and love crept into them again, "My father has re-entered his winter sleep. I could not come before he did."
"What news do you have?" He asked.
Tears welled in her eyes, "Your friend Langia is dead. We found him with secret messages and when we tried to arrest him, he was killed by an evergreen like myself."
Morelin's heart shattered again, "It was not their mission. They came because they were my friends." His voice became hoarse with pain, "What of Dorel?"
A faint smile touched her lips, "He has so far alluded my father's traps, but the trees will tell us if he passes southward."
"He will not go southward. He will use the rebel ways to go to the northern wastes and buy passage from

there."
Lucarnia looked down, she seemed frail now.
"Why do you wither?" He asked her.
She looked back at him, "Once again winter has brought me sorrow." She said, a tear clinging to the roots under her eyes, "I ask Morelin. Was I just another tool to reach your goal?"
"No my love." He replied and the word brough forth waiting tears from her eyes and the power of Krun answered, loosening the branches of Morelin's cell, "You were one part I did not expect, and I wanted desperately to believe that I would have nothing to report. My love for you could then have been untainted but the truth I could not hide."
"What did you learn?"
"The rebels that have harassed both of our lands are not so leaderless as we expected." He replied and her eyes widened. She went to turn away but stopped.
"Do not speak of such things." She said coldly.
Morelin's hand went to reach towards hers, but the branches moved, trapping his arm, "Please Lucarnia." He begged, "You are not blind to this world. Your father pays these rebels, just like his grandfather did by the plea of the lord of Cradlin. He does it to pull people like me away from my home. Our kings are both liars, using us as pawns to wage secret wars with eachother."
"You lie." She said desperately.
"You know that I do not. Look into my eyes and see it." She did and her white lips quivered. The branch released him, and he took her hand, "My heart is yours. Like Umoria and Aradtoria in the sky, we are

The Sundering of the two moons.

destined to be together, and I will let nothing keep me from you."
She was silent and Morelin thought then that he had lost her, but she soon grasped his hand tightly, "I have seen things my love. My father's secret meetings, his advisors taking trading trips to the frozen north or the apathy towards the tower of my mother's birth."
"You know what I say is true." Morelin's eyes were firm, "We cannot let this escalate further."
She nodded, "My father talks of war in spring. The trees of the north shall move southward and shall surround Melkin."
"They will find fire." He replied, "For Anglin is nervous and scared in his rule. He has long prepared for such an assault. Tell him of my imprisonment. We must get the kings together if we are to stop this war."
Her hand released his, "I cannot betray my father."
"If we do not, then our worlds will crumble."
"This will doom my people." She said sadly, "Anglin will come with an army and will not stop until the woods burn."
"I will beg him not to." Morelin assured her, "If Anglin gains my release, he will see it as a victory, as will king Nargir, for I shall be banished from his realm."
"If you are banished, then our time together ends."
He smiled, hearing the love he thought lost in her words. He leant forward and the branches opened so that he could kiss her trembling lips. She locked him in a firm embrace, letting go of the fear and the pain. When they broke apart, he stared into her eyes, "I did not say it in jest. We are like the moons of heaven, and we can never be separated. If we stop this war, the

Gods will reward us, and they will grant my desire to never be parted from you again."

She kissed him again, "I will do this thing." Her eyes seemed to grow sad, "But I see only bad things and our separation coming from this. The Gods will curse our treachery. Farewell my love, I will soon see you freed."

The tree limbs closed back in around him and Lucarnia vanished into the upper boughs. Morelin sat reinvigorated in his cell, waiting for his chance to win his freedom.

The Sundering of the two moons.

3. A long punishment.

Morelin woke late in the night as a vicious wind blew snow through the gaps within the tree's branches. He was shivering, covered in a gentle blanket of white flakes. He had given up using his power to keep him warm unless at the absolute need.
Far below him bells rang out and voices were shouting but he could not see anything below the blizzard.
"Guard." Morelin said to the lone sentinel stood just beyond his cell.
One of the Krun-graul turned towards him, "Yes?"
"What is happening below?"
The guard seemed troubled, "I do not know. The lords are being woken; they will soon clear the storm. It is feared that fires have been spotted on our borders."
Morelin sat back, wondering whether he had been wrong and with his imprisonment, the rebels had seen a chance to strike at Elmlin Itself. As the lord's below brought a wind that drove the snow southward, he knew that this was no rebel force. The forest itself looked like it was lit by thousands of torches. Some within the city but most beyond, creating a circle of threatening flames.
"You fool." Morelin whispered to the wind. He knew now that Lucarnia had achieved her mission. In his rage, Anglin had acted without care and had moved his forces to surround Elmlin. That was quite a display of force for just himself.
Resolve flooded through Morelin and with it some strength. He stood on stiff legs and walked to the

edge of his cell, "You must get me down there."
"If our enemies want you, then they should climb this tree to your cell." The guard said angrily, "None would have the strength."
"You are wrong." Morelin said, trying to place desperation into his voice, "Not since the days of Crio has one had such power over the earth as Anglin has. He will raise a mountain where Elmlin stands to reach this cage if he must."
"Is that a threat?" The guard asked, his eyes narrowing.
"No." Morelin sagged, "If Elmlin fell, then a beauty would be lost from the world more devasting than the burning of Fasurasuta. I would see the forest stand."
The guard seemed troubled, "Someone will summon you if you are needed."
Morelin nodded his head and leant against the tree. He seemed to be pulling strength from it and every breath cured the cold from his limbs. Beneath him the two peoples yelled at eachother, but it seemed war had not yet broken out.
Morelin watched from his high place, until the sun crested on the eastern horizon, breaking through the cloud, so that its morning rays seemed to set the forest ablaze. It seemed like a dark omen for him. The branches of the cell opened and Morelin stared in shock at king Nargir. He still seemed weak as he leant upon a staff of hard wood, but Morelin saw new buds growing in his hair.
"Word of your imprisonment has spread. You must be dear to king Anglin for him to muster such a force."
"No my king." Morelin said bowing, "But he is vain

The Sundering of the two moons.

and would use his love for me as a smokescreen to conquer." Nargir regarded him carefully and Morelin got on his knees to beg, "Please your grace. Allow me to go down and speak with him. I can talk him down."
"Present your hands." Nargir said ominously.
Morelin did as commanded, and a vine rapped tight around his wrist. He winced as roots bore into his skin and he felt it pull at the fire in his veins that kept him warm. Morelin went to create fire and the roots grew, tightening around his hands. King Nargir smiled at that and then he beckoned for Morelin to follow. They entered the platform that slowly lowered them to the floor. On the ground a tired army of Krun-graul and Ilma were assembled. Only some, the evergreens, looked in any condition to fight.
His eyes fell onto Lucarnia, stood beside a group of lords. Her head was bowed, and he could see that she grieved for her treachery. The sight of her filled him with joy though. He knew that by his pledge, war would be averted this day. Her eyes looked up, sensing his and a smile crept upon her lips. She charged towards him but stopped by her father, "A moment please?" She asked and he gave a disgruntled nod.
Morelin walked on stiff legs towards her, and she took him in an embrace that she quickly broke off at a glare from her father. Her hand brushed through his long blonde hair, "You look terrible." She smiled as she spoke.
"I am not an evergreen." Morelin whispered, "And winter has bitten me to my bones."
Suddenly her smile faded, "You said war would not

come and yet we are surrounded."
"That is not war." He replied, "We still have a chance to stop this turning into a battle. Your father must relent. He must give me over to king Anglin."
Lucarnia's eyes filled with sadness, "That, he will not do."
"ENOUGH!" King Nargir bellowed. Morelin was grabbed by a gust of wind that locked him in place. The gates opened before him and he was pushed in front, unable to fight back against it. He looked back over his shoulder at a tall member of the Ilma, dressed in the garb of the rebels of the north. Morelin gritted his teeth as he was pushed through the gate. The army of Melk surrounded him, but he had eyes only for Anglin. Even though they were family and had spent many years together, the king still frightened him. He was almost black of hair, with tilted eyes and a bulbous nose. He would never be called handsome, and his looks matched his attitude. He was obeyed through fear. Fear of his power and fear of his anger. The almost brown eyes of Nargir examined him closely and Morelin felt his gaze drop, "Are you well cousin?" Anglin asked.
"I am." Morelin deadpanned but he was cut off by king Nargir.
"You should talk first to me."
Morelin turned. Compared to Anglin, Nargir looked beautiful but exceptionally frail. Almost like Anglin could call upon a small gust of wind to knock his opposite over. Nargir, of all the people of the wood, stared Anglin in the eyes, "How dare you come in force into my land?"

The Sundering of the two moons.

Anglin gave a cruel, malicious smile, "You hold one of my kin captive."

"A spy in my land."

"So you claim." Anglin stepped forward and brinlon drew, arrows pointed at the king, but Anglin seemed not to notice it, "What news has he learnt that you would accuse him of such?"

"I will not speak of it." Nargir spat.

"Then what will you speak of?" Anglin lifted his hand and behind him, Ilma lords took fire and placed it as a wall behind Anglin. They would consume the arrows if any were stupid enough to fire, "I will burn this forest false king and cut off the rebel's routes. Already a force marches to claim Linkrun, and they will burn as they go."

Morelin's heart stopped as Lucarnia gave a small moan from behind her father. He knew it was a feint, a show of power but he hoped Nargir would think it genuine and would not push his cousin to anger. For a moment Nargir stood taller and then he sagged, leaning on his walking stick, still weak from winter's hold. Maybe in summer, when the people and the trees were at their strongest, he would have fought on, but he knew it was folly.

"We must end this peacefully." Nargir said slowly, "To stop our people dying."

Anglin smiled coldly, "My cousin shall be returned to me, and you will pledge spring forces to crush the rebels that infest this forest."

Morelin and Nargir locked stares and Morelin smiled but that created a spark of anger in the king's eyes. He seemed to stand taller, "It shall be done."

"I want a guarantee." Anglin said and Morelin knew he was playing on Nargir's weakness, wondering what he could gain in his moment of strength.

Morelin's stomach tightened as Nargir smiled a malicious smile, "You are un-married king."

His heart shattered as the realisation set in. He looked at Lucarnia, whose eyes grew wet with tears.

"I am." Anglin said in surprise at the statement.

"We must create a union between our lands as it should always have been between the houses of Krim's children. I present to you my daughter, for marriage."

"Father." She said but a stern look stopped her speech.

A dark gleam grew in Anglin's eyes, a vicious greed to claim the daughter of the wood that none had yet claimed. Morelin's legs felt like sagging as he sensed Nargir's victory. The wood king could not win by force, so he would win by cunning. Morelin could see it in Anglin's eyes. He would be besotted with Lucarnia and would do all he could to win her affection, weakening him greatly and the child of the two would be king to both realms. The wood would take the precedence for the people would love Lucarnia, where none loved Anglin.

"I welcome your kind offer king." Anglin whispered. The fire behind him died away as he stepped towards Nargir and Lucarnia. The wood king held out a hand that Anglin took, "Our families have long been friends." He said, his voice full of lust, "This affair should not affect that. We should be in union again."

"I hope it shall be so my friend." Nargir smiled as he

The Sundering of the two moons.

stepped aside, presenting Lucarnia to the king. In front of his hulking frame, she looked as slender as a flower, and she was more beautiful in comparison to his garish features. Her eyes swept towards Morelin, but he saw no pain in them, only resignation for the fate she had predicted in his cell.
She bowed to Anglin, "Pleasure to meet you, your grace."
"You as well my lady." Anglin said as he kissed her hand. She shuddered at his touch.
Nargir's eyes once again caught Morelin's, and his dark green wells were full of triumph.
Anglin stood tall, "My forces will depart until the wedding in spring, but I would have some of my soldiers remain, in case you turn back on your word."
Nargir seemed unhappy about this, but he eventually nodded, "Fine but none may hold the name of Diactra."
So, the armies departed and the vines around Morelin's wrists fell to the floor. Morelin and Lucarnia shared one more desperate glance, before he turned to follow the king.

Morelin spent the first two days of his march with men he knew from the warriors at Angralin but late into the third day, Anglin requested his presence. The king did not ride a brokin like Morelin did. He sat upon a slab of rock that moved with only the gentlest use of his powers.
"Cousin." He said, beckoning Morelin forward.
Morelin bowed, palm pressed to his head, "My king."
"How was it that you were caught?"

"Not by my lack of vigilance. We used secure methods, but I fear I was watched for other reasons beyond people suspecting my treachery." He did not tell the king of his affair with Lucarnia, and the king asked no more.

"Alas for poor Langia." Morelin deadpanned, "Was his body returned?"

The king shook his head, "I did not know he had passed. If I did, I would have ordered it. What of Dorel?"

"He has passed northward. He should return soon." They rode in silence for a while and Morelin watched faint smiles appear on Anglin's lips. It made his appearance more disturbing, "What of Lucarnia?" He asked finally, "You spent time with her. She did not seem weak like her father."

"She is an evergreen." Morelin replied, trying to keep his love for her out of his voice, "She does not wither in winter."

"Is she kind?" He asked, like it would make a difference to the man who ruled through fear.

Morelin thought back to their first meeting under the light of the two moons, "She is kind, gracious and powerful also."

"Good." He said, "I wish her to bear me many children and she will need strength for that."

A vicious hatred and jealousy filled Morelin. He did not care for her, or her spirit. He would force her to weakness just to increase his lineage. Morelin was in a hopeless state, wondering whether to kill the king and run off to find her but it was not in his spirit. He was a warrior, loyal to the Gods and his king. He knew he

The Sundering of the two moons.

would need to bear this pain until a battle claimed him at last.
That night, Morelin asked leave to return home and he departed. He crossed barren fields, walled off from the raids of rebels and came across valleys to the town of Minagrin, where he dwelt in his sorrow and turned his rage upon the rebels of Angralin.

The weather in the north let go of winter slowly but as the year grew older, spring flowers bloomed in the gardens of Minagrin, and birds returned from their southern migration. It was on a frosty morning when the summons to the wedding of king Anglin and Lucarnia came. Part of his heart wished not to go but he was heir to this town, this town that Mina had built, and he had position within Anglin's court.
The thought of kneeling beside Lucarnia and swearing fealty to her as his queen made him feel sick.
He set off for Melkin that afternoon and they arrived to find the dark walled city, surrounded in blooming blossom trees and full of people who had come to attend.
The wedding happened the following evening. Lucarnia looked beautiful in a dress of dark green, laced with white spring flowers and blossom fell from her hair. Anglin looked regal, in colours of dark green, laced with gold. He also looked dark. A king come into his full power, a power that cast a shadow over him. Nargir seemed reserved behind, but Morelin saw a strength in him, concealed and yet coming to bloom, like a budding flower.
A member of the church of Gadrika joined the pair in a

union of life. Lucarnia kept her name as was her choice and Anglin seemed not to care about it. His heir would take the name of Diactra. Once the pairs ceremony was done, the lords came out in order of rank, to swear fealty and to present gifts. The high lords came forth and Morelin followed his parents. They presented Lucarnia with mindane. A plant that grew in the gardens of Minagrin. They smelled beautiful and gave vibrant golden flowers. Morelin's mouth went dry as he knelt before her, hand upon his forehead, "Queen Lucarnia of the great wood." His throat went tight, and he was sure he could hear the quickening of her heart, "I swear featly to you and your king, from now until the ending of the world." Lucarnia's hand reached towards his face but stopped short. A tear lay upon the roots under her eyes, but she spoke as the queen she now was, "I accept your fealty." Then she whispered so only he could hear, "It seems the two moons have been parted."

Morelin looked down and nodded. Slowly he stood up and left. A great party happened afterwards and Morelin partook in the square with the residence. Only during a dance between the king and his queen did Morelin join the main festivities. During that dance, only Anglin must have thought this marriage real. Lucarnia did not look into his eyes, and she danced like a rigid oak against a wind she cannot change.

After the dance, Morelin went to look over the large sprawling city. It stretched as far as the eye could see with streets building upwards between its dark wood and stone walls. Wind riders were performing in the

The Sundering of the two moons.

sky and Morelin watched them eagerly. The moons came up into the sky, but they were veiled in a layer of cloud so only part of their radiance could be seen.
He heard footsteps behind him and knew the soft fall of Lucarnia's slippers. He breathed in her scent, like a meadow after a short burst of summer rain.
"There are few trees in this town." She said, her voice full of sadness and longing for her home.
"It is a fine city." Morelin said to comfort her, "And with your power, you will bring a beauty more elegant than any object of gold or stone."
"What of Minagrin?" She asked, "Are there trees in your home that would take me?"
"There are." He replied, wishing she had not mentioned his home. His love was a memory and a life with Lucarnia was a dream that could never happen, "The power of Mina runs through it and we have many orchids."
She seemed to look distantly towards the bright city before her, "I will ask my husband." Her voice faltered at the term, "If I can visit one day." Then she wept and turning to him she took his hands in hers, "Oh Morelin please take me away. Hide me from this horrible fate that I have been assigned. I do not love him and do not think I ever will. My heart burns only for you."
Morelin looked at her and he desperately wanted to do as she said. His heart yearned for her, but he grew cold inside, knowing that only in the frozen north would that life be possible and in that dark and terrible place, they would find happiness only in eachother. Even Lucarnia the evergreen might wither

in a land shrouded in cold and darkness. He would not lead her to that fate, "These words you cannot say." Her eyes filled with sadness and tears. He needed to carry that hurt, "We are now on different paths and our love is forbidden."
She nodded and left him, steeling herself for the life that had been forced upon her.

Morelin grew restless as summer approached and the orchids of his home began to swell with fruits. He was wandering through the groves, as Graul picked the ripened fruit. A large tree, unnatural in the grove, stood in the middle and beneath it grew the red flower of livora. A smile crept upon Morelin's lips and as he walked towards it, sweet singing reaching his ears, "Come down wood daughter." He said while looking into the thick bunch of leaves beyond.
"Or you come up." Lucarnia's sweet voice sent his heart fluttering. He had told himself lies to ease his pain, but that voice brought all feeling back to him. Morelin leapt into the tree and was caught by a smiling Lucarnia. Seeing her filled him with warmth. He had no time to dwell on it before her lips met his. She was trembling as he pulled away from her. She tried to cling to him, to hold onto the moment but he withdrew.
"You should not have done that my queen." He said while every fibre of his body begged to kiss her again.
"I am sorry lord." She said formally, "But I wished to kiss the lips of one who I love and not whom I am forced."
Morelin could understand her pain, "How is life with

The Sundering of the two moons.

our king?"
Her eyes filled with hurt again, "He is not as kind as I was promised. He rules with an iron fist and trusts no one."
Morelin felt a pain in his chest. Was the fate of the north worse than that? He dared not think about it, "Why are you here my love?"
A smile flickered onto her lips and Morelin thought she looked more beautiful than he had ever seen her. The leaves in her hair were full grown and the roots under her eyes stretched all the way to her lips. Her dark green eyes were vibrant.
"I am on my way to visit my father. He will be in his fullness now and I go to dine at his table, but I thought first to see the gardens of Minagrin."
Morelin looked from the tree to the garden, "Who comes with you? I do not believe the king would let you wander alone."
She smiled cheekily, "The tree is my protection and I travel with only soldiers and handmaids from my own realm."
Morelin's heart plummeted, "Now not even these gardens will bring me peace, for they will be filled only with the memory of you. Will none of the land be untainted by our separation."
She rubbed at his cheek, bringing his eyes to meet hers, "I do not want to leave you. I am travelling slowly, and I plan to come to the woods edge as the festival of the water comes. I ask you now Morelin, who promised me that like the moons we would never be apart, on that day, will you meet me in the glade of our first meeting?"

"I want nothing more." Morelin said, his voice hoarse, "But I do not know if it is possible, our fate is sealed." She did not look sad. Maybe in summer it was hard for her to truly feel that emotion for long, "I will wait for you there. If you do not come, I will understand but my heart will long ever more for you."

They kissed one more time in that tree before Morelin leapt down. At her command the tree moved and climbed over the palisade wall of the town and disappeared into the north.

Without hesitation, Morelin planned his own march. He rode on a stout brokin that had once belonged to Dorel. His friend had not yet returned from the north. He came at last, as the festival of waters came, to the edge of the forest. He was alone now. Dorel was far to the north and Langia was dead, buried somewhere within these woods. Once again, the two moons were close to their fullness as he stepped into the shadow of the forest. The woods seemed full of life; every tree full of green leaves that danced in the warm summer breeze. Morelin walked through the trees, and he caught their wakefulness, their awareness of him, in the song on the wind. He came to the glade, and he saw the one he loved. She was uniquely beautiful, unrobed, basking in the warm summer night, her skin reflecting the mingling lights of the moons.

"My love." She whispered as she smiled at him.

Blossom of bright red flowers grew in her hair, and she seemed more alive than he had ever seen her. She stood and Morelin strode towards her.

"Lucarnia of the great wood, bane of winter." He said and then he kissed her, and she returned it with

The Sundering of the two moons.

vibrant passion.
They parted slowly and she giggled, "Bane of winter." Her fingers ran through his hair, "I thought for a time that you would not come. The trees brought me news of what I had hoped for."
"My life is a web of cruel twisting of fate." He shook his head, "Since the king sent me to the great wood, I have been cursed. I would beg all the Gods to have your vows removed so that you could be mine."
"You are mighty lord." She said in a husky voice, "But not even you can ask that of the Gods." She took his hands in hers and Morelin felt the strength of summer within her, "Tonight Morelin my love, let us forget our vows."
They became one again in that clearing, underneath the two moons and together they planted a seed that would one day unite the realm of Krunmelkin.

4. The Sundering of the Two Moons.

They lay together for a long while in that clearing, until the moons had moved passed the western horizon and dawn approached in the east. He relished the feel of her skin on his, the beating of her heart beneath his hand. She was his everything.
A cool wind blew through the clearing, and she suddenly went rigid. She sat up sharply, listening to something in that wind. She stood, pulling a gown onto her as Morelin heard the sound of marching feet.
A tree parted and Morelin's heart sank. King Anglin stood menacingly; his eyes full of fire. Behind him one of Lucarnia's handmaidens screamed.
"My king." Lucarnia said, kneeling to a bow.
Morelin went to step forward, but earth rose up his legs, holding him in place. "TRAITOR!" The king yelled. Lucarnia, unfearful of anything, ran towards him, "My king, my love. Your lord Morelin has protected me from brigands along this road."
He turned dark eyes towards her, "Do you think me blind child?" He said through gritted teeth, "I have always known who holds your love. I know the words you whisper to your handmaidens and the way your heart flutters at the sight of him."
The idea of her love gave strength to Morelin and the stone around him crumbled. He took a step towards Anglin, arms outstretched in peace, "I will not deny any of this my king. My eyes have been blinded by love. She is more than the heart that beats beneath my chest. She is my moon and I wish never to be

The Sundering of the two moons.

parted from her again."
Anglin's eyes seemed to burn, and he barred his teeth as he bellowed, "SEIZE HIM!" To his guards. Earth clawed at Morelin again as Ilma wielding fire came to arrest him.
"Why should I not kill you where you stand?" Anglin asked.
It was Lucarnia who answered, and she grabbed at the king's face, forcing him to look at her, "I will come with you my king and will be dutiful to you till the end of my days. I will bear you many children and they will be as great kings among both the realms of the wood and sky. This will only happen if Morelin lives. Kill him now and my grief will be too great, and winter will take me at last and I will become as a snow drop, clinging still to winter as the new spring comes."
Anglin's eyes softened as he looked at her and he turned to Morelin with some hurt in his face,
"Morelin. My cousin, my friend. You are banished from this kingdom. You are stripped of land and title, and should you ever return, I will put you to death. Go now and wander in all your loneliness."
A white brokin was brought for Lucarnia and with one last despairing look at Morelin, she mounted, and was escorted out of the woods. King Anglin gave him one last wicked smile.

The stone around Morelin crumbled and he sat until noon came as he wondered upon his next path. He could not go south; he would be dead before he reached the kingdom of Kuratex. That left only the north and the perilous journey through the woods.

There, in the far north, was a land meant for outlaws like himself.

He set out at once and kept to the un-inhabited areas of the realm of king Nargir. The forest was menacing and from above him, he was sure he heard the calls of sentinels as they stalked his footsteps. On that long march, Morelin's mind went to Lucarnia, the love and bane of his life. He wondered in what prison Anglin kept her and wondered whether in the height of summer, when her strength would be greatest, was she held, and her beauty diminished. It was thinking about Lucarnia that nearly proved the doom for Morelin. In a time of hopelessness, where he was starving and mind sick, he came to the edge of a large waterfall. He looked down into the foaming fall, jagged rocks showing from the bowl at its bottom. He wanted to drop, to fall where no power could help him and rid his mind of that pain.

"Jump lord and end your suffering." Said a familiar voice that made Morelin turn sharply.

King Nargir looked nothing like when Morelin had last seen him. His brown hair reached far down his back and many green leaves grew within. The roots under his eyes covered most of his face and Morelin saw other growths over his arms. His eyes were bright and full of strength and knowledge.

"Or you could push me king." Morelin said hopelessly, "For I have broken your banishment."

King Nargir smiled, "This I know well. You have been watched since you entered the woods and I know all that my daughter and the king said." He regarded Morelin closely, "Where are you going?"

The Sundering of the two moons.

"To the north. To live out my life in those wastes."
"The reason for your banishment is the same reason my daughter now abandons the woods?" He said questioningly.
"It is your grace. My love betrayed me and so I betrayed my vows."
"It seems it is in your blood." Then the king grew angry, his voice full of power, "Continue your march forward fool. I would not have the lands of the woods tainted with such blood as yours." From a nearby tree, provisions were dropped. King Nargir pointed at them, "Go Morelin Diactra and never step foot in my woods again."

Morelin soon found himself in the far northern wastes. Beyond the woods and the power of Krun, the land became barren, covered most of year in snow. There were a few towns, but many were only small, found where people could make a living for themselves. The lordless people here mostly fished and there were few Ilma. Morelin was hungry and footsore as he found one of these small towns, but he was lucky, for a roaming band of brigands took him in, seeing the strength of him. It did not take him long to become the leader of these brigands and they roamed the countryside, settling disputes and stealing from those who wished to make themselves kings of these lands. It was on these journeys, that Morelin and Dorel became re-united and together they became great captains of a band of ruffians and Morelin carved out what life he could without Lucarnia.

Lucarnia gave birth to a boy nearly a year after Morelin's banishment and it was clear, even to Anglin, that the child was not his. The king accepted it however, knowing that Morelin was gone, and he had won. The boy's hair was cropped often, and mother and child were hidden away from the eyes of his people but as ten years passed, sickness began to take Anglin. Agral whispered words of vengeance and deceit in Anglin's ears. Setting into him a power that would bring forth the greatest tragedy of the Ilma days and would bring true retribution for the slight Morelin gave to the king.

Ten years of wandering in the northern wastes had laid heavy on Morelin. He was not the lord he had once been, and all vanity had left him. His hair was cropped short, his golden eyes dulled by years of hardship. His face carried scars and his soul carried the greater. With the help of Dorel, he now commanded a large company of a hundred men, who settled nowhere and earnt money settling the disputes of the land.

In a dream one night, as the company were camped on the northern edge of Elmkrun, Morelin saw Lucarnia again. It began like a message from the trees, caught upon the wind. The message was a long wail of pain. He seemed to fly, like he had in his youth, over the great wood and the fields of Minagrin, towards the coast. He flew towards Cradsuta, a great cape filled with many ships, manned by the twisted figures of Graul. Beyond that place, on a pinnacle of rock, sat a light house. Its white walls suddenly became bathed

The Sundering of the two moons.

in red as Aradtoria rose over the ocean. Towards the lighthouse, Morelin fled, and he came below the great lamp that lit up the ocean. Underneath he found Lucarnia, in a bed chamber locked by a great iron door. She was chained to the wall, her hair roughly cut, the roots ripped from her cheeks. She screamed but it was cut out by the yells of Anglin. Morelin flew towards her but before he could touch her, a gleaming knife pierced her breast and he was powerless to save her.

Morelin woke with a start, the dawn sky blood red above him. Around the camp, soldier stirred, and fires were built high for the morning meal. Dorel snored blissfully beside him, but he listened beyond that. On the wind, that came up from the south, he caught or thought he did, the sound of a scream. He kicked Dorel awake, who stared angrily at him. Morelin ignored the glare to say, "Continue upon your mission."
Dorel looked at him in confusion, "And where will you be going?"
"Krun calls me back across the wood."
His friend had concern in his golden eyes, "What madness is this? Has the cold finally broken your mind?"
Morelin stared southward, where far away, the light house of Cradsuta stood, "Krun has sent me a dream. The wood daughter is in peril."
"You fool." Dorel barked, "Your heart is simply troubled for one you love. To go back now, to break your exile, will only mean death for yourself."

"That was no simple dream." Morelin looked at the wood and the wind changed, coming from the north, ready to lift him and carry him back to his home, "I have never seen the light house of Cradsuta and yet I saw it as clear as day. It is a message, a warning from a vassal for one who shares his blood."
He waited for no reply and before Dorel could argue, he launched himself into the air, pulled by the wind and his powers of the elements. He followed the course of his dream and like in his dream; the wind did not alter its course. He flew high over a lintran tree in the middle of the forest, its leaves beginning to turn silver. He flew beyond the wood, over the fields of Krunmelkin as Graul worked on the coming harvest. He flew for five days and as night began to come and his strength ebbed, he came to the sea and Aradtoria rose over the ocean, bathing it in a vicious red light. He landed, almost at the point of collapse, on the outskirts of the lighthouse but he knew then that it was more than that. It was heavily guarded, and shouts came from the prison in its depths. Like a whisper in the wind, Morelin moved through the light house, using the many tricks he had learnt in his exile, and he incapacitated the two Graul guards who watched a locked door at the top of the lighthouse. He stepped over the unconscious guards and shattered the lock in his rage.
The chamber was dark, silent, and still. A fire burnt low in the hearth but gave off little light. Morelin's heart sunk, she was not chained to the wall and there was no sign of the king. The room contained only a large bed, made of a strong wood. Morelin breathed

The Sundering of the two moons.

deeply and his heart fluttered at the scent of a damp bed of leaves. Morelin's heart rose as he took several steps towards the bed. There he noticed two bundles, huddled together within. Morelin could not stop a noise escaping his lips as he looked at the smallest bundle. He was in Lucarnia's arms, short blonde hair ruffled from his sleep. Roots climbed from red scales under his eyes and Morelin recognised his own sharp features in the boy's face.

With a start the boy stirred, and he stared with brown eyes, full of fear, at Morelin, "Mother." He whispered. Lucarnia woke slowly and looked up at Morelin but in the darkness, changed as he was, she thought him nothing more than a threat.

"Halt sir." She said.

Morelin went to speak but the air seemed to have been sucked out of his lungs. He looked at her, the evergreen, grown ever more in strength and wisdom and in sorrow it seemed.

The bed, that Morelin realised was made from the twisting limbs of a tree, began to move towards him, to seize him in its boughs.

Suddenly he found his voice, "Stop wood daughter." His hand sprang up and flames went flying into the hearth, that suddenly seemed to roar, spreading its light onto his face.

She stopped, staring at him as tears began to form in her eyes. She ran to him, her hand coming down his face. Her eyes seemed full of pity, "The years lie heavy on you Morelin."

He stroked at her hair, feeling the leaves within, "But not on you, my love."

The child stepped out of bed, confusion written on his face, "Mother?" he said questioningly.
She held her hand towards him, "Child." She smiled, "This is your father, your true father, the one I have told you about. The one we do not mention in front of the king. Morelin meet Lincon, your child."
Morelin dropped to his knees in front of the boy, his legs unable to hold him up any longer, "How?" he asked.
"The night in the glade, when we were parted."
Lincon and Morelin met eyes for a second and then the child was in his arms, and it felt to Morelin like a world of missed love was suddenly bestowed upon him. After their embrace, Morelin found his feet again and he looked with concern at his love, "I dreamt that Anglin had you imprisoned, that harm was coming for you."
Lucarnia's eyes widened in fear, and she began to shake. Her eyes went to the door, and she whispered, "Oh Krun protect us."
The door opened and Anglin was stood within the doorway, the fire flickering against his white skin, revealing a vicious smile.
"So." He said in a menacing voice, "At last all truths are revealed. You came when I called Morelin, as I guessed you would and now the truth of my heir is revealed."
The tree began to move towards Anglin, but the king smiled, and the stone floor swallowed the bed, "Long have I dreamt of your betrayals." He whispered and Morelin caught a mad look in his eyes, "Agral has come to me and has given me his strength to redress

them."
The ground came up, locking Lucarnia in place. Morelin went to step forward but stopped at a primeval noise from Anglin.
"Let her go." Morelin begged, "You cannot win her love with chains."
Anglin laughed like a man crazed, "It seems I can never win her love." The king lifted his hand and part of the outer wall collapsed. The sound of crashing waves met them and the red light of Aradtoria bathed Lucarnia, but it no longer looked beautiful, now it was the colour of blood, "It seems you can never be separated in life." Anglin's eyes seemed to turn black, and his skin glowed with a sickly green light, "Agral has spoken to me, and he works through me."
Then Morelin thought he saw a ghostly shape emerge from Anglin. His opaque white skin carried hints of black and he was garbed in faintly green chain mail. At his waist was a sword, broken at the hilt.
"Wood daughter." Agral smiled, "For the treason of betraying a king, second only to the vassal's themselves, I bring the doom of Agral upon you."
Morelin and Lincon screamed as Lucarnia's body dissolved away until only her spirit was visible. It glowed red like the flowers of livora, and her skin seemed like the bark of the trees of her home. Her green eyes studied both her loves, and a silver tear fell from her eyes. Agral, his own ghostly shape looking grotesque compared to hers, grabbed her arm. The light of Aradtoria grew and swallowed them both. Then Aradtoria seemed to flash a violent red and the waves crashed the harder against the lighthouse. The

power of Lucarnia the evergreen, strengthening the moon.

"What have you done?" Morelin asked, anger, sadness, and pure desperation flooding through his voice.

"Treachery of the highest order needs the highest punishment." Anglin said, his body sagging like he had endured a great strain, "For eternity now will Lucarnia rest, imprisoned on Aradtoria, to look down upon you and your kin until you wither in the northern wastes."

Then Morelin collapsed at Anglin's feet, and he lamented, "Please my king, show some mercy. I will give everything to have her returned to me. I have an army in the north, and we will fight for you, defeat all your enemies and extend your lands if at the end my love could be returned to me."

A dark light kindled in Anglin's eyes and a voice whispered to him, "What better way to win victory than to accept this plea." It was Agral's voice, "Lucarnia will watch as Morelin kills innocents to earn her back. Or she may watch him die in the endeavour and so their separation would be complete."

"I accept this plea." Anglin replied, a cold gleam in his eyes, "My enemies shall you defeat and then I will order Agral to return her to you."

Though Morelin knew that he had indeed lost, hope made him kiss the ring of his king and hold himself for the grim tasks ahead.

So Morelin set to work killing the enemies of Melkin. By order, his company came from the north and became the legion of the flower, for they fought

The Sundering of the two moons.

under Morelin's banner. In those battles, many of his soldiers earnt renown and were pardoned of past crimes. The Ilma that followed Morelin became lords after and were given lands to govern but they all remained loyal to the flower and not to the karma bird of Melk.

As he grew, Lincon went with Morelin, and he became a great captain among the men, and he took after his mother in the power of the trees, and they went into battle with the power of the forest on their side.

As they fought, Morelin's mind was ever turned towards Aradtoria. More beauty was in the light of that moon now and Umoria was diminished, pulled off its course slightly by the pull of the dusk moon. It seemed her power pulled against Camara's, and the sea became more forgiving except when both moons drew close, and her power pulled violently at the tides. When she became full, Morelin would lay awake and would hear on the wind her lamenting song, so that he never tired of his mission or thought of forsaking it.

The company of the flower fought on the borders of Kuratex and against rebels in Elmkrun and drove the forces of Angralin all the way back to their fortress, that soon became the only refuge for the enemies of king Anglin.

Morelin amassed a great force for the final assault of that tower and the end to his mission. Before they departed, king Anglin held for the army a great feast. There Morelin hoped to gain a promise for that which he sort.

"My king." He said, finding Anglin alone.

Anglin looked towards Aradtoria that was waxing, coming nearly to fullness, "You have picked your day well." He said ominously, "She will be full by the time that you get your victory."

Morelin's heart lifted in joy, "So you have not forgotten your promise?"

"I have not." Anglin's voice was full of scorn, "You will have your reward."

As Morelin departed, Anglin grew angry, and jealousy filled his mind. Agral whispered dark words in his ears of how lord Morelin, with his wife returned, would seek to supplant him. These soldiers did not fight for him, they fought for the flower. These words fuelled anger in Anglin, and he sort out Dorel. Through torment of the mind, derived by Agral, Dorel fell to disaster, and he took the poison Anglin gave him and as Morelin made a toast to the king and to his soldiers, Dorel slipped him the poison.

It worked slowly and not until the battle was fully met at Angralin did it truly take hold and there in the barren valley, Morelin could not summon his power and he was mortally wounded. At the last, Lincon took up the charge and trees from the wood and Minagrin, came down upon the tower and the rebels were destroyed. In victory there was sorrow, and the army came to kneel beside Morelin as he drew his last breaths. Aradtoria and Umoria shone down upon his form as Lincon came to his side.

"My son." Morelin said, "Our victory is won. Make sure that Anglin does as he said, and your mother is returned to us."

Then Dorel collapsed by Morelin's side, and he wept,

The Sundering of the two moons.

"What a foolish thing I have done." He cried, "I poisoned you lord. King Anglin put the fear of Agral in my mind and I could not fight his nightmares till I had done his bidding."

Many arms seized Dorel and he did not fight back but raising a bloodied hand, Morelin ordered him to be released, "Then Anglin is cursed. He broke an oath made before the Gods and he will wither. All those who make pacts with Agral lead themselves only to ruin. Have no fear friends, for I go to the home of Gadrika, where I can wait for Lucarnia to join me."

Then Morelin drew his last breath and all his companions cried but Dorel was the loudest. In his despair, he grabbed a fallen blade and placed it within his chest before anyone could stop him and as his life's blood poured before Morelin, he cried, "Gadrika, send to me your vassal. Have him take my body and spirit and give life back to the one I love and have betrayed."

Then to his shock, he beheld Krim, and he knew it was not just the delusion of a dying mind. The vassal was dressed all in white and he knelt down beside Dorel. He placed a hand against his breast and healed the wound.

"Why?" Dorel asked.

Krim smiled and turned his attention onto Morelin, who seemed to be sleeping peacefully in death.

"For there is no need for you both to die this night." The voice of Krim was musical and all who heard it felt wound and weariness vanish, "Agral has ever whispered in king Anglin's ears, twisting his mind. Agral sort for one as strong as the vassals, as Anglin truly is. Counselled better, Anglin may have been the best of the Ilma and Agral could not allow that. What Anglin promised your lord, he could not give, as Agral knew well. By taking her spirit, Lucarnia became a vassal herself and she cannot be returned to the world of the living."

"What of Morelin?" Dorel asked, "He has lived a hard life and I would not have it ended by my hand, for my mind was clouded."

Krim smiled again, "He made a pledge to her upon the two moons and like them he shall not be separated from her. The power of Aradtoria has grown too strong with her presence and will in time destroy Umoria if equilibrium is not brought to the two moons."

He sang in a language foreign to Dorel but there was a hint to the words he knew. Like the words of the north were derived indeed from the language of the Gods. Then Morelin's body dissolved, and his spirit was like silver, and it stood slowly and Morelin pardoned Dorel.

Krim took Morelin's arm and in the growing light of Umoria they departed. The silver moon shone brighter, and balance was returned to the night sky. All the company sang upon the battlefield as on the wind, the twin voices of Lucarnia and Morelin were heard.

That song Anglin heard as he lay in his bed chamber, overcome by sickness. He cursed the two moons, seeing his best plans laid in ruin. Then Agral came and he was bathed in a wicked green light, "Still you can

The Sundering of the two moons.

separate those who wronged you, for the moons are just mountains pulled from the depths in the fashioning of the world and mountains you have the power to control." Then Agral led Anglin to the balcony, and he pointed to the stars of separation and said, "Long ago Livella placed those stars in the sky and yet she did not know what separation they foretold. The separation of the moons I wove into the tapestry and now shall it be so."
Anglin nodded and he lifted his hands towards Umoria. Then he and Morelin did battle like they never had before. Anglin held Morelin in place, while he desperately tried to follow the moving Aradtoria, who drew ever further from him. The waves crashed against the sea and the tides of the world changed as the orbits of Umoria and Aradtoria were altered. So much of his strength did Anglin put into that battle, that he aged beyond recognition and as dawn crept in the sky and the separation of the moons was complete, Anglin died. His last breath sounded as Aradtoria set with the rising sun, singing farewell to Morelin, as he desperately tried to bathe in her red light.

So Morelin and Lucarnia were separated from eachother but in the act they were made vassals of the moons and lived forever upon them, guiding the world from above. Many wept for the separation of the moons but hope remained, for in the battle Umoria's orbit was altered and he circled Ilmgral faster than Aradtoria so that in time they would again draw closer together and at that time there would be a great festival but none went to the sea that became treacherous in the mingling of their light.

From their son, Moreliag, first king of the united realm of Krun-Melkin would come and many years later Gadrikan Diactra would be born. He would give his undying spirit to give the Graul their powers, starting the first great war. Also, from this line would be born Infeon Diactra, child of the vassals and the greatest ever hero of the Ilma, who would use the gift of Gadrikan to divide the darkness and lay the Abgdonese empire in ruin until the time of the knights of Earth.

The Sundering of the two moons.

Authors notes.

Thus ends this volume of the History of Ilmgral. These events are the spring of the Ilma, where they waxed in their power and majesty and soon, we will come into their summer. Where in the full strength of their power, the working of Agral brought them almost to ruin. After these events, the Ilma became dark, and their minds turned against the vassals and the Gods. War brought forth the kingless times and beyond that, the great cataclysm that tore Ilmgral apart.

Jacob Bower

Language

Amora- Doom
Anita- Guard
Ara- East
Aradtoria- Dusk
Ash- winter
Bane- Home
Besuda- Arm
Brin- Three
Calerou- Former name for Kuratex
Cali- Land
Carano- Tavern
Crad- Two
Crio- Ore
Derna- North
Grin- Field
Krun- Woods/forest
Krim- Health
Kura- fear
Langeline- Valley
Lerou- South
Liano- Chasm
Lin- Tower
Liv- Light
Livine- Star
Melkin- Sky
Minton- iron
Mirta- Heart
Orna- Earth/mountains

The Sundering of the two moons.

Remain- Maiden
Satomen- Lake
Sika- Pass/gate
Sira- Diamond
Sita- River
Suta- Coast
Tex- Hall
Tuka- West
Thera- Ocean
Umoria- Autumn/silver

Animal, Plants and tools of Ilmgral.

Animal

Grignin- A wolf like creature, known to roam in packs around the forests of Scaraden.
Karma- Large birds. Extremely intelligent that make them excellent message carriers.
Brokin- The steeds of Ilmgral. They have long horns upon their heads and long, flat faces.
Gupin- Large fat animals. Hunted for their meats and thick hides.
Culdra- The great beasts of Kuratex and Scaraden. They were nearly hunted to extinction but are now farmed in huge ranges. There meat feed many and their bones form the base of most Grauls armour.
Trillon- Like the sheep of earth, they produce wool for clothing. They also produce milk for cheese but are prized for their large skulls that are often turned into helmets.
Tularp- Small rodent like creatures with spiked tails.

Farmed as cheap meat for most Graul.

Plants
Livora- A red flower with many petals. It grows only in the lands of Drage.

Mindane- A gift from Mina to her kin. This flower has a sweet, reinvigorating aroma and gives off many golden flowers.

Lintran- A tall tree with a bell-shaped canopy of leaves. Classed as one of the great trees of Ilmgral.

Aroral- Tall trees used for hardy word work.

Tools
Shruda- A small spear with a leaf shaped blade. Used for thrusting and throwing.

Lucrax- A large, curved spear with barbs designed to pull riders from brokin. Many Ilma weild them made of the metals of the Minton's to channel their powers.

Lon- A box like earth bows, made simply of one limps of a tree.

Brinlon- A long bow made of special wood from Brinsita and the great wood. This combines three times of wood to give greater distance to the archer.

Map available at the official website.
www.Knightsofearth.com

The Sundering of the two moons.

<u>The Knights of Earth Saga.</u>

<u>Book One:</u>

THE ESCAPE FROM HUMANITY.

Thomas Lita is no ordinary child; his vivid dreams of a strange world and a people unlike those of Earth led him to the discovery of a power within himself which sets him apart from all others. He kept his ability to manipulate fire, water and more a secret, until his dreams led him to four others, each with a power of their own. When they find clues to the origin of their powers on a school trip, they unintentionally release an evil presence that threatens not just the island but the entire future of the universe. The friends must use their powers to defeat this threat, learning who and what they are in the process, unaware that what they will find will change them forever.

Jacob Bower

The Knights of Earth Saga.

Book Two:

VENGEANCE OF THE GODS.

Three months on from the tragic events of Curamber. Thomas Lita tries to cope with the truth about his origins while his friends attempt to return to their normal lives.
Across the universe councils are held, for the first-time discussing humanity as a threat to the status quo. Something that seems destined to bring war back to Earth.
Urgarak, orchestrator of Cirtroug's release, seeks vengeance for his loss and with the Power of the Devil on his side, he thinks nothing can stop him.

The Sundering of the two moons.

Printed in Great Britain
by Amazon